Ellie had never before been so conscious of a member of the opposite gender.

Nick Tanner filled her vision, tall and rugged. He was not like the other men living on her ranch.

Suddenly she caught her breath, dragging in the scent of him. Light and tangy, and utterly male. Overwhelmed by Nick's flagrant masculinity, she stepped back.

Immediately she knew this particular guest was more than she'd bargained for....

* * * *

Praise for Barbara McMahon:

"Ms. McMahon has a super talent for drawing her readers into the hearts of her characters, the action of the plot, and the beauty of her settings."
—*Rendezvous*

"Ms. McMahon is one of the top writers of ranch romances today...."
—*Affaire de Coeur*

Dear Reader,

Welcome to Special Edition...where each month we offer six wonderful new romances about people just like you—striving to find the perfect balance between life, career, family and, of course, love....

Those dynamic MONTANA MAVERICKS are back with brand-new stories to tell! Reader-favorite Christine Rimmer launches Special Edition's continuity, MONTANA MAVERICKS: RETURN TO WHITEHORN. In *Cinderella's Big Sky Groom,* a virginal beauty enters into a pretend engagement with the prince of her dreams. Then in December, the passion—and peril—continues in our 2-in-1 Special Edition book, *A Montana Mavericks Christmas,* featuring 2 brand-new novellas by Susan Mallery and Karen Hughes.

Also this November, look for *The No-Nonsense Nanny* by Penny Richards, about the trials and tribulations of a feisty nanny looking for a fresh start *and* a second chance with the town's sexy sheriff.

Silhouette's majestic five-book cross-line continuity, ROYALLY WED, begins with *A Royal Baby on the Way.* In this first installment by Susan Mallery, a headstrong princess searches for the missing crown prince...and finds herself in the family way! Follow the series next month in Silhouette Intimate Moments. And sparks fly in *Cowboy Boots and Glass Slippers* by Jodi O'Donnell when a modern-day Cinderella finally meets her match.

Rounding off the month, *Yours for Ninety Days* by Barbara McMahon is an evocative story about a mysterious loner who finds sweet solace with an enticing innocent. And an unlikely twosome find themselves altar-bound in *Pregnant & Practically Married* by Andrea Edwards— book three in the adorable THE BRIDAL CIRCLE miniseries.

Enjoy these unforgettable romances created *by* women like you, *for* women like you!

Sincerely,

Karen Taylor Richman
Senior Editor

Please address questions and book requests to:
Silhouette Reader Service
U.S.: 3010 Walden Ave., P.O. Box 1325, Buffalo, NY 14269
Canadian: P.O. Box 609, Fort Erie, Ont. L2A 5X3

BARBARA McMAHON

YOURS FOR NINETY DAYS

Silhouette®

SPECIAL EDITION®

Published by Silhouette Books

America's Publisher of Contemporary Romance

To Tina Colombo—for going the extra mile.
I'll never forget it.

With heartfelt thanks, this book is for you!

SILHOUETTE BOOKS

ISBN 0-373-24282-4

YOURS FOR NINETY DAYS

Copyright © 1999 by Barbara McMahon

This edition published by arrangement with Harlequin Books S.A.

® and TM are trademarks of Harlequin Books S.A., used under license.
Trademarks indicated with ® are registered in the United States Patent
and Trademark Office, the Canadian Trade Marks Office and in other
countries.

Visit us at www.romance.net

Printed in U.S.A.

BARBARA McMAHON

has made California her home since she graduated from the University of California (Berkeley) way back when! She's convinced she now has the perfect life, living on the western slopes of the Sierra Nevada, sipping lattes on her front porch while she watches the deer graze nearby and playing "what if" with different story ideas. Even though she has sold over three dozen books, she says she still has another hundred tales to tell. Barbara also writes for Harlequin Romance. Readers can write to Barbara at P.O. Box 977, Pioneer, California 95666-0977.

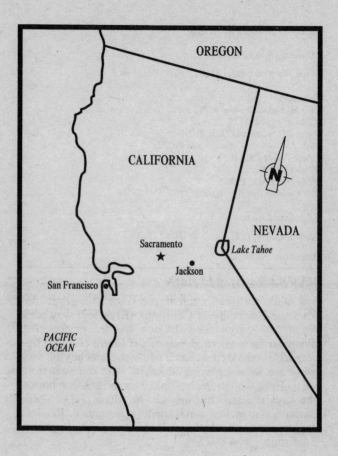

Chapter One

Ellie Winslow was definitely worried. She peered through the front window, checking the empty driveway once again. Still no sign of the deputy or her new guest. Glancing at her watch, she frowned. It was after four. No possible way they could join the others. Well, that couldn't be helped now. Why were they so late? She'd expected them around noon. Had there been an accident? No, she would have been notified.

The delay gave her time to get a few more accounts brought up to date. She'd much rather be outside with the others, moving the small herd of cattle from the lower winter pastures to the higher, summer fields. Riding, feeling the sun on her face. Joining in on the wisecracking and smart-mouthed remarks the boys delighted in making.

She and her new guest should have been there with them! She had planned the weekend that way—to ease him into the routine, to meet the others in an informal manner, to have a chance to relax. All her plans were shot to bits, now.

The worry mingled with her jitters—which was nothing new. She always seemed nervous with the arrival of each new guest. She considered it a kind of stage fright. Surely she knew what she was doing after fourteen guests.

Providing help to those that needed it, wasn't that the entire purpose of Helping Hands? To provide youthful first offenders a second chance? To provide the kind of help that her brother Bobby had never found?

For a moment the old anguish surfaced. She tried to damp it down. Regrets would change nothing. The past, with all its sorrow and pain, was gone. She'd been much too young to make a difference back then.

Now she did the best she could to offer alternatives, helping others the way Bobby should have been helped. If she had let nerves stop her, where would Pete and Manuel be today? Or Carrie? Or Trisha and Consuela? Or the others? She was making a difference—had in fourteen young lives thus far.

She raised her head straining to hear. Was that a car?

Dashing into the living room, she peered out the front window. Yes, the sheriff's emblem blazed on the side of the white cruiser. Finally.

Ellie took a deep breath and hurried out the door.

"Miss Winslow? I'm Deputy Carmichael. I believe you're expecting us." The rumpled deputy sheriff's uniform showed the effects of the heat of the day as the man climbed from the car. He stepped up to the porch and held out a sheaf of papers.

Ellie nodded. "Yes, I'm Ellie Winslow." She smiled and reached for the familiar forms, scanning the transfer papers. They appeared in order. She scrawled her name at the bottom of the transfer form to acknowledge the arrival of her guest and handed the sheets back to the deputy.

She peered around him to the patrol car. The windows were tinted, so she couldn't see her new guest.

"Y'all are several hours later than I expected. Did you

have car trouble?'' she asked as she waited impatiently while he tore off the top sheet and handed it back.

"Yeah, flat tire on my way there,'' the deputy answered. Ellie skimmed across the papers again. Nicholas Tanner, she read. Briefly scanning the pages she noted the conviction had been for accessory to embezzlement. White-collar crime, she mused. Would he fit in with the others?

While the deputy sauntered to the car, Ellie continued to read the summary report on the referral sheet which gave her the name of her new guest and how long he was required to stay at her place: three months. At the end of three months, his prison term would be over and he would be free to go wherever he wanted. Until then, he was under a kind of house arrest at her place.

And it was up to her to make sure his transition back into society went smoothly. To give him the maximum chance to succeed.

She'd known this program was something she had to do from the first time she'd heard about Helping Hands at her church, which was one of the sponsors. She'd been selected as soon as she'd applied. There were never enough volunteers. She was happy to be able to give back a part of what she had so much of—now. And only sometimes did she rail against fate for bringing the solution too late to help her brother.

Nick Tanner sat stiffly in the back of the hot patrol car. Since stopping, the air conditioner had been off and the sun blazed down on the car. The least the deputy could have done was roll down a window. He held tightly on to his control as if the tension coiled within him could act as an impenetrable barrier, shutting out the hellish memories of the past three years.

Outwardly he appeared calm, controlled. He'd perfected that demeanor over those years. He had sat without moving for the entire trip, staring straight ahead. Ignoring the attempts at conversation from the deputy, he focused on the knowledge that he was finally out. Bars and concrete floors and arbitrary rules and regulations were behind him. His throat ached and he swallowed hard, his heart pounded heavily.

No matter what it took, he was never going back. He'd bow and scrape and promise anything before he'd ever be sent back. It had been a shocking, wretched, endless three years. Dark anger flared when he thought about it, if he let himself think about it. Best not to dwell on it, that never got him anywhere. It was over. Or would be in three more months.

He didn't know what to expect from this work furlough program. He hadn't thought beyond getting out. His profession was lost to him. He'd stupidly seen to that. And the woman he thought he'd loved hadn't been whom he'd thought she was. Everything had changed. Nothing would ever be the same.

He'd never trust another soul. He learned that the hard way first from Sheila, then from being incarcerated. He was truly on his own. The only one he knew he could depend upon was himself.

He looked out the window. The deputy blocked his view of the woman who had come from the house. Now he turned and headed for the car. Opening the door, he motioned for Nick to get out.

Nick did so with as much dignity and pride as he could muster. His gut, his hands clenched once, then he forced himself to relax. He didn't like the cynical look in the deputy's eye, but he'd had years of practice hiding his emotions. In only three months he'd be a free man. Able to go anywhere, do anything. Rebuild his life. He could summon the patience needed to get him through.

Nick stared at the woman who would be his jailer for the next three months. He hadn't given much thought to her or the others on the ranch when told of his pending release. He hadn't cared a lick—his only thought had been what he'd be leaving behind. And he couldn't get out fast enough.

He found himself surprised at how small the woman seemed, actually petite. Her eyes were bright-blue behind blue-framed glasses. They stared at him almost apprehensively. Her honey-colored hair scraped back in some sort of ponytail at the nape of her neck looked hot and heavy on her slender frame. She wore faded jeans, not particularly stylish, and a plain white shirt that looked as if it belonged to her older brother, or father. While she had a trim figure, it was not one to lose any sleep over, Nick thought.

His eyes skimmed down her again and he reconsidered. She was the first woman he'd seen in almost three years. Maybe he'd lose some sleep after all. She looked to be in her late twenties—and scared to death. He glimpsed the uncertainty in her eyes, her beseeching look at the deputy. Maybe she was the daughter of the place and her parents ran the ranch. That made sense.

For a moment a gut-wrenching pain hit. She wasn't afraid of him, was she? His lips tightened. He didn't want anyone *afraid* of him. He thought that by doing his time, he'd paid his debt and could move on. Maybe he'd been wrong.

Ellie watched as the deputy opened the back door and ordered the man from the car. Her new guest reached back inside the car and drew out a duffel bag.

The man straightened and frowned at something Deputy Carmichael said but he refrained from speaking, merely nodding.

Ellie held her breath, her eyes wide in startled surprise as she looked at her newest guest. Standing almost arrogantly beside the deputy, he topped the older man by several inches. His feet firmly planted on the dusty ground, one hand holding that packed duffel as if it weighted nothing, he turned, his eyes sweeping the front of the house. His gaze settled on her. With an impassive expression he stared at her through steel-grey eyes, narrowed as if assessing what he saw. His jaw was firm, his lips tight.

There must be some mistake, Ellie thought, dismayed, unable to drag her eyes away from his piercing gaze. This was not some cocky young teenager she'd expected. This was not some confused young boy of eighteen or nineteen needing a helping hand like the others, needing assistance to ease the transition from prison back to the real world. To be given a chance to learn something new, make a difference in his life before going out on his own.

Instead, she looked at a tall, self-contained man who appeared to be in his early thirties. And who from the looks of him knew all there was about the real world and then some. He could probably teach her a few things, and still come out ahead.

Tentatively she tried a smile, hoping her dismay didn't show. Something was wrong. She was to be assigned a young man, a teenager, not this…*this very male adult.*

Her heart began to pound as he continued to stare at her through those disturbing grey eyes. Ellie felt tendrils of awareness slowly seep through her body. She had never been so physically conscious of a member of the opposite gender before. Not even Dr. Merrill when she'd had such a crush on him. Breathing grew more difficult, and a small curl of fire and unexpected excitement built deep within her.

Aghast at her reaction, she dragged her gaze away, looking in near panic at the papers in her hand. Quickly she read the first section again. The age line had been left blank!

The deputy indicated Nick should head toward the porch. Ellie swallowed hard, her thoughts spinning. She wasn't prepared to deal with this! She'd been expecting a much younger man.

"Deputy, I think there's been a mistake," she called tentatively.

"Mistake, ma'am? I don't think so," the deputy said. "You got all the paperwork, if there's a problem, you have to take it up with your own coordinator. My job is just to deliver him." He looked at Nick then back at Ellie and shrugged. "I've done my part."

He nodded once and returned to the patrol car. Before she could formulate an argument, he climbed inside and quickly drove away, spraying dirt and gravel from the drive as he accelerated.

Ellie tilted her chin, trying to look poised and assured, hoping the frantic beat of her heart wasn't evident. Whatever was wrong, it was too late to fix today. She took a deep breath, doubts rising, but she ignored them, smiling tentatively at the man before her.

"Nicholas Tanner. I'm Ellie Winslow. How do you do? Welcome to the Lazy K Ranch."

She offered her hand. She noticed that he hesitated a second, then he stepped close enough to shake briefly, dropping his gaze to their linked grip. Then up to her face. Ellie almost yanked her hand away in shock. His hand felt hard, callused, and his touch sent spiraling tingles along her arm. She turned away, visibly squaring her shoulders, hoping he didn't notice her reaction. What was wrong with her? Nerves?

"What mistake?" Nick asked.

His voice was deep and dark. Ellie hesitated when hearing it. Was there a trace of the south in his own spoken words?

"Helping Hands is for youthful first offenders. I think you're over the age limit," she said heading for the door. Biting her lip, she wondered how to handle this turn of events. The deputy had been no help. And the offices were closed on Saturdays. She'd have to wait until Monday to straighten things out.

"What's the age limit?" he asked, stepping after her. "There was no mention of age limit when I applied." His voice was hard.

For a moment, Ellie felt a hint of intimidation. Deliberate on his part? That she wouldn't put up with. She straightened as tall as her frame would allow.

"Let's get one thing straight from the get-go, Mr. Tanner. I run this place and I make the rules."

"As you go along?"

"No. They're written down." She felt her ground slipping beneath her. Had there been an upper age limit? "But I'm set up to deal with teenagers, not older men."

"Thirty-two is not that old. I'm a first offender. The counselor at the prison made no mention of an age limit."

"You're years older than the others here."

"Others?"

"I have four others in the transition stage, two girls and two boys. They're all within a few months of being the same age, nineteen. That makes you more than a decade older."

She tried to keep her emotions level, even. Tried to take charge of the situation that seemed to be spinning beyond her control. Nick Tanner was not like the others staying with her. Nor was her reaction. She'd never felt like this before. He filled her vision, tall and rugged. While she might feel some affection for her temporary charges, she'd never felt this gut-level physical awareness!

She caught her breath, dragging in the scent of him, light and tangy, and utterly male. Overwhelmed by his flagrant masculinity, conscious of him as she'd never been around other men, she stepped back. Magnetic, disturbing, blatantly virile, he radiated a curious leashed energy. She took a shaky breath, her mind going blank. She wasn't afraid of the man—but she began to fear her own reactions. What was wrong with her today?

"This entire program is geared for troubled young people,'' Ellie said. ''Part of what we do is work toward finding jobs, by teaching new skills. Some of our participants don't even have a high school diploma, so we work on schooling. You're old enough to know how to live, how to shop for food, clothes, a place to live. Why did you even apply for the program?''

''To get out.''

''Oh.'' He was honest at least. Then she frowned. Not totally honest or he wouldn't have been in prison.

She forced herself to concentrate on the problem at hand, trying to ignore her awareness of the proximity of his muscular jean-clad legs only inches from her own, of his broad shoulders which seemed to be a yard wide, of the easy way he held the heavy, sagging duffel. The slight breeze tossed his hair and Ellie found herself instantly curious about how it would feel beneath her fingertips. Shocked at the wayward thought, she schooled her features, desperately hoping nothing of her reflections showed in her expression. What was the matter with her? She'd seen good-looking men before and never been so affected.

It had to be first-day jitters, nothing more. She'd been successful at this many times before. If she let him stay, this time would prove the same. Though she had doubts when she wondered how she'd get through the program if every thought revolved around touching his hair, or more.

He gazed over the open fields. What was he thinking? The dark-green of the live oak that dotted the hillsides was the only break in the golden-brown color, except for the deep-blue sky. Late spring in California meant there wouldn't be any rain until fall. The green winter grass had dried and turned golden. Excellent fodder for cattle. And beautiful in its own way.

Would he find the same fascination with the place she had when she'd first found out about it five years ago? Inheriting the ranch had been the catalyst that moved her to join Helping Hands.

Her initial training had whirled by. Pete Concannon and Manuel Lopez had been her first guests. Both had six months left on their sentences. They'd been a handful. Without the help of Gus, her foreman, and Gus's wife, Alberta, who was the cook, she might never have managed. But now, four years into the program, she thought with pride, it grew easier with each new arrival.

Pete now worked on a ranch near Redding, went to church on Sundays and was dating a nice young girl. He still called once in a while just to check in.

Manuel Lopez had been more difficult, a real challenge. A Latin charmer who caused Ellie to wonder if he'd ever leave, even after his sentence was complete. But he was settled now, working as a veterinary assistant in Davis. He planned to start at the university in the fall and train to become a vet—a far cry from robbing liquor stores.

Even before her first two guests had left, she'd taken in more. A maximum of five—the most she felt she could handle at any one time.

Nick would be the fifth of the current guests.

His room was ready. She'd spoken to people in town who would be willing to help with appropriate job opportunities depending on her guest's interests. The other guests knew of his planned arrival.

Only, she hadn't expected a grown man. She expected a teenager.

Nick drew in a breath and wondered how long it would take for the woman to make up her mind. The hot smell of drying grass assailed him—infinitely sweeter than prison air. The wide spaces and openness already began to ease some of his tension. If she was serious about this being a mistake, he had to find some way to convince her to let him stay.

Awareness of Ellie Winslow gradually increased despite his efforts to ignore her. Her scent mingled with the dry grass, a soft fragrance like a bouquet of spring flowers. Her hands were those of a worker, brown and callused, yet small and delicate. Odd that she held his future in those hands. He wondered how someone so petite successfully ran a cattle ranch. How much help did she have? He was surprised to find for the first time in years he was curious about someone else.

What did she get out of the program? He knew that no one did anything unless they got something out of it for themselves. Any idealistic dreams he'd once had ended when reality struck.

Nick grew uncomfortable with the delay. She seemed to be arguing with herself, glancing back to the papers and skimming across them as if looking for an answer. Or an out.

Nick counted the seconds ticking by. She needed to make a decision. With the deputy gone, it had to be harder to kick him out. There was nothing she could do before Monday—by then he could convince her to let him stay.

Finally, she looked up at him.

"Come with me. I'll show you your room."

Relief swept through him like hot fire. He almost sagged with it. But he kept his expression neutral. He'd become good at that. It had been the only way to survive these last years. Keeping a distance, he followed her into the house.

The place needed a lot of work. That was obvious even from the outside. Yet it appeared solidly built. Huge, it must have a dozen rooms or more. He followed Ellie as she bypassed wide wooden stairs that led to the second story and headed for the back of the house. Doors opened from the hall into large rooms. Their footsteps echoed on the wooden floor. Rugs or carpets would soften the sound, but he saw no signs of any.

The kitchen appeared bright and airy with large windows over the sink which overlooked the yard. A round, worn oak table stood in the center, four chairs circling it. The sink looked new, as did the appliances, but the scuffed and uneven floor showed its age. A bright red barn rose behind the house. Obviously new. Nick wondered why she poured money into a barn when the house needed so much work.

As he followed her, Nick allowed himself to begin to relax. He was relieved she hadn't crossed-examined him endlessly. He suspected that would come later, but in the meantime he could almost pretend he was a boarder in a rooming house. Not that he'd ever been a boarder any-where. His family would have a fit to even consider such a thing.

Of course they would have an even a greater fit if they knew where he'd been the last few years. They thought he'd been too busy to come for a visit. With the help of a couple of friends, he'd made sure the news of his arrest had never traveled back east. Answering machines, call for-warding and other technological inventions perpetuated the image even after he'd been convicted. He wondered if he'd ever make a trip home now. Prison changed a man. And he didn't want his family to see that change, and know.

A large German shepherd dog scratched at the back screen door, tail wagging.

Ellie crossed to the door and hesitated, turning to Nick. "This is my dog, Tam. Are you afraid of dogs?"

Nick shook his head.

She opened the door and the big dog bounded inside, dancing around Ellie as she fussed over him, then darting across the room to Nick. His tail whipped back and forth as he greeted the stranger.

"He's really quite nice, though don't tell any burglars that."

She blushed when she realized what she'd said. "I'm sorry," she murmured, clearly mortified at her slip.

A glimmer of a smile touched Nick's eyes as he looked at the dog.

"I won't tell a soul."

Nick held his hand out to let Tam sniff, then slowly scratched the dog's ears while he looked around.

"Your room is here, off the kitchen," Ellie said as she opened a door to a large bedroom, with its own bath beyond. "It's all yours. I won't come in. You'll have to take care of it yourself, but that way you'll know you have total privacy. If you wish, you can move to the bunkhouse in a week. That's where the other two boys are staying. For the first week, male guests stay here. The girls have rooms upstairs with me. The upper level is off-limits for men."

Nick passed her and paused at the door. The room had a high ceiling and two tall double-hung windows on the back wall, he noticed. A queen-size bed with carved oak headboard dominated the room; against the wall to the right was an oak dresser, a chair and a nightstand. A colorful braided rug covered the hardwood floor while various watercolors adorned the walls. Through an opened door he glimpsed a bathroom. The color scheme of blue and brown appealed to him.

Ellie pointed to the front of the house. "We passed the dining room, where we eat most of our meals. I have a cook, but she's out on the mustering now. We also passed the parlor and TV room. Use them whenever you wish. If you need anything, towels, soap, whatever, let me know. This will be your home for the next three months."

Nick nodded, setting his duffel down. He reached for the door and glanced at the knob.

"No lock?" he murmured, his eyes clashing with hers as he raised an eyebrow in question.

"You're perfectly safe here, Mr. Tanner. I said I would not trespass. None of the others will, either. We all respect each other's privacy," Ellie replied primly, tilting her chin slightly.

Nick's head jerked up in surprised amusement. "I meant for me to be locked in at night, not to lock you out."

"We don't lock people in here, Mr. Tanner. The screening process ensures we aren't matched with dangerous or violent offenders. You could walk away at any time, but I hope you won't."

He stared at her thoughtfully. Then nodded. "Since I'll be here for a while, could we dispense with Mister and Ms. and go to first names? I'm Nick," he said.

"Of course. I'm Ellie."

She should have suggested it—she was supposed to be guiding him. And everyone on the ranch used first names. How could she have forgotten?

Or had she been trying to keep the more formal Mr. Tanner appellation in hopes it would keep a distance between them?

He nodded, looked around, tense and uneasy. *Why,* she discovered with sudden insight as he closed the door, *he's nervous, too.* Just like the others had been when they first arrived. Of course most of them also came with a chip on their shoulder the size of a redwood, but that gradually wore off. Once they were comfortable at the ranch, her guests began the task of changing to fit in.

Would Nick ever fit in? He seemed totally different from anyone she'd expected. And she wasn't sure she liked his being here. First thing on Monday, she'd call Alan Peters at Helping Hands to discuss the situation with him.

She rubbed her forehead. It was getting late. She had to feed the animals and see to fixing something for supper. "I'll have some lemonade on the front porch in a half hour, if you want some," she called as she left the kitchen. Normally the chores were the tasks of her guests, but she didn't mind doing them tonight. With most of the horses gone, feeding the few that remained was a snap. The chickens, ducks and pig were easy.

Finished in no time, Ellie prepared fresh lemonade and headed for the front porch.

She'd hung a big wooden swing on the wide front porch

right after she'd moved in and her greatest pleasure was to sit there in the late afternoon and watch the activity around her small ranch. Sometimes one or more of her guests joined her. Or Alberta sat for a while discussing meals and gossip from town. Even after five years, Ellie still marveled at her good fortune in inheriting the place.

But the small, familiar pang about her brother Bobby hit again. So much, but so late.

Chapter Two

Ellie had finished half her lemonade when Nick pushed open the screen door and paused in the doorway.

She pointed to the pitcher and second glass. "Help yourself."

"Thanks, it sounded good." It had been a long time since he'd had fresh-made lemonade. He poured the cold, tart liquid into his glass then glanced around for a chair. None in sight, only the swing or the railing. Sitting gingerly beside her, he carefully left a lot of room between them.

Silently they moved to and fro, sipping the refreshing beverage, eyes on the distant hills.

"How big is the ranch?" Nick asked, curious about the setup and his hostess. He'd been told what to expect for himself, but not about the people he'd be living with for three months. Who was Ellie Winslow? How did she wind up volunteering for the program? How many people were involved? Was she divorced? Widowed? He glanced at her hand—no ring.

"About a thousand acres deeded land. We also graze cattle on BLM land—Bureau of Land Management—government owned."

"Has it always been in your family?" Nick could see the house was old and in need of some serious work. While his room was fresh and newly decorated, the hallway and stairs needed attention. It looked as if the outside hadn't been painted in decades.

"I inherited it a few years ago. Before that I didn't know it existed. It's wonderful, isn't it?" she said softly.

Nick looked at her, wondering at her apparent delight in a place that needed so much. A place located far from a city, from stores and theaters. Her blue eyes seemed to shine, and soft color stole into her cheeks. She looked almost pretty when she smiled. Nick felt a tightening inside and turned away. He didn't want to feel anything. He'd put in his three months, follow the rules of the place and then leave.

"There's still oodles to do yet," she said. "I'm taking one project at a time. We did the barn first, so I could house the animals. Then we renovated the bunkhouse. The bedrooms and kitchen came next. By the end of next year, I hope to have the house completely redone. Then we can concentrate on building the herd."

"Why are you in Helping Hands?" He needed to know what her motives were. He liked things orderly. And she was difficult to place, different from the women he was used to. Different from Sheila. Or was she just good at hiding her true colors? Sheila had been an expert. Would Ellie Winslow lie, too? Or have some convincing tale that sounded good?

Ellie's gaze dropped to the glass in her hand. She watched as the ice swirled around when she tipped the glass this way and that. The ranch had belonged to her father and during all those years she'd cared for him he'd never mentioned it. All that time it had sat here, a refuge for

Bobby, for her and she'd never known about it. So much wasted time and opportunities. Could she explain about her brother? She didn't as a rule talk about Bobby. Or her father. Or anything that happened before she moved to the ranch. Did she even know why she felt so strongly she had to do this? Would Nick understand why she hadn't just hidden away, worked on her paintings and ignored the rest of the world?

"Let's just say for now that I have strong reasons and am blessed with a way to help. To make a difference in young lives."

"You make it sound like you've been doing this for decades. You look pretty young to me," he said, wondering how old she was. The glasses and hairstyle did nothing to enhance her looks. But she had traces of real beauty. Especially her eyes. They were expressive behind those glasses. He'd like to see her when she wasn't wearing glasses.

"I'll be thirty-two in a few months. You are my fifteenth guest."

"Hardly ready for the old folks home," he answered, suddenly not wanting to be drawn into a personal discussion with her, not wanting to learn more about her or the damn program. She would be the same age as he. It gave them a bond that he didn't want to explore. He was a loner now. He'd chosen to stay away from people he knew, to find a new line of work, and avoid problems that any kind of relationship caused.

Restless energy filled him, threatening to spill out. He rose to his feet, draining his glass.

"I'm going for a walk." It wasn't a question, but he paused as if awaiting an answer. Or permission.

"Fine." Ellie's voice was soft. She checked her watch. "I plan on supper at six-thirty, if you're not back by then, I'll hold yours."

She kept silent as he strode off down the driveway, heading for the quiet country road. Tam stood, his attention on Nick until Ellie touched his shoulder.

"Go Tam, go with him. Walk."

The dog needed no further urging, but tore off after Nick, catching up and settling down to a slow trot, sniffing the grass at the side of the drive, darting back and forth.

Puffs of dust rose with each step. Nick noted his shoes would be covered by the time he reached the road, but he didn't care. For the first time in years he was free. The big dog caught up with him, prancing alongside. Nick smiled, a small triumph for his first day. He could go anywhere, do anything he wanted. As long as he lived here for the next three months. For now the walk was enough. He glanced back but didn't see Ellie. He was truly on his own and it felt glorious.

Turning onto the country road, he stretched out his legs and picked up his pace. He wanted the exercise. And to taste the freedom of choice.

She had let him go without a protest.

He looked at the deep-blue sky overhead, the golden hills gently rising around him. In the distance, he could see the tips of the mountains still covered with snow. But there were no other houses in sight, no cars. He was truly alone. What a difference from prison. From his place in San Francisco.

Yet this had been what he'd requested. He couldn't go back. There was nothing about his old life he could return to. Better to change everything and go forward. His pace increased as he stretched out his legs, drew in the hot dry air. He picked up his speed until he was running.

Ellie watched Nick and Tam head up the quiet country road. If it had not been so late, they could have taken the truck to the meadow where the rest of the crew planned to spend the night. But the only way to get where they would be camping was cross-country and she didn't relish driving when the shadows were so deep she couldn't tell a rut from a ravine.

They'd stay home tonight, eat here. She would explain the routine and rules and let him meet the gang tomorrow. Rising, she gathered their glasses and headed for the kitchen wondering what to do about dinner. It was almost six. Would Nick return soon? Should she wait, or start cooking?

For an instant, she faltered. What if he just kept going? What would she do in a case like that? She'd never had a guest skip out on her before. But then, she'd never had a guest like Nick before. He didn't appear to need anyone or anything. He could definitely cope in the outside world without any assistance.

Which made him quite different from her usual assignments. Dangerously different? Only to her own peace of mind.

A quick knock sounded on the screen door some time later. Nick opened it, stepping inside. Tam came bounding in beside him.

"Hi, fellow, did y'all have a good walk?" Ellie leaned over to ruffle the fur around Tam's neck, smiling up at her guest, trying not to notice how his eyes seemed to look deep into her soul. She constantly felt as if he were assessing her. Did she come up wanting? Flustered, she cleared her throat.

"Nick, this is your home while you're here. No need to knock or anything. At night we lock up. But that's after bedtime. During the day I don't lock up. There's no crime around here and with Tam and all…"

She'd done it again. How could she keep harping on crime? She hadn't mentioned it around her other guests on their first days. It was the last thing Nick needed to hear. Flushing slightly in embarrassment, feeling awkward, she hoped he'd attribute her heightened color to leaning over the dog. She pushed her glasses back in place and stood.

Nick moved near the sink and leaned against the counter, folding his arms across his chest. He gazed at her as if she were an intriguing puzzle he could solve if he studied her long enough. His staring kept Ellie on edge and she didn't like the feeling.

"Do I help with dinner?" he asked as Ellie opened the refrigerator.

"Dinner tonight could be a small problem. I thought we'd be eating with the others, so didn't really plan a meal. Since I thought you'd be younger, I mean, I thought my new guest would be younger..." She took a deep breath. "I could always throw together some hamburgers—not the most nutritious meal for your first night. But Alberta is a much better cook than I am. She has a mothering instinct."

He tilted his head to one side. "Is that something you're trying for? The reason you pull back your hair to make you look older? Wear no makeup, and dowdy clothes?" he asked. "To give an impression of being someone's mother?"

"Actually I always dress this way." She turned back to the refrigerator, trying not to let his words hurt. Did she look so awful? Her hair hung heavy down her back, but it was neat and tidy. And who had time, or the inclination, for makeup when dust and perspiration would only make it run?

Still, his words wounded.

Ellie knew she wasn't pretty, but no one had ever told her in so many words before. And it especially hurt that the drop-dead gorgeous male standing in her kitchen had said it. She took a deep breath, eyes staring blindly into the refrigerator. What was she doing?

"I have all the fixings for hamburgers, fries and milk shakes. But I don't know, would you rather have ham or roast beef? I can warm up something quickly," she said, proud her voice remained steady. She wasn't here to interest some man. It didn't matter what he thought about how she looked.

Nick moved away from the counter and came to stand beside her. His hands gently touched her shoulder and he turned her to face him, his finger lifting her chin so he could see her eyes. "I didn't mean to hurt your feelings, Ellie Winslow. I appreciate the opportunity to be here. I'll make it work, you can count on that. And I'd love a hamburger and fries." His voice was soft, deep and as sweet to Ellie's ears as honey.

She nodded, the heat from his finger spiraling through her just like earlier that afternoon when he'd taken her hand.

Stepping away, breaking contact, she took a deep breath. Ignoring the pounding of her heart, she turned back to the open refrigerator. She spied a bottle in the back.

"Oh, I have a small bottle of sparkling cider. We could celebrate the start of your new life. Would you care for any?" Her voice came out breathless, and she refused to look over her shoulder at him. She didn't keep alcohol on the premises, but they usually made a fuss to celebrate a new guest's first day of freedom.

"That would be good."

Ellie heard the note of sincerity and was glad she'd remembered the dark-green bottle. She found glasses and filled two before she began to cook.

"To your future success, Nick." Ellie offered a toast.

"May they all be honest ones," he replied wickedly.

Ellie choked on her sip, and burst out laughing. So much for the concern about watching her tongue.

"Nick, how awful!" She relaxed at last. Maybe it wouldn't be so bad after all. She'd been awkward around Pete and Manuel at first, she remembered. And absolutely floored when Trisha had arrived. But she'd never felt as

self-conscious around them as she did around Nick. Never
so aware of herself as a woman. Of vague yearnings...

Stop it! she admonished herself. He was no different
from the other guests.

Liar, a small voice whispered.

He chuckled at her amusement, then paused, looking at
her in surprise.

"That's the first laugh I've had in a long time," he said
slowly in dawning awareness.

"I've been worried to death every time I open my mouth
that I'll say something to embarrass you," Ellie admitted,
testing the tentative rapport she sensed.

"You would have already if I'd been a burglar," he
teased.

Ellie swallowed hard at his look. His eyes had softened
to silver, his grin was a trifle lopsided, as if rusty. She felt
her insides begin to melt. She'd already thought him gorgeous,
but with that smile he looked terrific! Did he have
a clue what his smile did? He should come with a warning
label.

"It's harder than I expected. I don't want to say anything
that will offend you, so if I do, just tell me," Ellie said
turning back to get out the meat. It was past time to start
cooking if they wanted to eat any time soon.

By the time dinner was over, Ellie grew confident Nick's
visit would become as successful as any of her other
guests'. He ate everything she put before him, asked questions
about the ranch, listened carefully to her review of
the rules and explanation of assignments. And he even
helped with the dishes.

When she'd put the last glass away, Ellie suggested coffee
on the porch, although it was already growing dark.
The temperature had dropped and the evening air felt cool
and pleasant—refreshing after the heat of the day. A brief
time outdoors before retiring always helped her sleep.

They sat in silence in the growing twilight, the only illumination that which spilled through the tall windows from the living room lamp. The hills blended into a muted silhouette as the light faded from the sky, stark trees outlined on the horizon. There was a hush across the land while the birds and animals settled in for the night.

Gently Ellie set the swing in motion, sipping her coffee. She was physically aware of Nick's sitting close to her. His shoulder only a few inches away. His long legs stretched out, bending and flexing as the swing moved back and forth.

She frowned, afraid to look his way. This was madness. She couldn't be attracted to her guest—she was here to help him, to be a kind of mentor, not develop some kind of romantic fascination.

"Where are you from, Ellie?" Nick asked. "Not California. The south somewhere, obviously."

"The great state of Georgia, suh," she drawled, making the words stretch to several syllables each. "Though not recently," Ellie said in a more normal tone.

"Lived in California long, then?"

"Almost twenty years. It was so long ago when I left Georgia that I can scarcely remember it. I had just started middle school."

"So how did a Georgia cracker come to California?"

"My mama died," she said flatly, staring off to the dark hills. "My father and she divorced when I was a baby. I never met him before coming west."

"That's tough."

"It wasn't easy." And that was all she had to say. The words so commonplace, reflecting none of the turmoil she'd experienced. None of the bewilderment when her Aunt Caroline had put her on a plane and said goodbye. None of the desolation she'd felt when first moving in with her father. And reflecting none of the joy of her brief time with Bobby.

Ellie remained quiet. It had been years since she'd

thought of her mama. She'd been only a few years older than Ellie was now when she'd died. It was a shock to realize she'd been gone for almost two decades.

"Do you ever go back? To visit?" Nick asked.

"Nope." Ellie stopped thinking about her past. It was best forgotten. "How about you? I hear a trace of the south in your speech. Where are you from?"

"I'm from the East Coast, too—Maryland. I came to California for graduate school at Stanford. Got a job in San Francisco after that."

And then went to prison, she finished silently. What had happened? And, how had he ended up this program? With a college degree—and a graduate degree—he didn't need Helping Hands. But he'd signed up for it. Why? Just for an early release? Or did he truly want a new start?

"Tomorrow we need to map out a strategy for your time here," she said.

"Such as?" he asked cautiously.

"What kind of job you want, how to look for a job, get some clothes, all sorts of things," she said briskly.

"Not yet," he murmured.

"What?" She tried to see him in the dim light, but could only make out his silhouette.

"I'd like a little time just to get used to being out, being free again."

That sounded reasonable, Ellie conceded. It was a big change. A few days couldn't hurt, though the program urged immediacy. He could start out with chores around the place, get to know the others.

"We'll plan on making plans." She frowned. She was the one supposed to make the decisions—why did she suddenly feel he was taking charge? Maybe she wasn't forceful enough for this kind of work. *Or against this kind of man?* She hadn't had any trouble dealing with the others. Had become quite adept actually, in getting them to go along with her plans. But the others were younger, and looking for a fresh start. Nick was not in the same league by a long shot.

"Have you always been a rancher? Why did you agree to sponsor people in Helping Hands?" Nick's curiosity had not been satisfied. Just what did she get out of all this? What was her angle? He knew she had to have one—everybody did. No one did things that didn't get them something they wanted. Only, he couldn't figure out hers. He didn't see any big payoff in taking prisoners. The place was falling apart. Her clothes were clean and neat, but certainly not stylish.

"I've only been ranching for five years. My primary income comes from illustrating children's books. My friend Margot and I are a team. She writes them, I illustrate. We've done more than two dozen. You'll see my work all over the place."

"The watercolors in the bedroom are yours?" he asked.

"Yes. Those I did for fun. They aren't in any books."

"I like them. They're restful, pleasing to the eye." The various paintings were done in shades of blue. They were different from what he thought of as watercolors—bolder, dramatic. Unexpected. Like his hostess.

"But why are you involved in Helping Hands?" he persisted.

"I told you, so I can make a difference."

"Most people have a personal investment when they do something," he countered.

"Is that what you think?"

"That's what I know."

"Umm, maybe. But in this, I just want to help."

He looked out over the darkening landscape. The hills showed nothing but grass and a few trees. He hadn't seen the cattle she spoke of. It seemed a lonely place. He wondered why she lived so far away from a town. Didn't she miss the advantages of a city?

"Do you ever get lonely here?" he asked, curiosity rising again despite his vow to keep a distance.

"How could I? Normally this place is teaming with activity. I have a foreman and two cowhands. A cook. And my guests. Margot comes by several times a week to work. There's too much going on to get lonely."

Ellie glanced at Nick. "I lived with my father until he died five years ago. He was chronically ill with crippling arthritis and then Alzheimer's—needed constant care. I didn't really have much chance to do a lot when he was alive." Purposefully keeping quiet about how domineering the man had been, how demanding, she thrust the memory of those years away. They were gone forever and she was free.

"Upon his death I inherited this place. It requires a lot of work, so who has time to miss anything?"

Nick listened for more. Something was missing. The tone of her voice was careful, deliberate.

Her summary was brief, leaving out details. Had she ever married? Did she have any children? Want any? He thought briefly of his sisters. Both had married young—their children were already in school. He'd missed three years of their lives. And would probably miss a lot more. He had no plans to return to Maryland. He could imagine how appalled his family would be if they ever learned where he'd been during the past three years.

When Ellie rose and said good-night Nick remained on the swing, still savoring the feeling of freedom. What would happen if he just walked down the driveway and kept going? Would the sheriff be called? Or could he just disappear and never be found?

There were only three months left.

Once Nick went to his room, Ellie slipped back downstairs to lock up the old house. She took a book to sleep. Keyed up from the day's events she needed something to make her drowsy enough to sleep, and to forget about her new guest. Had he gone right to bed? Or was he lying in the dark savoring the difference from prison? She wondered what he thought about on his first night of freedom. Was he glad he'd come to the ranch? Or did he wish he'd gone straight back to San Francisco? What would his future hold?

She drifted to sleep with the light still on, the forgotten book in her hand, thinking about her newest guest no matter how hard she tried not to.

A soft rap at her door brought Ellie instantly awake. Nick thrust it open and stood in the frame, tall and dark, fully dressed. His eyes glittered in the light. For a shocked moment panic washed through Ellie as she raised up on one arm. What did he want? Why was he here in her room? She had told him men weren't allowed on the second floor. Especially when she was alone in the house. The nearest neighbor lived miles away. The rest of the ranch crew was now high in the hills. For the first time she was conscious of the isolation of the ranch.

Throwing a quick glance at her clock she saw it was 3:00 a.m.

"Nick, what is it?" Ellie took a deep breath, resisting the strong temptation to draw the covers to her neck. Gripping the edge of the sheet tightly, she tried to remain calm. Her heart began to race.

Nonsense, she told herself, the guests in the program were not violent offenders. They'd all been carefully screened before being accepted. She had nothing to fear. Anyway, Tam would protect her.

Maybe, she amended as the dog leaped up from the rug beside her bed, tail wagging to greet his new friend.

"Sorry, I saw the light beneath the door and thought you were awake. Do you always sleep with the light on?" He stared down at her in the big bed, yet saw the entire room from the corner of his eye. Totally feminine, with lacy white curtains at the window and dainty French provincial furnishings, he felt as out of place here as he had in a cell. His gaze remained on Ellie. Her cheeks were rosy from sleep, her eyes a deep-blue. Her hair swirled like a cloud around her face, down her shoulders. It was almost too much hair for her small frame. But it looked silky soft and tantalizing. Nick felt the stirring of attraction. It had been a long time since he'd wanted a woman. And she was infinitely appealing with that pink gown that so clearly left her arms bare, her skin gleaming like ivory in the lamplight.

Ellie shook her head, eyes wide with uncertainty until she saw the book across her legs. "I guess I fell asleep reading."

"I didn't mean to wake you. I know you don't want men on this floor. But the other girls aren't here and I did think you were up. I heard something in the yard. Not knowing the set-up here, I didn't know if you could have a fox in the henhouse."

"Good grief." Ellie pushed back the covers and stood, snatching her robe from the nearby chair. "Probably a coyote. We're bothered with them from time to time."

"The chickens are squawking. I couldn't see anything in the yard. Is there a light out there?"

She nodded as she looked at him. "You're dressed."

"Haven't gone to bed yet," he stated.

"It's the middle of the night," she said, hurrying down the wide stairs. In seconds, she was through the kitchen and she switched on the outside lights. Ellie flung open the door and hurried out to the yard.

A blur of yellow fur flew by, Tam in hot pursuit seconds later, barking loudly as he ran after the coyote.

"Damn!" Ellie stared after her disappearing dog. "I hope he doesn't catch him. I don't want him in a fight."

Nick stood beside her. "Shall I check on the chickens? I have shoes on."

Ellie looked at her bare feet and sighed, thankful she'd remembered her robe. "If you would, please. I see several from here and both ducks, but hate to think there are any injured or dead.''

In two minutes Nick had checked the coop and reported all was well. Tam came trotting back, his tail wagging.

"Good boy, you chased him away." Ellie patted her dog, checking him over for any injuries. She straightened and looked at Nick. "Thanks for raising the alarm. A few more minutes and I expect I would have lost a few hens."

He nodded and looked up at the sky. For a long moment the silence stretched between them. Ellie grew cold. "I'm going back in," she said.

"Is it possible for me to stay outside for a while?" he asked, turning to look at her. "It's the first time I've been outside at night in three years."

"Sure, if you wish." Slipping back into the kitchen, she closed the door. She knew how it felt to never be able to do what you wanted when you wanted. Knew he'd relish the taste of freedom as she had when her father had first died. She enjoyed being on her own, not at the beck and call of a querulous, sick old man. She relished being her own boss, doing what she wanted. Making her own decisions, seeing how things turned out. Nick had been in one kind of prison, but she'd lived for more than fourteen years in one of another kind. She shivered. If Nick wanted to stay out all night, it was fine with her, as long as he didn't leave. She peered from the window, trying to see him, wondering what she would do if he didn't return.

Chapter Three

Ellie awoke at her normal early hour the next morning, her light still on, the book fallen to the floor. Had Nick stayed out all night? Anything could have happened. How could she have slept with the house unlocked and her newest guest who knew where?

Quickly dressing, she tied her hair back remembering what Nick had said last night about her looks. She stared at her reflection. He was right. She did appear dowdy. Lifting her heavy hair, she tilted her head. Maybe she should get a haircut, start wearing a little makeup. Pick out some clothes that fit, rather than going for total comfort.

Slapping on her glasses, she left the room. Foolish thinking would get her nowhere. There was no need to go changing anything about her life for the sake of a few words from a man she'd met yesterday. She looked fine just the way she was. And it wasn't as if a bit of makeup would transform her into a raving beauty.

The door to Nick's room was closed when she passed

through the kitchen. Had he returned in the night and taken Tam in with him? Or were they still out? Where could he have gone in the middle of the night? The trucks were still parked near the barn. Her car on the far side.

Ellie let the screen door close slowly, softly, so as not to awaken Nick if he was sleeping. She could have peeked into his room, she supposed. Yet that would violate their privacy policy.

She moved quickly to the barn built the summer before last. Sliding open one of the tall doors, she stepped quietly inside to get the food for the chickens, ducks and her pig, Penelope. The donkey and horses would be next. A few flakes of hay would hold them for the day. She supplemented their feed in the winter months or when strenuous work was required. With the majority of the horses on the mustering, she had little to do this morning with the few in the corral but heave in the hay.

Tam came racing around the side of the house, barking in delight when he spotted Ellie.

"Good morning, fellow, how are you? Have you been out all night?" Ellie ruffled the fur around his ears and petted his head as Nick rounded the corner. Had they been walking for almost four hours? She straightened, relief and a sudden warmth spreading through her at the sight of him. Darn it, she couldn't keep reacting like this every time she saw him.

He looked tired. There were circles beneath his eyes. A day's growth of dark beard covered his cheeks. It made him look even more dangerous, especially dressed in the dark jeans and black sweater. Dangerous and sexy. His eyes constantly assessed, watched. Ellie wondered what he thought about.

Stopping when he spotted her, Nick's gaze roamed across her, then moved to examine the barn.

"We heard you. Tam took off like a bullet when you crossed the yard," he said.

"It's time to feed the animals. Ready to help? Scoop some grain into this tin, up to here." She pointed to a black mark on the can and nodded toward the bin. "Scatter it outside for the chickens and ducks. Then we'll feed Penelope."

"Penelope?" Nick took the can and looked at it a moment as if he'd never seen one before.

"My pig."

Nick's startled eyes met hers, the grey lightened to silver. A slow smile began to tug at his lips.

Ellie paused, fascinated by the change. Her insides began to melt. It was as if every nerve ending in her entire body tingled just from being near him. His smile was lethal.

"I can't wait to see Penelope," he said with that lopsided, casual smile.

"Feed the ducks and chicks then come on back."

Ellie moved to the rear of the barn. The stalls for the horses were empty, primarily used in inclement weather. In the back, a pen opened to the outside through a small door. Pacing beside the low rail fence was her large black-and-white Hampshire pig. Ellie called to her and Penelope came over for a scratch. Knowing it was almost time to eat, she stood on her short hind legs and placed her front ones firmly on the rail of her pen. Squealing a high-pitched, loud greeting, she nuzzled Ellie's hand.

"What a commotion. Is she always so loud?" Nick came to stand beside Ellie, gazing in disbelief at the pig.

"Always when it's feeding time. Awful, isn't it?" Ellie laughed, then turned and opened a nearby bin, scooping a bucketful of oats and grains. These she dumped into the pail inside the pen. Penelope grunted, dropped down and began eating, snorting and snuffling as she inhaled the food.

"Eats like a pig, doesn't she?" Ellie murmured, affectionately.

Nick watched the animal for a moment, then shifted his gaze to Ellie. Shaking his head slowly, he murmured, "This is the farthest thing from what I imagined. I've never been any place like this.''

Ellie grinned up at him, stepping back in hopes of minimizing his magnetism. ''It's different from the city, isn't it? You'll soon become used to everything. As I said last night, we all pitch in on the chores. You can feed her later. Are you ready for breakfast?''

''Yes, and I promise to keep quiet while you fix it,'' he said, glancing back at Penelope.

Ellie laughed and replaced the pail.

Leading the way to the kitchen, Ellie had to step past Nick—close enough to feel the radiant warmth from his body. Nerves tingling, Ellie drew in a deep breath. She couldn't remember when she'd last felt this way. Had it been for young Dr. Merrill so many years ago when he'd started caring for her father? What a crush she'd had on him—though her father had put an end to that quickly enough. But even so, she didn't remember feeling precisely like this.

Of course she didn't have a crush on Nick. It was probably just heightened awareness of another's presence. Once the others returned, things would return to normal. Her purpose was to help Nick reacclimatize himself to society, not to develop a crush on the man.

''Eggs and bacon and biscuits okay?'' she asked, entering the back door, firmly in control of her feelings.

''Sounds great.'' He walked right behind her, caught the screen door before it slammed and slowly closed it. He wondered if he had time for a cold shower. Watching Ellie's hips sway as she walked in front of him caused a reaction he'd not experienced in a very long time. He wanted her!

She wasn't sleekly sophisticated as Sheila had been. Wasn't trendy or flirtatious like the women where he used to work. But there was something about her that drew his eye, that made him curious to discover what made her tick.

And to find out if that hair was as heavy as it looked, and as silky.

"Orange juice's in the fridge, utensils in that drawer. You can set the table," Ellie directed washing her hands. As she pulled down the flour and shortening Nick made an attempt to get his libido firmly under control. The last thing he needed was any complication of that sort. Hadn't he sworn off women with good reason?

When breakfast was on the table, they ate in silence. Ellie watched him surreptitiously. She was intrigued with the firm line of his jaw, the dark beard that bristled on his cheeks, the muscles moving as he chewed his food. He caught her gaze on him and she looked away quickly, though she found it almost a physical effort to keep her eyes averted.

She wished the others would hurry up and return home before she made a blithering idiot of herself.

"If I can use the phone, I'll call my lawyer and get clear on where I stand with a few things. He's been handling my finances for the past few years," Nick said when they finished eating.

"I said before, while you're here, you're to treat this as your home. Call whomever you like, whenever you like. Invite friends over, raid the refrigerator, help with chores. You need to get used to freedom. This is not prison."

"It's an extension, and you're my jailer," he said bitterly.

Ellie blinked at his tone, disappointment piercing at his words. Had she secretly hoped for more?

Gently she said, "This is not a prison, Nick. You can come and go as you like. You just have to check in with me." She didn't like being thought of as a jailer. She had never thought of herself in that light. Did the others resent her? Resent the time they spent here?

Maybe initially. But every boy and girl she'd helped were now leading lives vastly different from what they had expected when in prison. She raised her chin determinedly. She would not be hurt by any imagined slights. And she'd do her best to make sure he benefited from the program as the others had.

He looked at her, eyes narrowing. "The state pays you for my keep, right?"

She nodded, not mentioning that the money the state paid for each one in the program barely covered food, much less her increased costs in other areas. He didn't need to know that. Her painting provided her ample means to take on an additional expense with her guests. And the ranch almost operated in the black.

"So, consider yourself a boarder. Look on this as your home," she said briskly.

He glanced around noting the cheery room with gleaming appliances, warm wooden cupboards and bright-blue gingham curtains fluttering in the light morning breeze. She'd made it a warm, welcoming place, totally different from the sterile condo he had in the city with its modern furniture and sleek design. He liked Ellie's place. And that surprised him.

"Thanks." Suddenly Nick felt awkward. She was being kind to him. He wasn't sure how to proceed. He shouldn't be here. He should never have been such a fool in the first place to end up in jail. But he couldn't change the past, he could only accept it and go on.

"As soon as I do the dishes, I'll leave you the kitchen. This is the only phone I have. You want to track down eggs while I'm washing?"

"Track down eggs?"

"The hens lay them all over. It's like an Easter egg hunt every day. There's the basket we use. They lay them under plants, in the barn, all over, just look where you think a hen could fit. Want to give it a try?"

"Sure," he said, shrugging. "A new experience."

Which was exactly what he was looking for—he sure didn't want to repeat the old ones.

He pushed open the screen door and left.

Just as Ellie finished the dishes, the phone rang. She dried her hands and answered it. Her friend and writing partner Margot greeted her.

"Well, *chérie,* how does it go? Is the young criminal behaving himself? Does he want to be a cowboy yet?"

She'd long ago gotten used to Margot's French. Eight years in the States and Margot still spoke with a strong accent. And Ellie was used to her friend's teasing her about her involvement with Helping Hands.

"He's behaving." For a second Ellie remembered her foolish scare of last night when Nick had appeared in her doorway so tall and dark. He'd only wanted to tell her about the coyote, but her imagination had instantly supplied much more.

"Margot, this one's lots older than the others. And he seems very together, if you know what I mean."

"No, *chérie,* I don't know what you mean. How is he together?"

"Well, he doesn't seem worried about the future. He's had a lawyer handling his finances while he was in prison. If he has finances to handle, why does he need Helping Hands? And then, I don't know, he has a kind of a presence about him." She paused, trying to explain how she felt to Margot. "He's very much a man—virile, actually. I feel out of my depth. His being here is a mistake. I was expecting another teenager, but I didn't know how to turn him away. I guess I can call Alan tomorrow and find out how to handle it."

Margot laughed. "*Bien sûr, chérie,* most men are virile. Your problem, *enfante,* is in not being around men much. Why send him away? Let him stay and maybe explore some of that virility. Time you got something from that program."

"Oh, right. I can see the situation now. The coordinator yanks my approval. All my guests leave because of inappropriate behavior. Besides I'm constantly around men. There's Gus and Rusty and Tomas. I see Philip almost as often as I see you," Ellie protested, aware of what her friend really meant.

"Those cowboys work for you. And Gus is old enough to be your grandfather. It's not the same, *chérie*. You don't give men a chance."

"I have too much to do to become involved with anyone," Ellie said stiffly. She knew better than to let her heart become tangled up. Didn't everyone she love leave? Hadn't the lessons of the past been enough to prove to her she needed to guard her emotions? And even if she was willing to risk her heart on love, she was not willing to give up her independence. She'd waited too long for it, and had paid too high a price to let it go.

"Live a little. How old is he?"

"My age. What does that have to do with anything? He's years older than he should be to be in the program."

"Still, you let him stay?"

"I did yesterday. And I guess the longer he's here, the harder it would be to refuse." Had she subconsciously already made her decision? Would she really call Alan Peters in the morning?

"*Eh bien,* we'd like to stop by today, especially if Alberta will prepare something delectable for us. Primarily to discuss the *petit* pond you wish to build. I've talked to Philip about it and he'd like to see the place you want it."

"Alberta will be delighted to see you, as always. Your compliments make her feel like a cordon bleu chef."

"She could be. Until six? *Au revoir, chérie.*"

"Till then." Ellie hung up.

"I found eight eggs, does that sound right?"

Ellie spun around. Nick leaned against the counter. He

watched her with that unnerving gaze. Beside him on the
counter sat a basket of eggs.

"I heard part of your conversation," he said, his eyes
never leaving hers.

Ellie's face grew warm. What had she said? She swallowed hard, hoping he had not heard it all. She'd die of
embarrassment if he heard her comment about his virility
or Margot's recommendation! The mere thought caused a
wash of heat over her face.

She looked into the basket, trying to regain her balance.
"It's hard to say if these are all. Some of the hens lay every
day, others only every few days. Eight sounds fine." She
still felt flustered. Thank God he couldn't have heard Margot's suggestion.

When she reached to take the basket, her fingers brushed
against his arm. The touch was pure electricity. It was all
she could do not to jerk her hand back as if she'd been
burned. The shock went clear through to her toes. Watching
him warily, she cleared her throat. Was she the only one
effected? Or did he feel something unusual as well? His
impassive expression gave nothing away.

"That was my partner, Margot. She and her husband will
be coming for dinner. They'd like to meet you. Of course
you'll meet the rest of the crew when they get back this
afternoon. Dinner will be a lot more hectic than last night."
Anxiously, she glanced at him to see if he noticed her reaction to his touch.

Nick's expression hardened instantly. A muscle jerked in
his jaw as he withdrew, as if pulling a shade down between
them.

He looked out the back door, out over the rolling hills,
aware of Ellie like he had never been aware of another
woman. Her small figure was downright sexy in her jeans
and the loose cotton shirt that draped her high, firm breasts.
Her hair shone in the sunlight spilling in through the window. Her eyes behind her glasses seemed puzzled.

His lips tightened. He didn't want to meet anyone he didn't have to. Didn't want to see the speculation, the curiosity, the distaste. Her other *guests* were in the same boat, the cowhands and foreman part of the package for this half-way house. But not strangers. Not her personal friends.

"Nick?"

She reached out and put a tentative hand on his bare forearm. He felt a jolt. He turned back to her, staring down at her slim fingers. Her hand was small and warm. She was petite all over, with too much hair and tinted glasses that hid her pretty blue eyes. Slowly he searched her face, seeing her again as he had last night with her glasses off, her hair swirling around her shoulders. He drew a deep breath. He did not need this awareness!

"I'm uncomfortable meeting anyone I don't have to," he said, hating to admit it. His anger flared at her for forcing him to say it aloud. "I don't want to meet your friends."

"Why not?"

Frustrated, he dragged his hand through his hair, dislodging her fingers. "It's tied up with being in prison. Everyone here knows about it, of course, but one reason I came here instead of going back to my own place was to start a new life without everyone tiptoeing around my past. Your friends would know, of course."

"Of course. But that's behind you now. You have to go on. Sooner or later anyone who plays an important part in your life will know about that time. You've got to acknowledge that it happened, learn from it, but go on. Forgive yourself for the wrong and strive to do right."

"Is this a lecture?" he asked, his eyes narrowing as he faced her.

"No, just a suggestion."

Nick stared bleakly at her. What she said was true. He was a fool if he thought he could put it behind him and ignore it, as if changing the place he lived would change the past. It would haunt him forever. Maybe someday he would forget. But forgive? He didn't think he'd ever do that. Not himself, and certainly not Sheila!

"I'll be here when your friends come," he said at last. What choice did he have?

She smiled and he looked away. He was starting to look for Ellie's smiles, watch the way they made her eyes seem even a deeper blue, the way her entire face seemed to light up. He'd be glad when the others who lived here returned to act as a buffer. He didn't need this close one-on-one time with Ellie Winslow.

"I'm finished in here. You can call your lawyer now," she said. Whistling for Tam to join her, Ellie went to the front of the house, giving Nick all the privacy he needed.

Nick continued to lean against the counter for several moments, staring after her, a forgotten longing building despite all his attempts to halt it. Try as he might, he couldn't ignore the sensations he felt when he watched her. He wondered what her skin would feel like against his. Was her hair as soft and fine as it looked? Would her taste explode on his tongue, or be subtle and alluring? Dammit, everything about her was starting to seem alluring.

Not that she'd ever given a sign that she saw him in any way other than a temporary guest she was trying to help. What woman would want a relationship with a man like him? And what kind of fool did that make him to even entertain such a thought? He'd already been down that road once.

"Blast it!" he exclaimed, reaching for the phone.

Ellie spent the morning sketching and painting. She and Margot had another book in progress, and she worked on the scheduled illustrations in the upstairs bedroom she had converted to a studio. The day was bright and sunny. A soft warm breeze blew from the west, tossing the airy Priscilla curtains, keeping the room cool.

She kept an eye out for the return of the hands and Gus

and Alberta. Kat and Ariel had to get home early enough to get their clothes ready for work this week. And she wanted to hear how everyone had liked sleeping outdoors. These city kids were as awestruck as she had been about working on a ranch. But they adapted well. Extremely well in the case of Jed and Brad. Who would have expected the two boys to become so horse mad?

As she lost herself in her painting, she could think about things. Foremost today was her new guest. With a college degree, he certainly didn't have the same background as her other guests. Why had he embezzled funds? Trying to get rich quick? Most likely. He appeared angry and bitter, but that was to be expected. He'd have to work through that to resume the semblance of a normal life. The program arranged for counselors if the guests wished. Maybe she could suggest it. Or maybe he'd open up later when he grew more comfortable being here.

It was almost one o'clock when her hunger grew strong enough for Ellie to think of lunch. She had expected Alberta and the others to be back by now. Hoping they had not run into problems, she went downstairs to fix herself a sandwich.

Had Nick wished to eat earlier? Would he have fixed himself something if he'd been hungry? When she reached the kitchen, she saw no signs he'd been there. His door was closed. She washed her hands and began to prepare sandwiches. She'd leave a couple covered on the counter for him.

"Can I help?" Nick's deep voice startled Ellie. She turned to find him right beside her. Involuntarily, she stepped back, her pulse racing. He moved so silently. It was another thing to get used to. The boys clunked around; Nick moved as quietly as a wolf on the prowl. But it wasn't his silence that caused her heart to skip a beat.

He stood overwhelmingly close, emitting an aura of strength, determination and physical power that attracted her. She was not used to such blatant masculinity, and didn't know how to respond to the feelings he aroused. He'd think her an idiot if he ever suspected.

"I'll have sandwiches fixed in a few minutes. You can get plates and napkins," she said breathlessly.

"I spoke with Matt, my attorney. He'll drop by tomorrow, if that's all right." he said, breaking into the silence.

"Wow, that's service! First to reach him on a Sunday and then have him drive all the way out here." She set the sandwiches on the table and went to get iced tea from the refrigerator. "What time is he coming?" she asked as she plopped the pitcher on the table and drew out her chair.

"Early afternoon. He's not so accommodating to everyone. We were personal friends. Before."

"No problem. You'll have plenty of privacy. The girls both have jobs in town and dinner won't be until seven. I'll make sure everyone stays out of your way when your lawyer's here. You'll have the house to yourself—except the kitchen. Alberta spends most of her time in here. Would you like him to stay for dinner?"

"No," he said, toying with his sandwich.

Ellie watched him, her heart beginning to ache. He seemed determined to be self-sufficient, yet somehow it made him seem all the more lonely. She hoped being here would help.

"Something wrong?" she asked gently.

He looked up, his eyes showing the familiar bleakness when he met the gentle sympathy in her gaze.

"I'm not looking forward to seeing Matt," Nick said at last, surprising himself. "He'll tell me again what a damn fool I've been. Then he'll try to talk me into returning to San Francisco. I'm not ready for that. In fact, I don't know what I want yet. That's one reason I'm here."

Ellie became intrigued. After the arrogant display of assurance, this hint of vulnerability was the last thing she expected. Her heart beat against her breast as she wished she could erase his haunted look, make things easier for him. But he had to handle his life, his future, himself. As well as not invading privacy, the training has stressed that each guest had to do his own growing and learning. The host was not to become a crutch.

"Well, it's academic, anyway, for another three months," she said gently, trying to find a way to ease his problem.

His face closed and he nodded. Another reminder that he still wasn't totally free. He was in limbo for another three months, required to remain here. Or return to prison. But after three months he could do as he wished. What would it be?

Ellie sighed softly and resumed eating. She'd just lost whatever ground she'd gained by reminding him. She should have kept quiet.

They had scarcely finished lunch when the yells and thundering sound of hooves echoed in the quiet afternoon. Ellie hastily tossed the dishes into the sink and headed outside, the warmth of her feelings surprising her. Grinning widely, she watched as the crew headed for the ranch yard.

Jed led the way, riding the big bay gelding as if he'd been born in the saddle. The fact he insisted on wearing his baggy cargo pants, tattered tennis shoes and baseball cap didn't alter the fact he'd picked up more horse lore in his five months here than anyone.

Ariel came in a close second. Riding like crazy, she was trying to pass Jed, and Ellie could see the girl's fierce determination from where she stood. Holding her breath in fear of Ariel's falling, she made a mental note to discuss her riding with Rusty. The girl was competent, but if she continued to attempt daredevil stunts like racing, Ellie wanted her to be even better.

In just moments, the entire group reined in. The boys slid off the horses and hurried to Ellie, talking about moving the cattle, about the meals Alberta had prepared—on an open fire no less. Their unabashed enthusiasm made Ellie laugh as her heart swelled in delight. This was what the program was about. And for Jed and Brad it was working. She had introduced them to an entirely new way of life. And they had both embraced it with all the enthusiasm of young minds and hearts.

"Wait until you try it in the rain," Rusty said good-naturedly as Brad expounded on how well he'd learned to move cattle, and how he'd brought some stragglers into line.

Ellie grinned affectionately at the boy. He'd taken to ranch life as avidly at Jed, but had gone whole-hog. His boots were showing wear, no longer as shiny as a few weeks ago. His hat was covered in dust, his Wrangler jeans and western shirt showed signs of the work he'd been doing. But it was the open smile of sheer delight on his African-American face that heartened Ellie the most. Brad had all the makings of a fine cowboy.

"I hope this isn't something we'll be required to do every weekend," Kat's petulant voice said. She dismounted and wrinkled her nose at her horse. "It was hot, there were flies, and if I wanted to sleep on hard ground, there're city streets that don't have bears prowling."

Jed and Brad laughed and hit each other on the shoulder. "Gus told us about the bears late last night."

"I wasn't afraid," Ariel said, tossing her head. The five earrings in her right ear caught the sunlight. Her short auburn hair gleamed. Her eyes narrowed suspiciously. She rounded on Ellie. "I think he just made it up to scare us. Right?"

"Ever the cynic, Ariel?" Ellie asked gently. "Bears usually keep to the high country. And the campfire would have kept them away."

Nick stepped out on the porch and everyone stopped talking to turn and stare.

"Who's that?" Kat asked, her eyes sparkling with sudden interest. Standing taller, she moved a step closer.

"Our new guest, Nick Tanner," Ellie said, warily wondering if there was trouble looming. She hadn't considered Nick's effect on others; she'd been too busy worrying about her own reactions.

Alberta walked over and stood by Ellie, eyeing Nick suspiciously. "A bit old, ain't he?" she asked quietly.

"Older than most, but as he told me, he's still young and a first offender," Ellie defended.

"Nick, let me introduce everyone. You'll get a chance to know them better at dinner. Alberta is our cook."

The older woman nodded, her suspicion clearly showing in her expression.

"Her husband, my foreman, Gus," Ellie said, pointing out the whipcord-thin man still calmly sitting in the saddle. He tipped his hat, but remained silent.

"My hands, Rusty and Tomas."

Both cowboys slouching in their saddles touched the brim of their hats.

"And our other guests, Jed, Brad, Ariel and Kat."

Nick studied each one in turn and nodded. When the introductions were over the cowboys began riding toward the barn. Jed pulled his horse along, as Ariel and Brad followed. Only Kat remained where she was standing.

"So, Nick, how long will you be with us?" she asked, her eyes sparkling with interest.

"Three months," Nick said evenly.

Her smile widened as she nodded. "I'm here another four, myself. Maybe we can hang out together."

"After you take care of your horse," Ellie said firmly. She met Kat's glare and calmly stared her down. Only after the girl left in a flounce for the barn, did Ellie relax.

"Trouble, I'd say," Alberta muttered, tugging gently on her reins, as she glanced sharply at Nick.

"Maybe," Ellie commented, turning to Nick.

"Not from me. Don't you think she's a bit young?" he asked, raising one eyebrow.

"Of course she is. She's just nineteen. But she wants independence so badly she can taste it. And she thinks she's all grown-up."

"Even if she were, she's not for me. I'm not getting involved with another woman in this lifetime!" That said, he turned and entered the house, the screen door slamming behind him.

Chapter Four

Ellie faced Alberta. "I didn't expect someone so old," she admitted softly. She was worried about Kat's reaction to Nick.

"Problems will probably come from that young miss, I expect. You letting him stay?"

Ellie nodded. Hadn't she really made up her mind on Saturday? "He can use this time, just in a different way from the others. And he doesn't have as long. He'll be gone before Kat's term is up."

"Staying in the house?"

"I gave him the bedroom off the kitchen. He can move to the bunkhouse if he wants. Or maybe being older, he'd rather stay apart from the others."

"Might be safer for all concerned if he moves," Alberta commented with a wise shake of her head.

"Why?"

"Watch Kat. You're right in saying she thinks she's grown-up. And she's dying to test those feminine wiles you and Margot are showing her. She flirted with Jed and Tomas the entire weekend. I kept my eye on her, I can tell you.''

''Great, another problem.''

''Life would grow boring without them, right?'' Alberta said cheerfully. ''I'll be glad to get back to my own kitchen. That trail cooking is a chore.''

''I'm sorry I missed it, however. You work magic on an open fire. Margot and Philip are coming for dinner, will that be a problem?''

''When did two extra mouths ever present a problem? I'll make beef stroganoff—it's fast and filling. A nice salad.''

''Take your horse, Alberta?'' Brad asked, coming out of the barn.

''Thank you, son. Don't mind if you do.'' With that, Alberta headed for the small cottage she and Gus shared. Ellie knew as soon as the older woman showered and changed she'd be back in the kitchen. Ellie had better have those dishes washed and put away before then!

Margot and Philip Templar arrived shortly before six. Ellie awaited their arrival on her swing. She could hear the normal afternoon activity around the house. The boys were in the barn, doing evening chores. Their voices mingled with those of Rusty and Tomas. It was Ariel's turn to help Alberta, and her sassy comments could be heard through the screen door. Kat had said she wanted to soak in a warm tub for hours to get all that range dirt off. Ellie smiled remembering her comment. This from a girl who had lived on the streets in Oakland for months on end.

Another who was benefiting from Helping Hands.

A warm glow of satisfaction filled her. Now if she could find the key to helping Nick...

Nick leaned against the fence and watched the two cowhands brush the horses, assisted by Jed and Brad. He knew starting tomorrow he'd be assigned daily chores. It was no more than he signed up for. He wondered if he could convince Ellie that he wanted to be a cowboy. Learning the trade would keep him ranch-bound. Less likely to run into anyone. And give him the time he needed.

At the sound of the car on the gravel, Nick sighed and pushed away from the fence. Ellie's friends had arrived. Slowly he walked toward the front of the house. Ellie was sitting on the swing and he looked from her to the approaching car.

Those few minutes watching the boys in the barn proved they would have little in common. Not only was there an age difference, they seemed to talk an entirely different language. If he was to rejoin the human race, he might as well get the first meeting over with. But he was angry with Ellie for forcing the issue so soon.

Ellie smiled at him, the smile fading when he glared at her.

"Don't worry, they don't bite," she said gently.

He'd had years to perfect an impassive demeanor. One day here and he'd obviously blown it if she could assess his feelings.

"Come meet my friends. If you can't stand them once you've met, you can slip away. I wouldn't force them on you."

Margot was tall and slender, with short dark hair. Philip topped his wife by several inches. His hair had begun to turn grey, giving him a distinguished appearance. He had kept his physical prowess even though he looked well into his forties.

Briefly Ellie's gaze switched to Nick. How would he appear to her friends? Dark, forbidding, aloof? Ellie saw the strain on his face and moved to stand near him, as if to lend moral support.

"Hello, *chérie*," Margot said, giving Ellie a kiss on each

cheek, and turning to greet Nick, an assessing look in her eye.

"Margot, Philip, I'd like you to meet Nick Tanner, Nick, my best friends, Margot and Philip Templar."

There was a moment of awkward silence after the introductions and handshakes, which Philip broke when he turned to Ellie.

"If you want to discuss this before dinner, we'd better get going. Show me where you want it."

"Want what?" Nick asked, curious as the others turned to look over the yard. It looked like dirt and dried grass to him.

"Ellie has another grand scheme on which she wants some advice. Haven't you told him?" Philip teased her.

"Not yet. Though I did mention you were going to help me with a project." She turned to look at Nick. "I want to build a pond for the ducks. I thought I could have it over there, so I can see it from the porch." Ellie pointed to the slope on the far side of the house where she'd marked out the perimeter of the artificial pond she wanted.

"Build a pond," Nick repeated, staring out over the drying grass in disbelief.

"Dig a hole, cement it, and fill it with water, so I can watch the ducks swim," Ellie explained patiently.

Margot and Philip laughed. "You'll get used to her—and her reasons for doing things. Always for what she wants as an end result, like watching ducks swim. Never for the projects themselves." Margot turned to Philip. "Remember the barn?"

"How will I ever forget? The barn started out as a house for Penelope, it just evolved into a structure large enough to house the horses and store hay. The old one would have done with some repairs. Except there was no room for Penelope."

"Well, how was I to know how much work it would take? Anyway, it's great now. And look how much Rob and Jason learned from building it,'' Ellie defended. Two of her earlier guests had found new skills wielding hammers and saws. Both now had promising jobs with construction crews in Sacramento.

"You could have repaired the older one. Come on, *chérie,* do you have a cola, I'm parched,'' Margot said, nudging her friend.

"Sure. Anything for you guys?''

Philip and Nick both nodded and requested soft drinks which Ellie quickly got. Settling on the swing, Margot and Ellie watched as the men moved to the place Ellie wanted her pond, deep in discussion. Both were tall and well built, but Nick seemed harder, more solid. Probably tempered from his experiences, Ellie thought, unable to keep her gaze away from him. She delighted in the chance to watch him without his knowledge.

"*Chérie,* he is *formidable.*''

"Nice, huh?'' Ellie said, enjoying the sight of the man. What would it have been like to meet him before? Or after his three months were finished? Would they connect in any way, or was their only tie the program?

"You didn't tell me he was gorgeous. How do you keep your hands off him?'' Margot asked, sipping her drink as she studied Nick over the rim of the glass. "Maybe I have to rethink this Helping Hands deal.''

"Margot, don't be ridiculous.'' Ellie sighed. If she only knew.

"Try it, *chérie.*''

"Margot! That's impossible! He's here for the program. Once his time's up, he'll be gone.'' Why did that thought bring an ache?

"Ellie, we've been best friends since we both started working together eight years ago, *vrai?*''

Ellie nodded, forever grateful her art teacher had put her in touch with Margot. Her art classes had initially kept her sane during her father's last difficult years. The fact she had been able to work in her chosen field had been an extra bonus. Painting illustrations for Margot's stories while her father slept had provided her with the strength to see to his demands.

"You need to liven up your life," Margot said seriously.

"What?" Ellie swung around, staring at her friend.

"You heard me. Get a new look, get a new outlook. Have your hair cut, get contacts, buy a tight tank top and change your image." Coolly her friend surveyed her. "You've got a great figure, but you never show it off. Fix yourself up a little. Get Kat to help you. She has great clothes sense."

Ellie stared at her in amazement. Whatever was Margot thinking?

"Are you crazy? Margot, I'm almost thirty-two years old! I'm trying to offer a helping hand to kids who need it to get back on track. Not vamp some man!"

"I know that, Ellie. But think, all those long years your father was ill, you missed what the rest of us had—dates and parties and fun. You're still young, you look young. Grab for some fun before it's too late."

"Really, Margot, I'm fine. I like my life the way it is. I certainly can't throw myself at Nick, if that's what you're suggesting." Ellie blanked out the image that sprang to mind—Nick kissing her, touching her with the sweet promise of love, his body pressing against hers. She couldn't let anything like that happen, even in her dreams.

"I'm not saying you should throw yourself at anyone. But who knows who you might meet while doing this Helping Hands? Police officers, lawyers." She gave a Gallic shrug. "The possibilities are there, *chérie*. You must be ready for them."

Margot could have a point. Ellie had already met several people she would not have known except for the program. Alan Peters who started Helping Hands; some of the deputies who brought her guests; Joshua Bennett at the ranch where Pete, one of her former guests, now worked. That nice vet in Davis.

"I'll give it some thought."

"Don't think, *do!*" Margot urged as the men turned and headed back.

"Ellie, Nick has a great idea, one you'll love," Philip called.

She looked at Nick. "Really? What?"

"How about a waterfall into the pond? If you move it just over to the left a few yards, the slope steepens. We could dig the pond there, get some rocks and build a waterfall. The pump recycling the water would be hidden in the rocks so it wouldn't be a threat to your ducks."

"What a great idea! Can we do it?" she asked Philip excitedly.

"I don't know why not. Nick's volunteered to help. I'll sketch some plans. Nick said he'd get estimates for costs. If it's what you want and can afford, we can be ready in a few days to start digging."

Philip smiled at his wife. "I think Nick's as nutty as Ellie," he said. "Instead of trying to talk her out of building a pond, he complicates it with a waterfall."

"It's a great idea," Ellie defended stoutly. "I'll have you know I'm not nutty. I only draw the pictures in the books— your wacky wife thinks up the stories."

"*C'est vrai.* But let us not discuss who is crazier. Can the pond be built?" Margot asked, flicking an interested glance at Nick as he watched the easy interchange among the three of them.

They discussed the proposed project until Alberta called them for dinner.

Ellie chatted excitedly about the pond at the table, capturing the imagination of Ariel and Jed. Both wanted to help with the work.

"Can we go wading when it's filled?" Ariel asked.

"If you want to walk in duck poop," Kat returned, wrinkling her nose. "I think it sounds gross."

"But think of the pleasure we'll have watching the ducks swim. And I love the thought of hearing a waterfall from the porch," Ellie said, stepping in to avoid another confrontation. She wanted the meal to progress peacefully, especially with Margot and Philip present. Sometimes her guests got a bit heated and it took a lot of skill to prevent a minor riot. But part of learning new skills included how to behave in public and in various social situations.

"So it's a new project—who wants in on it?" Ellie asked.

Jed and Ariel quickly jumped at the chance.

"I don't mind being a part of it," Nick said. "I can at least do some of the digging. When I was in college, I worked summers in construction."

"Then, I'll help, too," Kat said quickly, smiling at Nick.

Margot looked at Kat and Nick, then at Ellie—raising her eyebrows in a silent question.

The phone rang. Ellie hurried into the kitchen to answer it. She was surprised to hear the man on the other end request Nick.

Handing him the receiver a moment later, she smiled at his surprise. Was it the attorney calling back? A moment later Nick relaxed. Obviously not bad news.

Ellie knew she should return to the dining room, give him some privacy, but she stayed just where she was, her curiosity keeping her in place.

"Hello, old man, how are you?…I was going to call, wanted to get settled first.… Now Steve, I had to talk to Matt about business.… Yes, you were.… Yes, again.…No, I didn't go back to the city, I'm east. Near Jackson… Whenever you want.… Sure, wait a moment."

Nick covered the mouthpiece and turned to Ellie.

"An old friend. Is it all right for him to come out next Saturday for a short visit?"

"Sure. Invite him to come for dinner. We'll barbecue,"

she said casually, trying to impress upon him he was free to do what he wanted at her place.

Nick hesitated, then nodded.

"Steve, how about around four on Saturday? We'll catch up and have dinner here, barbecue or something. It'll be a madhouse with all the people who live here, but we can get a spot to ourselves. Hold on."

"Can you give directions?" he asked, holding out the phone.

Ellie took the phone and gave concise, easy directions.

"Tell Nick that Sally's coming, too. I want them to meet," the man said before hanging up.

"I'll tell him. See you Saturday."

"Tell me what?" Nick asked when she hung up.

"Sally's coming, too."

"I expected she would. I haven't met her."

"Who is she? Who called?"

"Steve Davis."

"A friend," she said, glad he had friends who wanted to see him.

"My closest friend, maybe my only remaining friend," Nick stated bleakly. "I've known him for years. He, uh, he was the only one who stood by me enough to visit me in prison. Sally's his wife, though only of a few months. We haven't met yet."

Ellie paused, struck by his tone. She longed to reach out to touch him, to ease some of his pain if she could. But it was important her guests worked through their past and adjusted to the present on their own.

"I'd like to be your friend, Nick, if you'd let me," she said softly.

It was a long time before he answered. His eyes hardened as he stared down into hers. He slowly shook his head. "It wouldn't work. I don't want or need a woman for a friend." The bitterness in his tone surprised her.

Swallowing the flash of regret, she stepped back into the

dining room. She had the others to see to and weekly assignments to give. And her dinner to finish, she thought, trying to ignore the sting she felt at his rejection. She'd enjoy Margot's visit and plan her pond with Philip. And try to ignore the question that clamored for an answer: What had happened to Nick to make him so bitter toward women?

Ellie knelt at a flower bed in the front yard the next afternoon when a metallic gold BMW turned carefully onto the gravel drive and drove slowly to the house. This had to be Nick's attorney. Kat and Ariel were at work in town. Brad had ridden out with Tomas to check on a stretch of the endless miles of fencing.

Had Nick been taking riding instructions from Gus? Were they finished yet? He'd said he knew how to ride, but just the basics. Her foreman was going to work with him to assess his level of expertise.

A tall man in a three-piece charcoal grey suit climbed out of the car, adjusting aviator sunglasses. He reached back inside the car to draw out a slim leather briefcase, slammed the door and started for the house. When he saw Ellie, he veered in her direction.

"Good afternoon," she said wishing she'd had time to wash her hands. Nattily dressed and sporting a thin, dark moustache, he represented the epitome of a successful lawyer. He could grace the cover of any business journal. Had Nick once dressed the same?

"Good afternoon. Nick Tanner here?" Even his voice sounded polished.

Ellie nodded, pleased to note she felt no reaction to him. Since Nick's arrival she had wondered if she was going to be attracted to every man in her age group she came into contact with.

But that particular sensation seemed to be limited to Nick. And something she had to get over fast.

"Come inside, I'll find him for you. I'm Ellie Winslow."

"Matt Helmsley, Nick's attorney. Nice to meet you, Miss Winslow." He looked around, his expression hidden by his glasses.

He followed Ellie into the cool house, surveying the sparse furnishings and decorations in the living room with a critical eye as he took off his sunglasses. Motioning for him to have a seat, she went through to the kitchen.

Alberta was rolling pastry for pies. She smiled when she saw Ellie.

"Come for a snack?" she asked.

"No, I'm looking for Nick. His attorney is here."

"Is that a fact?" She sprinkled a bit of flour on the dough, dusted the rolling pin.

"Nice when you can have a busy attorney drive all the way from San Francisco just to confer with you, don't you think?" Ellie glanced at the door to Nick's room, partially ajar.

"Makes me wonder a bit more about Nick, that's for sure," Alberta said, pressing on the dough evenly. "I think Nick's in the barn with Gus. Saw them both ride in a while back."

Ellie pushed through the screen door and let it bang behind her as she walked to the barn. It was cool in the shadow of the big building. She heard voices in the back.

"Nick?"

"In here."

"Matt Helmsley is here."

Nick strode from the back of the barn, his step even and deliberate. Wiping his hands on the sides of his jeans, he nodded when he saw Ellie.

"Where?"

"I put him in the living room." She turned to fall in beside him as he headed for the back of the house. "I can get y'all something to drink if you like. Beyond that, you're on your own. Alberta is cooking, but you'll have privacy.

She won't go into the living room while your attorney is here.''

Nick paused as he opened the door, glancing down at Ellie. "It's a business meeting. We don't need drinks."

Ellie was dying to know what Nick had to say to his lawyer. What could be so important he couldn't handle via the phone? Or what would cause the man to drive all the way out to the ranch? But it was not her business. If he wanted her to know, he'd tell her.

"Yell if you need anything," she said, heading around the house to the flower beds.

Ellie walked slowly back up the driveway from the mailbox sometime later, ruffling through the mail. The weeding complete, she couldn't put off the office work much longer. Hearing voices, she glanced up and saw Matt and Nick walk out of the house and go together toward Matt's fancy car, still deep in conversation.

Nick watched as his friend carefully backed his expensive car down the driveway and drove off. He shifted his gaze to Ellie.

"Have a nice visit?" Ellie questioned, walking toward the house as Nick stood waiting for her. Did he regret coming here? Did he wish he was back with his friends, his old life in San Francisco? While all her guests came from urban environments, she knew Nick's former way of life vastly differed from Jed's or Brad's.

"I was able to get some business attended to."

"He looks very successful."

"In material ways, he is. I wonder if it's enough." Nick looked thoughtfully down the drive as if looking for answers. "Different people need different things. I prefer this place to San Francisco," Nick said. "At least for the next few months." Without another word, he turned and headed for the barn.

* * *

Nick lay on top of his bed. One arm behind his head, he stared at the ceiling. His muscles felt strained from the work he'd done today. He'd practiced saddling a horse until he knew he could do it in the dark. But the damned saddle must weigh seventy pounds. Lifting it up on the horse and taking it off two dozen times had been hard.

Still, it felt good to be doing physical labor. Different muscles used today were making themselves felt. But a small twinge of pride also rose. He could saddle a horse with the best of them now.

Who would have thought an ace accountant would become comfortable around horses? Around men who worked outside most of their lives. Rusty and Gus had a wealth of knowledge about cattle, horses and ranching. Brad wasn't the only one interested, Nick thought wryly.

But that probably was not Ellie's plan for him. How long could he stall her? She wanted him to conform to the guidelines, get busy planning the next stage in his career. He knew he had to do something, or be ineligible to continue in the program. But rather than waste her time and his, he needed to stall. To see if he could make it his own way.

Rising, he felt the pull of stiff muscles. Padding silently across to the window, he raised it and looked over the silvered landscape. The bright moon illuminated the barn, Gus and Alberta's small house, the bunkhouse. Ellie locked the back door at night, but anyone could climb out the window without a bit of trouble. Had no one tried to escape?

Yet why would they? Most of these kids probably thought they'd died and gone to heaven after their experience in jail. He'd picked up enough at dinner to know picture-perfect families were not a part of their backgrounds.

Nor Ellie's with her mother dying so young and her father an invalid. He still wondered what made her tick. Why did she spend so much time and effort on society's misfits? Why wasn't she married with a bunch of her own kids at her knee? He remembered her that first night without her glasses, with her hair swirling around her face, that feminine pink nightgown enhancing the color in her soft skin. No hardship to make love to. Were the men who knew her blind?

He clenched a fist. Ellie was the white-lace-and-wedding-bells type woman, not someone to get thrills sleeping with an ex-con. She'd be horrified at the notion.

And he'd be a damn fool to get tied up with any woman. Hadn't he learned his lesson?

The night air felt cool against his skin. He drew a deep breath—held it and slowly let it go. Dried grass, a hint of hay, horses, chickens and dust. What made this place so appealing to a woman like Ellie Winslow? What made her tick?

He had three months to find out.

Chapter Five

At breakfast the next morning, Alberta broached the subject of shopping.

"I need supplies. These guests eat like the famine is coming," she said, heaping another three pancakes on Brad's plate. Even Kat ate like she didn't know when her next meal would arrive.

"It's not my turn," Ariel said quickly.

"The way I figure it, it's Nick's. He hasn't had a turn yet," Jed said, placing his fork on the plate and leaning back in the chair. "That was good eating, Alberta!"

Ellie smiled and sipped her coffee. One of the things she tried to teach these young people was manners. When they first came, they never thought to thank Alberta for her cooking. Pleased with his progress, her gaze moved to Nick. He ate steadily, said little. He looked at Jed when he spoke.

"My turn for what?" Nick asked.

"Shopping," Brad answered. "A man's got to learn how

to shop for himself, according to Ellie here. So we take turns buying the groceries. Of course unless you plan on having a household of ten, I don't quite see how shopping for the ranch prepares you for having your own place." He slanted a glance at Ellie.

"It's the theory," Ellie said, smiling. This was an old argument with Brad. He truly hated to shop. Of course lately, he didn't want to do anything not from the back of a horse.

Nick's gaze moved to her. Studying her, he finished the last of his pancakes and reached for the coffee. "Shopping?"

Ellie swallowed, and nodded, glad she hadn't choked. When he looked at her like that, it was all she could do to sit still. Her heart sped up, her hands grew damp and she felt as tongue-tied as a young girl. Heat coursed through her, blood thrumming in her veins. Glancing around, she fervently hoped no one else noticed her physical reaction to the man.

Nick had to start some of the steps of the Helping Hands program. Just because the man was older than her other charges, didn't mean he could skip the different stages of the program. At least she didn't think it did. Once he proved he could handle things, she'd back off. But favoritism wasn't in the game plan. The others had to take turns shopping, so Nick did, too.

"We can go into Jackson this morning. There're some nice stores where you can get some more clothes if you need them. Then we'll buy the groceries for the week."

"I could use a few things. I'd like some more jeans, for one." He looked at Brad. "And maybe some boots. Gus said I should get some for riding."

"And maybe a suit?" Ellie suggested. "For job interviews. Or do you have some in San Francisco you can send for?"

Nick glanced at her sharply, his eyes narrowed.

Jed hooted with laughter. "A suit? I've never seen a guy around here wearing a suit! What's Nick going to interview for—mayor?"

Ellie flushed and looked away. It was true, most businessmen around Jackson wore casual attire. But she couldn't envision Nick settling for a permanent job around here. When his time was up, surely he'd return to San Francisco, or some other big city.

"I'm not interviewing for anything," Nick said. "I'll get experience here like Jed and Brad."

Everyone at the table fell silent, staring first at him and then Ellie.

"We'll discuss that later," Ellie said quietly. He'd mentioned holding off on starting that first day. Was he deliberately resisting the program?

Kat leaned forward and smiled an invitation. "Stop by my store today, Nick. Come see where I work."

"Like he wants to buy some women's clothes. You can have a burger and fries where I work," Ariel said, glaring at Kat. "I'll give you extra toppings."

"We won't be there long enough for lunch, Ariel. And I doubt Nick needs any women's apparel. But I might stop by, Kat," Ellie said.

"Whatever." She didn't seem as enthusiastic with Ellie's proposed visit as Nick's.

By midmorning Ellie was ready to leave the ranch. She offered to let Nick drive the truck, but he declined.

"I need to get my driver's license renewed. It expired."

"We can take care of that whenever you're ready. It would be a good thing to have soon so you can drive. The others use the other ranch truck as needed. Ariel and Kat share it when driving to work," she said easily as they started their trip into Jackson. "You'll need transportation to a job, too."

"I have a deal I want to propose. I guess now is as good a time as any to do it," Nick said slowly.

"A deal?" Ellie became wary. "What kind of deal?"

"I worked in an office before. I was an accountant. But I'm not going to be able to go back to that line of work. I need to change careers."

Alert, Ellie knew he was watching her closely to judge her reactions. How did he think she would react? It was the first time he'd brought up his past. Was she supposed to say something? She waited. When the others had told her about themselves, they'd been able to explain why they had done what they'd done. Sometimes talking through it helped them see what other choices they might have made.

"Before I get a job, I'd need experience in that field. Right?"

She nodded.

"I have some experience in construction from my college days. But nothing recent. I can get experience here. Fix up whatever you want, build the pond, paint the house, renovate a room, you name it. And I've been working with Gus for a couple of days now. He's a fount of information about ranching. Another possibility. There are ranches all over the west, this would be good training if I wanted to do that."

"Is construction the field you want to work in?" she asked slowly. "Or ranching? Which?"

"I would have said construction, since I worked in that area years ago. But I like what I've learned so far about ranching. It may be a whole new field for me. Brad and I can hire out together."

She laughed softly and shook her head. "I don't know. This seems like a huge change for you. Aren't you going to miss San Francisco?"

"No," he said, looking away.

"I guess that's a step in the right direction, then. Deciding what you want to do," she said slowly. Something didn't feel right, but she wasn't sure why. Did a man with an advanced degree in accounting or business or whatever suddenly change careers and work on a ranch?

"Then jeans and work shirts are all I need," he said, satisfaction evident in his tone.

Ellie caught Nick's expression. It made her uneasy. Was he up to something? But what? He wasn't avoiding work. It was his decision as to what he wanted to do. If he was serious about doing the repairs and about learning about the ranch, she'd make sure he got all the experience he could handle.

"I'll explain it to Mr. Peters," she said at last, hoping the coordinator of the project would be satisfied. He'd been understanding when Jed and Brad evidenced interest in the ranch. Why wouldn't he feel the same with Nick?

As they drove into town, Ellie mulled over their brief conversation. It was the longest one Nick had participated in since arriving. He kept to himself even at mealtimes.

Glancing at him, she took a deep breath and tried to focus on her driving. His shirt was open at the throat, displaying the brown column of his neck, his pulse beating steadily at the base. The sleeves were rolled back to the elbows, exposing the tanned skin of his forearms. The muscles of his upper arms and shoulders filled the shirt. Even staring at the highway she could see him from the corner of her eye. And what a sight he was.

Maybe Margot had been right. She'd been alone too long. She needed someone to share things with. Not marriage—she didn't want to end up dependent on some man. But if she found a companion, she could keep her independence and still have more in life than just work and the ranch.

But not Nick. Not a man who would leave in three months. No matter how enticing the thought, she would not entertain fantasies about the man! She was paying far too much attention to him as it was. She had to stop!

He remained silent for most of the trip, but Ellie knew he watched her as she drove. He seemed to spend a lot of time watching her. Or was she imagining things?

Nick studied the old town as they turned on to the main street. He'd do better to watch the buildings and take his eyes off Ellie. She intrigued him. His former fiancée had loved fancy clothes, jewelry and stylish cars. Ellie wore faded jeans and dusty boots. Her clothes were always clean and fit adequately, but she did nothing to display her trim figure or enhance her looks. She made no effort with makeup beyond a touch of mascara. And scraping her hair back from her face added nothing to her looks.

Yet she seemed complete, content. There was none of the restlessness Sheila had always displayed. Was it an act? He felt a certain satisfaction when he saw the color rise in her cheeks, the rapid rise and fall of her breasts in reaction to his bold look. At least something got to her.

"Stop staring at me," Ellie said self-consciously. Heat washed through her whole body as if every nerve ending was attuned to him, seared by him. Yearned for him.

"I like looking at you," he murmured audaciously, not turning away.

"It makes me nervous." She threw him a quick look, frowning at the gleam in his eye.

Both windows in the truck were wide-open; the air whipped around in the cab. A strand of hair came loose from Ellie's ponytail and Nick reached over to tuck it behind her ear, his fingers lightly caressing her cheek, trailing fire and ice in their wake.

Ellie tightened her hands on the wheel, her heart pounding recklessly. Her breathing stopped. His touch was so light, so gentle and so disturbing. God help her, she hoped she could park the truck without crashing into something.

She pulled up behind the National Hotel, and parked in the covered lot beneath the police station. Jackson had been a gold rush town and the old buildings gave it a special charm missing from newer towns.

"As you can see, Jackson isn't very large. You can walk to the other end in only a few minutes. There're a couple of clothing stores that will have what you want along the way. We'll meet back here in two hours. Is that all right?"

If he wanted her to go with him, he'd have to ask. But she bet he wouldn't. She knew he had received some of his money from Matt Helmsley, so there were no problems that way.

"Okay. Two hours." Nick climbed from the cab and followed her across the short bridge spanning a creek to the main street. He started up the sidewalk, watching the people, checking out the cars and trucks that lined the road. There was parking on both sides and plenty of people were in town, yet it wasn't close to being crowded like San Francisco. Several nodded as they passed, offering a soft greeting. He nodded in return.

Ellie watched him go, wishing he'd asked her to accompany him. She sighed as he disappeared from view. There was more to this particular guest than she'd bargained for. Three months would pass slowly. Especially if she acted like a love-struck teenager every time she was around him!

Sighing softly, she walked up the sidewalk. She'd check out Kat and see her in action. The girl had obtained a job as a sales clerk for one of the dress shops on Main Street but Ellie had not yet stopped in while she was working.

"Hi, Ellie!" Kat greeted her as soon as she stepped inside the shop. An elderly woman browsed clothes on the sale rack. The owner stood in the back and waved when Ellie came in.

"Can I help you find something?" Kat asked.

"You sound very professional," Ellie said smiling. She was proud of Kat. Was this how parents felt when their child succeeded? "I'm just looking today. How are things going?"

"I love working here. Yvonne said I have a natural talent for fashion. She's offered to make the job permanent when my time's up. Think I should take it?"

"Why not? You like it, you're good at it."

"I guess I thought I'd be going back to Oakland."

"Only if you want to. You get to do whatever you want," Ellie said gently.

Kat fell silent.

"Show me what you think would look good on me," Ellie suggested.

"I'd love to dress you in pastels and trendy styles. Your figure is great. You can wear a lot of things I can't. How about this top? Lavender is pretty with your skin."

For the next half hour Kat offered different clothes, keeping a running commentary on why each one would be perfect for Ellie. Tempted, Ellie truly considered buying something. She couldn't forget Margot's suggestion. But she felt so conspicuous buying new clothes right after Nick arrived. Not that she'd be buying them for him. But she worried that others might think that was the reason.

"Let me think about this," she said at last. "I don't want to rush into anything."

"Don't be stodgy, Ellie. Live a little. You could be a knockout in that blue dress."

Smiling, Ellie let herself dream for a minute. She'd glide down the stairs at home, the dress fitting like a dream. Nick waiting at the bottom of the steps… Good grief, she was trying to forget about the man, not weave new fantasies about him.

"Later, maybe. I'll let you know." She crossed to the back and spoke for a few minutes with Yvonne, then headed for the drugstore. She had time to kill until she was due to meet Nick, and other things to do besides think about him.

An hour later Ellie started for the truck. She was surprised to find Nick lounging on the wide stairs leading to the old hotel, several bags beside him.

"Been waiting long?" she called as he gathered his things and joined her on the sidewalk. He seemed more relaxed than earlier.

"No, just a few minutes. I enjoy watching people."

"Get every thing you need?" she asked.

"Sure did. It wasn't so bad." He gave her a slow, lopsided smile and Ellie's heart turned over, her insides softening. She almost faltered, grabbed a quick breath and began walking briskly toward the truck, all the while praying desperately that he wouldn't notice how his proximity affected her.

"Next stop is the supermarket. Everyone takes turns buying groceries. Sometimes I send Kat and Brad or Ariel and Jed. The results are interesting, to say the least. But as long as they get the things Alberta writes down, I don't mind the other things they buy. You probably don't need much practice in shopping for food."

"Close by my condo there was a small store where I got bread and cheese and things," he said as they walked under the roof of the parking garage. "Usually I ate out. I'm not much of a cook."

"I can cook, but I hate it. That's why Alberta is such a godsend. I had enough cooking when I was a teenager to last me forever!"

"Your truck fits in here," he said as they pulled out of the parking lot and drove the short distance to the market.

"How?"

"The whole place is like a rowdy Western town, ranches and cowboys. Every guy I saw had a cowboy hat on or boots."

"What did you expect? This is the West. And ranching's one of the big businesses around here."

"San Francisco is nothing like this."

"I know. I lived there before I moved here."

He looked at her. "And you like this place better?"

"Much. Come in and help me get the food." She stopped before the local supermarket and jumped down from the truck.

"What about the packages?" Nick asked. She'd left her window down.

"They'll be fine. No one steals things here." She headed for the store, biting her lip. She had to be careful of how she talked to him. Yet she couldn't guard every word she said.

Ellie pushed a cart toward him, pulled one free for herself.

"Two?"

"Yes, and they'll be packed." Drawing the list from her pocket, she started down the first aisle. Nick followed, scanning the rows of food, picking out items and tossing them into the cart when she called them out. When extras went in, she kept quiet. Until his cart began to fill up when they were less than halfway done.

"Nick, we're not here to buy one of everything. A few favorites are all right. One of everything on the shelves is not!" she said in exasperation when he tossed in two boxes of cereal.

"Ellie, you wouldn't want to deprive me of a breakfast cereal I haven't been able to have in ages, would you? Or applesauce, or peaches?"

"What have you been eating all this time?" she asked as he piled more items in his cart.

"Bread and water."

She laughed softly. "I don't believe you. You can have one kind of cereal. Alberta makes a hot breakfast almost every day. Any more cereal will just get stale before you can eat it. You can have another kind next week. But we're not getting four different kinds today." She reached in the cart and began pulling out the boxes.

"Ah, cookies," he rumbled as they turned the corner of another aisle.

"That's it, you read the list and push your cart. I'll pick out the groceries." Ellie tugged his arm, thrusting the paper at him.

He gazed down at her, his eyes light with amusement, surprised to be enjoying himself with their nonsense.

"Be sure to get Oreo cookies, ginger snaps, graham crackers…"

"Enough, enough—you'll O.D. on sugar. Even Jed doesn't eat all that, and he's a bottomless pit. Besides, Alberta—"

"Bakes cookies all the time," he finished.

"How did you know that?" she asked, startled.

"Didn't for sure, but it figures. We've had fresh cookies for the past couple of days. She's a treasure. We get a huge breakfast every day and she made those pies for dinner yesterday."

"Well, you're right. But she doesn't make Oreo cookies, so you can have those if you want."

Shopping took a long time, but it was more fun than Ellie ever remembered. Nick grew relaxed enough to tease her on every aisle. He wanted some of almost everything he saw, except beets. He made a big scene about beets, obviously playing up to her own insistence they were good and healthy.

Ellie wasn't sure what was serious and what was for effect as she constantly limited his selections. But he kept her laughing. And every once in a while he stared at her with a puzzled expression as if he'd never seen a laughing woman before.

When they reached the produce aisle, Ellie paused. She loved vegetables, all kinds. Eagerly she looked at the selections.

"Let's skip this row," Nick suggested, noting her delight.

"Oh, no, you need veggies to counteract all the sugar you plan to eat," Ellie said primly. "Veggies are good for you."

She stood beside him, looking up. Tempted beyond resistance, Nick reached out his hand and captured her chin, cupping it in his warm palm. He leaned over and spoke softly and firmly, his breath brushing against her cheeks.

"I'm not a young kid like Jed or Brad, remember? I don't need a mother—mine is well and living in Maryland."

Ellie couldn't believe another person's touch would have such power. She felt weak, tingly, excited, giddy. Her stomach grew warm and her breasts began to fill with a heavy desire. Widening her eyes slightly, she almost lost track of what Nick said. She could feel the warmth from his hand along her chin, across her jaw. She tried a deep breath, almost strangled. His scent filled her senses, his touch short-circuited her brain waves.

What would it be like to have him touch her all over? If his fingers against her jaw could wreak such havoc, what would his lips all over her body do? His hands along her skin, his strong muscles beneath her fingertips?

"I don't like vegetables," he said.

"None?" she asked breathlessly. She should step back, break contact, but couldn't. He leaned over her even more and for one crazy moment Ellie longed to lean forward to meet him halfway, to touch him, to feel his skin beneath her fingers. To feel the strength of him, the warmth. Feel his lips on hers.

"Peas."

"Huh?" She blinked.

"I like peas." His breath puffed against her cheeks. His eyes were silvery, solemn as he gazed deep into her own.

"Oh." She was drowning in the silver pool of Nick's gaze, unable to think, to move, to even breathe.

Gently Nick traced her jaw with his thumb as he withdrew his hand. Straightening, his lips tightened. She felt so soft, so desirable. He turned back to stare at the peas on display. Ellie Winslow was too potent. She should have slapped his hands away. In the future, he vowed, he'd keep his hands to himself or risk losing what little self-control he managed so far.

"No other vegetables, only peas?"

"I'll eat some others." He continued looking over the display, avoiding her eyes.

He'd crushed the lighthearted atmosphere. He knew it but didn't know how to change it. Ellie moved to the peas. She filled bag after bag until Nick caught on and smiled.

"Enough, as someone recently said. What happened to moderation?"

They both worked to recapture the enjoyment of earlier. He was glad she still seemed at ease with him. He couldn't keep up the roller-coaster emotions he experienced around her. He wanted to get back to the ranch, close himself in his room. Or even take one of the horses out and escape Ellie's proximity.

He stared at her long and hard as she chatted with the checkout clerk before turning and looking away. For a moment his guard had dropped. That was dangerous. He'd not forget the lesson Sheila had taught so well. Ellie was just a woman like all others. In three months he'd truly be on his own, and that was what he wanted. All he wanted.

On Saturday Ellie enlisted Ariel's help in cleaning the house until it shone. Kat worked Saturdays and so was excused from a lot of the housework, a point Ariel mentioned more than once. Ellie tried to patiently explain to Ariel that she would one day have her own home and would want to know how to keep it clean. Experience was never wasted.

Alberta planned the barbecue for that evening when Nick's city friends were expected. Making the event festive, she had one of the boys stake out horseshoe posts and set up two picnic tables. Gus oversaw the huge barbecue pit, piling on the coals and monitoring them until they glowed red.

Ellie was curious about Nick's friends. She'd met his attorney, but she didn't think Matt Helmsley and Nick were close friends. They seemed more thrown together due to circumstances than common interest, she suspected.

But from the little Nick had said last weekend about Steve, Ellie knew they were true friends. Would this visit make Nick long for his old life? Or was he content to stay away from the pursuits he'd enjoyed before? Ranch life was not for everyone, she knew. Did he miss the excitement of the city?

When Ellie heard the car turn into the driveway in the late afternoon, she went to greet Nick's guests. Nick also heard the car. He came out a moment later. His longer stride enabled him to pass Ellie as he hurried to meet his friend.

"Steve!" The men shook hands, gripping with both.

Steve was taller than Nick, and thinner. He was dressed casually in brown slacks and a cream-colored shirt, his hair a reddish-brown, his face open, friendly. Nick wore a pair of new jeans and a dark shirt. With the deeper tan he'd acquired over the past few days, he appeared more vital than his friend, Ellie thought. Or was it just because he was Nick?

A tall, sleek blonde climbed out of the car on the far side, closed the door, and went to stand beside Steve. She wore white slacks and a bright-blue silk shirt.

"And this is Nick?" she said smiling at him.

"Nick, my wife Sally." Steve made the introduction proudly.

Nick greeted her gravely, then turned to nod to Ellie as she drew closer. "Ellie Winslow, my, er, hostess. Steve and Sally Davis."

Ellie smiled a greeting, suddenly feeling shabby in her jeans and yellow cotton top. She should have listened to Margot and Kat and bought some new clothes. There was nothing wrong with hers, but they were designed for work, not entertaining.

And Sally's short sassy haircut made Ellie all the more aware of her own long hair neatly plaited in a French braid. Staid and dull. Was that how Nick saw her? She tried to imagine the women he knew. She'd lived in the city for years, she knew how others dressed. It had never been important to her. Until now.

"We have things set up in the back. Nick can give you a tour and then join us there," Ellie said after introductions had been made.

Nick looked startled. Ellie almost smiled. "Don't you want to show them around?"

"Sure." A glimmer of a smile rose in his eyes as he turned back to his friend. "You'll never believe this, Steve."

After Nick had finished showing Steve and Sally the barn and corral and talked about the program, he brought them to the back of the house. Alberta had pitchers of lemonade and iced tea on one of the picnic tables, cans of soda sitting in a huge tub of ice at the head of the table. The rest of the ranch crew was already lounging around, soda or glasses of lemonade in hand.

"What's your pleasure?" Alberta asked when introductions were complete.

"Lemonade," Sally said. "I haven't had any since I was a little girl. And I remember loving it during the summer months."

"You go sit in the shade. It's cooling down, but still hot in the sun," Alberta said after handing around drinks.

Jed and Brad were playing horseshoes with Rusty and Tomas. Gus sat on the back porch, watching the younger men, and keeping an eye on the grill. Alberta sent Ariel into the house on an errand.

Nick looked at Ellie. "Coming?"

"Don't you want to visit with your friends?" she asked softly.

"No."

"Oh," she said, puzzled. She would have thought they would have lots to discuss. "Okay, then, if I won't be intruding."

Feeling a bit shy, Ellie walked with Nick and pulled lawn chairs into the shade. Tongue-tied, she felt out of place. What did she have in common with these people? She didn't know them or their interests. Nick was their only common tie, and he sat silently, his lips tightly closed.

The silence stretched out until Ellie almost began to talk about cattle just to introduce some conversation.

Steve made a wry face and raised his glass of tea. "Here's to freedom, Nick, long may you keep it!"

Chapter Six

Nick smiled grimly, raising his glass in silent acknowledgment. "No more damn-fool stunts."

"That's what Steve called it," Sally murmured to Ellie as she sipped her lemonade, eyeing Nick with uncertainty.

"Over and over, I have no doubt," Nick said easily, with a half smile at his friend.

"Well, it's true, man. No fool like an old one."

"I won't make that mistake again." Nick scowled down into his glass.

"What are you talking about?" Ellie asked, puzzled at their exchange.

"What Nick got sent up for," Steve replied.

"Oh." Ellie said quietly. She waited a minute, then took a breath. "What?"

Three pairs of eyes swiveled to her in surprise. Nick spoke first.

"Doesn't Helping Hands have all that information?"

"Embezzlement."

"No, I never embezzled a penny," he countered quickly.

"You don't know exactly why Nick was in prison? Or about the delectable Sheila?" Steve asked.

"Who?"

"Steve..." Nick said, his tone a warning.

"You needn't explain," Ellie assured quickly, curiosity raging. She was dying to know what happened. And just who was the delectable Sheila?

"Ask, if you want to know something." His voice was hard, his gaze firmly locked on her.

Ellie studied his expression for a long moment.

"All right, then, what did you do?"

"I made a damn fool of myself over a woman." He paused as if looking a long way back. "I thought we were in love. I asked her to marry me and she accepted. Only it turned out Sheila was only using me to cover for her own crime of embezzlement. By the time I had it all figured out, I was caught and tried as an accessory." Nick's tone was bitter, his face settling into the closed, withdrawn look Ellie saw so often.

Ellie glanced at Steve and Sally. Steve stared thoughtfully at his hands clasped loosely before him. He, of course, already knew the story. Sally's eyes were fixed on Nick. When no one spoke, Nick continued.

"We worked at a financial brokerage house. She was an account executive. I was the assistant controller. Just before the annual audit, I discovered a discrepancy in the books. I worked a couple of days on it and discovered it led back to Sheila."

Nick paused and took a long swallow from his drink.

"Did you call the police?" Ellie asked softly.

"No. That was mistake number one. Or mistake number two, actually. Having anything to do with Sheila was mistake number one. I confronted her with my discovery. At my place. She cried, gave me a song and dance about wanting to be worthy of me. Of not wanting me to be ashamed of her because of her poor background. She had only used the funds she'd embezzled to buy clothes to be able to be seen with me. You can imagine—it made me feel like a heel, as if I were so shallow things like that were important." He shook his head.

Ellie leaned forward. "Then what?"

"She talked me into giving her a little time. She'd get the money from somewhere, her folks, or borrow it or something, and pay it all back before the audit. She swore she'd never do anything like that again. She'd only done it for me. Now that she knew me better, she knew clothes didn't matter. Dammit, what a pack of lies!"

"But you didn't know that then," Steve said.

"I should have. She was only looking out for herself."

"Now you look back and see that, but at the time, I can understand how you felt as you did. If Sally said something like that, I'd listen to her."

Sally gave her husband a loving smile and patted his arm.

Ellie wondered how much Nick must have loved the woman to stand by her even when she'd confessed to a crime.

"I gave her the time she requested. We were both arrested ten days later for embezzlement. Once the story came out, I was charged as an accessory. You see, Sheila had continued her scheme during those ten days. She'd hoped to get enough to get clear out of the country. If she'd had a few more days, she'd have made it."

Ellie tried to sort through her feelings at the tale. She couldn't believe a woman would betray a man who loved her. "What about Sheila? What happened to her?"

Nick didn't answer. Steve did.

"She's one gorgeous, red-haired, green-eyed bitch. Lovely to look at, but rotten at the core—selfish and greedy. Not that you could convince old Nick here, he had to learn the hard way. She was sentenced to ten years."

"A very hard lesson to learn," Nick said bitterly. "But

one I learned well, extremely well. I'll never trust a woman again.''

"Hey, Nick, don't be hasty in that decision. One woman did you wrong, but don't let that put you off women for the rest of your life. Married life can be pretty good, with the right partner.'' Steve wrapped his fingers around his wife's hand and smiled at Sally.

Whatever lingering fantasy Ellie had imagined about Nick vanished with his revelation. She understood why he had such a strong conviction to remain apart. He was not ready for any kind of commitment to another woman. After a shattering betrayal by the woman he loved, he had erected barriers taller than anything she could scale. And she didn't blame him. How did anyone recover from such a blow?

In time he might meet someone he could trust, grow to love. Time, however, was not on Ellie's side. He wouldn't be here long, and once he left it was unlikely their paths would cross again.

Nick glared at his friend. "Easy for you to say. I'm glad you and Sally are making a good life together. I'd hoped to do that, too. But look where it got me. You tried it and succeeded. I tried it and went bust. I'm not willing to risk it again.''

"I am lucky and I admit it. I hope you will find the same luck one day, too, Nick,'' Steve said slowly.

"Ellie, tell me about this place. Has it been in your family long?'' Sally asked brightly, changing the subject.

"It belonged to my grandparents. When my father died a few years ago, it was left to me,'' she said quietly, refusing to look at Nick, refusing to dwell on the painful surprise his story had caused her. For one long moment she tried to imagine having a man love her so much he'd throw away honor and honesty for her sake.

She couldn't do it. She was not the type to inspire such passion. But the chasm between her and Nick seemed even larger than before. Sighing softly for a dream that never would see daylight, she turned her attention to Nick's friends and their interest in the ranch.

"As you can probably see, it was neglected for years. As time and money permits, I'm repairing it little by little. Nick's going to help."

In all the years she'd cared for her father, nursed him, catered to him, put up with his cranky nature, his caustic tongue, she'd never known about this property. With all the problems with Bobby, their father had never mentioned the ranch. It had graphically emphasized to her how little he'd really cared for either of them. She could never forgive her father owning this haven and denying it to Bobby. She could almost understand Nick's determination to go it alone. A person was safer on their own with no one to let them down when they foolishly relied on that person. She'd learned that lesson from her father. Independence was the only way to live. Respecting that yearning in Nick was easy. If only she could forget her own attraction to the man.

"*Nick's* going to help?" Steve asked with a teasing glance at his friend.

"That's right. Get another kind of experience behind me. I'm not going back to an office job. No one's going to hire an embezzling accountant. Thought I'd try construction or maybe ranching."

"But what about—" Steve caught the sharp negative shake of Nick's head and stopped. "Well, I guess it's as good a skill as any. I never figured you outside an office, somehow."

"Time will tell," Nick said.

A short time later, Alberta announced they were starting to cook and everyone should come and place their orders.

Kat arrived from work just as Alberta began to place the meat on the hot grill. Per requests, there were steaks for the cowboys, barbecue chicken and ribs for Nick and his guests and the ubiquitous hamburgers and hot dogs for the teenagers.

When it was time to eat, Ellie arranged the seating so Nick and his friends had a picnic table to themselves. Sally called her to join them. Hesitating only a moment, Ellie agreed, moving her plate from the other table. She was aware of Kat's frown, but ignored it. Nick's friends wouldn't want a bunch of teenagers at their table.

Dinner proved to be fun. Steve reminisced about his and Nick's early days together in San Francisco, two young bachelors out to set the world on fire. Sally talked about her job as an assistant television producer for a local station.

Ellie felt emboldened enough to speak briefly about her own life when she lived in San Francisco. She glossed over her domineering father and spoke more of the walks she liked to take in the parks near their apartment, of the fun she had in her art classes. And the excitement surrounding the first book she and Margot had sold.

As the conversation ebbed and flowed, Ellie picked up a new perspective of Nick. His conversation was sprinkled with funny anecdotes and knowledgeable insights to current events—with an overriding hint of biting cynicism. Had he been this way before? Or was the cynicism a result of his recent experiences?

It was growing dark when Steve announced they'd have to leave. "With a three-hour drive ahead of us, we won't be home until late."

"Y'all are welcome to stay the night," Ellie offered. "I have a spare bedroom."

"Another time, perhaps," Sally said. "I would love to come back and see that pond when it's done."

"And all the work around the place Nick is planning to do," Steve added, with a wry look at his friend.

Ellie walked to the car with the Davises and stood beside Nick in the quiet driveway watching the taillights disappear around the bend. The night had grown dark, silent, the temperature continued balmy. For a moment, if she let her imagination run riot, she could pretend she and Nick were a couple bidding farewell to friends. They'd turn and head back into the house together, talking softly about the evening, enjoying the lingering feeling of closeness and—

Nick turned and headed for the house, without saying a word.

So much for imagination, Ellie thought as she turned and caught up with him.

"Your friends are nice," she said.

"First time I met Sally. They had a whirlwind courtship, have only been married a few months. Steve told me all about her when he visited. Thanks for letting them come over."

"This is your home for the duration."

Nick hesitated near the porch, looking at her. He took a deep breath. "It's still awkward for me to meet people. You made it easier today. Thank you." He said the words hesitantly, as if they were hard to form.

Her heart ached. She was happy if she had helped—that was the purpose of the program, and she wanted him to succeed. But there was only so much she could do. Nick had to do the rest himself.

"I enjoyed them. Invite whomever you wish."

"Maybe." He raised his hand and tentatively brushed the backs of his fingers against her cheek. "Thanks again."

Startled, Ellie's heart stopped, skipped a beat, then raced. Things seemed to spin around. His touch had been unexpected, but her reaction was becoming commonplace around him. Instantly she wished for more. Wished he had kissed her. She wanted to meet his lips with hers, capture the magic of a first kiss with a special man. Her arms rigidly held by her side so she didn't fling them around his neck, she cleared her throat, wishing one of the other guests would come around the house, or Alberta would call her.

"I'm going for a walk. Want to go, old boy?" Nick

called to Tam, lying on the porch. With a joyful bark, the big dog bounded over to Nick, tail wagging.

"I'll see you both in the morning, then," Ellie said calmly as she moved toward the porch, holding herself erect, her emotions damped down. She wished Nick had asked her instead of Tam to go for a walk with him.

If she was wishing for things, she ought to wish she could control her feelings around him. She experienced none of these feelings with anyone else. Who would have suspected her new guest would wreak such havoc with her senses?

Immediately after breakfast on Monday morning, Ellie went to her studio. She had work to do on the current book and needed to get going on it. The weekend had been full of activities. Yesterday she'd gone riding with Jed and then spent part of the afternoon with Ariel. Kat kept pestering Nick until he excused himself and went to his room, firmly closing the door behind him.

Picking her paints, Ellie tried to work on her drawings for the new book, but felt too restless. Time and time again she looked out the window, trying to see where the others were.

Others? Or just Nick?

Throwing down her brush she rose and paced back and forth. This was ridiculous. Maybe if she talked to Margot, she could settle down. They could discuss the book, get her back in the mood for painting.

Instead of being in the mood for spending time with Nick Tanner, Ellie thought as she dialed her friend's number.

"Hello, *chérie*." Margot's friendly voice answered the phone. "What's up?"

"I just called to talk about the book. Do you have the first draft finished yet? If I can read it, maybe I can come up with some ideas."

"We already blocked out the ideas for the illustrations. What did you want to change?" Margot asked slowly.

"Nothing." She sighed. "Margot, I'm having painter's block."

Her friend laughed softly. "It's supposed to be writer's block."

"I just don't feel like painting today."

"So don't. Go herd some cattle."

"I have ranch hands for that."

"Speaking of hands, how are you and Nick doing?" Margot asked.

"In what?"

"In the friendship department, *ma chère,* what else?"

Ellie felt the stain of color flood her cheeks. Friendship wasn't exactly what she craved. But she dare not let anyone else know that!

"We're doing fine—like the others. He had some friends over on Saturday. They were nice." And trendy and more interesting than she could ever be.

"Have you cut your hair yet?" Margot asked suddenly.

"Margot, I don't think…"

"Ellie, do allow me the concession that I know fashion. You'd do well to follow my advice."

"Kat said that."

"When?"

"I stopped in her shop last week. She wanted me to buy a whole bunch of clothes."

"So do it."

"But it seems so…so blatant!" Ellie protested.

"What is wrong with looking one's best for someone, especially when the someone is so very male?"

"Margot, he's in the program. I can't do anything with him, even if he wanted to, which he doesn't." Not with her, not with any woman.

"You do not wish to marry, just amuse yourself. Really, Ellie, splurge *un peu.*"

Ellie played with the telephone cord. "I don't know—" She was so tempted.

"Ellie? Do it."

"I'll think about it."

When she hung up, Ellie wandered into the hall, surprised to find she was actually thinking about what Margot had suggested. Stopping before the mirror, she lifted the hair from her neck, trying to envision it short. It had been this length as long as Ellie could remember. It was so easy just to pull it back. How would it look short?

Would Nick notice if she got it cut? Would he like it?

Unable to paint, Ellie gave up trying and drove herself into town. Maybe she would buy some of those clothes Kat had recommended after she changed her hairstyle. Summer was coming and with it very hot weather. A shorter style would be much easier to care for, and cooler. Could she get something sleek and elegant like Sally? Or sexy and sassy like Margot's cut? Somehow she didn't see any of the adjectives applying to her.

Plain old country girl. Was that a style? It sure depicted her now. But she wanted a change.

The hairdresser was quick once she verified Ellie really wanted the length cut off. Ellie was pleased with the result. Without the weight, her hair curled. The cut was light and carefree and made her look years younger. She shook her head, delighting in the feel of the wispy curls.

The stunned expression on Kat's face when Ellie entered the boutique was worth the whole trip. Kat exclaimed over the new haircut and then insisted that Ellie had to buy some new clothes to go with her new look. Showing off, she picked out several outfits, and a handful of tops and shorts, expounding on the effects the new clothes would have.

When Ellie tried them on, she felt as if she were looking at a stranger. Was the woman with the tiny waist and long legs really her? The tops contoured to her body, emphasizing her shapely breasts. The shorts were very short and her legs pale beneath them. She wore jeans too much to acquire a tan. Maybe she should rethink that, as well.

Kat talked her into wearing the short pink top and new jeans home.

As she rang up the sale, almost bursting with pride for such a large order, Kat looked at Ellie with speculation.

"Isn't this a sudden change?" she asked suddenly suspicious.

"Margot has been ragging on me for a while to enhance my wardrobe," Ellie said easily. "She feels I let down my half of the team."

"I thought it might be because of Nick," Kat said as she slipped the last of the tops into a huge bag.

"Nick?" Ellie said, hoping the heat she felt in her cheeks didn't show.

"He's a real babe. I bet every woman who sees him, wants him."

"Well, he's a guest at the ranch like the rest of you. Only here for a short time, then on his way." Not for anything would she give Kat a hint of how she felt about Nick. Not that she was sure herself. Was it only physical attraction? Or something deeper?

"Wish I was going to be home when you show up. I bet they don't even recognize you!"

"Thanks for your help, Kat. I'm happy with the new clothes." Now if she could get home without shattering into a thousand nerve endings. The enormity of what she'd done was starting to make itself felt. Was she a total idiot?

In for a penny, in for a pound—Ellie stopped at the drugstore to pick up some new makeup then headed self-consciously back to the truck. With any luck, everyone at the ranch would be out working and she could sneak into her bedroom without anyone the wiser.

Of course they would all see her at dinner.

Nick brushed down his horse and turned him loose in the corral. Within seconds the perverse animal rolled in the soft dirt, coating himself with a dusty layer.

"Dammit, I just brushed you!" Nick called at the horse.

Gus rested his arm on the top rail of the corral fence and chuckled softly. "Horses are the very devil, aren't they?"

"Why bother to brush them if they immediately roll?" Nick asked in disgust.

"That cools them off. A man always takes care of his horse, never know when you'll depend upon him for your life."

"Surely that was in the Old West," Nick said, eyeing Gus suspiciously.

"Can be true today. A lot of ranching hasn't changed much from a hundred years ago. Of course, a lot has. There sure is a hell of a lot more paperwork. Poor Ellie, it's a struggle for her to keep up. Business isn't her strong suit. She's an artist at heart."

"Seems to be doing okay." Nick said shortly.

Gus shrugged. "Time will tell. But I know she subsidizes the ranch income with that from her painting." He took off his hat and hit it against his thigh to shake off the dust, then replaced it carefully. "Dinner be soon, time to wash up."

Nick watched the old man head for his cottage. Gus had to be seventy if he was a day—whipcord tough, wiry, full of energy. Nick didn't know how he did it. He himself was tired at the end of every day and he didn't do as much as Gus. Of course he'd been doing it less than two weeks and Gus had a lifetime behind him, but still, he could give the man forty years.

When he heard a truck, he turned toward the house. Were Kat and Ariel returning from work? No, they'd taken the old truck. The big one was usually reserved for Ellie.

It stopped and the door opened. Nick stopped walking and stared. A shapely rear was the view he got as the woman leaned into the truck. In a moment she straightened, her arms full of bags.

He looked at Ellie with astonishment, straightening to his full height. He almost didn't recognize her. She'd done something to her hair. The short curls were perfect with her small stature. He could see her eyes shining even behind her glasses and her color was high.

Damn, the reaction came fast and hard—pure desire.

For a moment he felt as if he'd been kicked by that dusty horse. Then his common sense took over. Lusting after Ellie Winslow was plain stupid, no matter how pretty she suddenly looked.

And she looked like a beauty. Amazing what a haircut could do. Or was it the pink top she wore?

She glanced at him, almost in panic, and whirled around to hurry into the house. Nick followed more slowly. He needed a minute to get his raging hormones under some kind of control.

He'd liked her hair that night he'd seen it swirling around her shoulders. Now he wished he could thread his fingers through those soft curls, feel the texture of that silky-looking mass, see if those curls wound themselves around his fingers. He jerked back, not liking where his thoughts were heading—where they seemed permanently lodged these days.

Ellie escaped to her room and dumped her bags on the bed. Darting to the mirror, she stared at herself, seeing the stranger she'd seen at the dress shop. Taking off her glasses, she gazed at herself, slowly smiling. Even if no one else noticed the change, she liked it.

She put her new clothes away and went to the bathroom with her new makeup. Slowly experimenting, she enhanced her eyes. Without her glasses, they looked mysterious and interesting. For several moments she studied her new appearance. Sighing, she put the glasses back on. She had no wish for Kat or Ariel to start speculating aloud at the dinner table on the reason for the sudden change. But just maybe she'd call her eye doctor about contacts.

Alberta made a fuss when Ellie came down to help set the table. Ariel immediately wanted her hair curled so it would look like Ellie's and Jed and Brad flirted with her as if she were their age. The only person who didn't make a comment at the dinner table was Nick. But twice Ellie caught him staring at her.

At the end of the meal, Nick spoke for the first time. "Gus has all the help he needs for the next few days. Want me to start on that pond?"

So much for his noticing her haircut or the new top. She ignored the hint of disappointment that he had nothing more personal to say and nodded. There was too much going on to interrupt the normal flow of ranch work, but she did want to enjoy the pond this summer if she could.

"If nobody has other plans when dinner is finished we can discuss it."

"Everyone?"

"What's to discuss?" Brad asked. "Aren't we just going out there to dig a hole and fill it with water?"

Nick shook his head. "There's a bit more involved with it. Advanced planning will make the project go more smoothly."

Jed wrinkled his nose. "Sounds like even more work, to me."

Nick nodded. "But planning at the beginning saves time in the long run. If we know what we're doing, there's no wasted effort. We don't want to run short of cement at a critical point, or find out we can't get electricity to the location when we're all ready to go with the pump. We need to check out the pricing of the supplies, get the best deal we can for Ellie. Same as you would for all the different supplies the ranch needs."

Brad looked at Ellie. "Do you do that for everything?"

"Of course she does," Nick said.

Slowly Ellie shook her head. "I haven't a clue what you're even talking about," she said slowly.

"What?"

"I don't plan things out like that. I just buy things when we need them and pay the bills when they come in."

"How do you know you're getting the best prices, that you are taking advantages of sales, or quantity lot discounts?"

She shrugged.

He looked around the table; every eye was fixed on him. Slowly Nick looked back at Ellie. It was hard to concentrate on business when she looked so damned enticing. Her eyes seemed huge behind her glasses. Her hair looked like a sunny halo around her head. Feeling the familiar reaction, he damped down the desire. This was important. For her anyway.

"Ellie, Gus told me you are always doing accounts and things for the ranch, I assumed that meant planning as well. How do you know if you have enough money to do the renovations you want, expand the herd, meet your expenses?"

"I'm not very good at that part of ranching yet. Really, when you think about it, I'm a painter, an artist. Business is confusing to me." She looked at Jed and Brad, then Gus. "Maybe we need some help with this."

Nick wanted to withdraw, to get up and leave. He didn't want to be drawn into her life any more than he had to be to make it through his three months. But he couldn't imagine just paying bills when they came due without having an idea of what was right, what needed to be budgeted for.

"You're an accountant, maybe you could give us some pointers," Ellie said firmly.

"No."

Brad looked at him. "Hey, man, if you can help, why

not? I'll show you how to hot-wire a car if you like. It's something I'm good at.''

"Thanks, Brad, but I think that's a skill Nick doesn't need to know," Ellie said dryly. "You'd do better to teach him some of that roping you've been practicing so long."

"Yeah, but if there's more to ranching than just riding a horse, don't you think we all should know about it?"

"Count me out," Kat said quickly. "I don't want to live on a ranch my whole life."

"But basic business guidelines would help you in whatever you did in the future," Ellie said. "Right, Nick?"

He shook his head.

"Yes, it would. It would help all of us and you have the expertise to teach us."

His jaw worked as he clenched his teeth. Damn the woman, she was deliberately putting him on the spot. "Not with my history."

She waved a hand as if dismissing it as trivial. "Nonsense, I'd take it as a personal favor if you'd show us where we could improve."

Surprisingly, he longed to do it. He loved bringing order out of chaos. He liked projections, analysis and searching for the best way to allocate funds.

"Besides, Ellie said we are all a family while we're here. Family helps each other, right?'' Ariel said warily. She looked at Ellie and then smiled almost shyly at the delight on the older woman's face.

Nick thought of his family, so far away. He'd hidden the fact he'd been charged, convicted and sent to prison from them. Through judicial use of an answering machine, and Steve's mailing letters for him, he'd covered his tracks. They would be horrified to know where he'd been for the past three years. He didn't think his idea of family was what Ellie had in mind.

Nor had Ellie anything to guide her, if the faint hints

she'd given about her own family life were anything to go by.

But she'd obviously impressed that notion on her charges.

He didn't feel any kinship with these teens. They were from broken homes, the wrong side of town. Street-smart punks who had been caught. But Ellie was trying to change that. Given the chance, he had an idea they'd make it. Maybe not all of them, but the ones who came through Ellie's place had a good shot at it. Because of the woman and her determination. And her loving care.

He'd be more interested in a different kind of loving. For a moment he saw himself drawing Ellie into his arms—

"Nick?"

Chapter Seven

Nick took a moment, to focus on Ellie. He nodded once. "What?"

"You will help, too?"

"I'm not doing this alone. Everyone has to pitch in."

"I'm not an accountant," Ariel protested.

"But you're part of this makeshift family, right? You can call around and get pricing on cement. Kat can call and ask about pipes and pumps for the waterfall. One of you can check with the city for building permits. Brad and Jed can help me stake out the pond. Rusty and Tomas can locate the rocks we'll need for the waterfall. And all of you can help when it comes to digging the hole and pouring the cement."

If they wanted family solidarity, he'd give it to them.

"And what about Ellie, what does she have to do?" Kat asked petulantly.

"Ellie and I will review the accounts for the ranch, make plans and designs she wants for improvements around here, create a schedule for implementing each project, begin list-ing building materials and estimate costs. When we get started, you can all help in that, too.''

Nick looked at the stunned faces and almost smiled. It was time they knew if they pushed him, he'd push back.

''And Brad, once we have things straightened out with Ellie's accounts, she ought to let you handle some of them while you're here. That would give you a broader base for ranching.''

'''And all experience is good','' Ariel quoted.

''Have you done this type of thing for a ranch before?'' Ellie asked. It sounded totally complex but thorough, con-trasting sharply with her own haphazard way of just wading in and figuring things out as she went along.

''Not for a ranch. But this is project management, pure business, nothing else. We'll apply the same rule to ranch-ing as to other businesses. We get cost estimates, itemize plans, set schedules and deadlines—then we'll be ready to go. We'll know how long it will take, what it'll cost. No surprises along the way.''

Ellie nodded, fascinated by this part of Nick. For the first time since his arrival, his tough-guy attitude eased. He seemed confident and assured. She felt the excitement around the table take hold. She could imagine him as he must have worked before, planning, scheduling, organizing. He probably had been tops in his field.

And he lost it all for the love of a woman.

She glanced around the table. The others were already talking back and forth with Nick, asking how to do the various tasks he listed, excitement sparking in each eye. This could be a godsend. She hoped it helped Nick as much as it would the rest of her charges.

He answered the questions that flew fast and furiously with a calm, even manner, treating each one as if it were important and meaningful. Nothing in his manner made the others feel ignorant or stupid. He could be a great teacher, she thought suddenly. Had he ever considered that? Of course with his record, that was impossible. But maybe in something like Helping Hands?

Over the next two days the activity around the house surprised Ellie. Nick had the other guests organized better than she'd ever seen them. With cost estimates being tracked down and discussions about the schedule of the project, everyone joined in with suggestions and ideas. They compared estimates and argued about who still had work to finish to bring in their contribution.

Gus kept them busy outside. Mornings he assigned tasks to Nick, Jed and Brad—primarily help for the two cowboys. Afternoons Nick spent in the office, going through Ellie's accounts and working to get a handle on her financial situation.

Thursday at lunch Nick announced they were ready to start on the pond. He wanted Ellie to approve the markers for the perimeter once he and Jed staked it out.

Nick placed the stakes where Ellie had indicated she wanted the pond, holding them while Jed pounded them into the hard ground. Brad watched, but didn't get in the way. Consulting Ellie on the location of the waterfall and drainpipe, Nick then staked where the water piping and the electrical wiring would go. The ground had been baked hard in the late spring sun. When he was ready to begin, Nick sent Ellie to find a pick and some shovels.

"Not today," she said.

"Why not?"

"This is a momentous event. Like when we poured the foundation for the new barn. We need to celebrate." Her guests had had little to celebrate in their short lives. Ellie wanted to expand their experiences, make major events out of commonplace things so they could see a difference in life.

"Tomorrow before Kat and Ariel leave, when the cow-

boys are still around, we'll have a groundbreaking cere-
mony with everyone.''

"It's a damn pond, Ellie, not a new bridge or shopping
center,'' Nick said in exasperation.

"Still, it's a new project for all of us and I want a cer-
emony.''

Nick stared at her for a long moment. "Fine, you're the
boss. If we're finished for the day, I'll head for my room.''
He walked away without a backward glance.

Ellie watched him go, feeling disappointed. They spent
so little time together. He'd expected her in the office while
he was working, but she told him to get things under control and then teach her how to maintain them. Her interest
did not lie in office work. He'd been surprised she trusted
him with her accounts. But faith and trust were tenets of
Helping Hands. Plus Ellie felt confident about Nick. He was
an honest, honorable man who had been caught up with
the wrong woman.

"It's hot, better to dig in the morning or late afternoon,
anyway,'' Jed said watching Nick walk away.

"Works for me,'' Brad said ambling toward the barn.

"I think you're right. Either of you want to share some
lemonade on the porch?'' Ellie asked. If she couldn't be
with Nick, why not one or both of the young men she was
growing fond of.

"I want to go riding,'' Brad said with a friendly salute.

"I'm all for sitting and doing nothing,'' Jed said. He
grinned self-consciously. "Uh, Ellie, I didn't tell you the
other night, but you look pretty with your short hair.''

"Why, Jed, thank you. You've made my day!'' She
beamed at the young man, touched he'd delivered such a
nice compliment.

"As soon as I get the lemonade, we'll sit and talk,'' she
said brightly.

Ellie went to the kitchen for the lemonade. She knew
Alberta kept an icy pitcher in the refrigerator.

Glancing at the closed door to Nick's room, Ellie wondered what he was doing? He spent a lot of time in his room. When everyone gathered to watch TV or play games in the evenings, he would excuse himself and retire to his room.

Had he always been such a loner, she wondered? Or had that changed with his recent past? She wished she felt comfortable enough around him to ask why he spent so much time alone. Maybe one day she'd gather the courage.

The hot spell continued into the next day. When Ellie rose she donned a pair of denim shorts and a cool top. She'd been wearing the skimpy tops Kat had chosen for her for several days now and liked them. Today was the first day for shorts. But if she was to be shoveling dirt, it would be hot work. She needed to keep cool, didn't she?

Leaving her glasses on the nightstand, she made her way downstairs. Everything at a distance was slightly blurry, but she could see clearly close-up and she didn't need the aggravation of them sliding off her nose as they worked.

They began work on the pond immediately after breakfast. Ellie had a camera and took pictures of all her guests, of the ranch hands and Gus and Alberta. The older woman insisted on taking a group picture with Ellie in the center.

Ellie ceremoniously handed Nick the pick and Jed and Brad each a shovel.

"I declare the new pond officially started."

"Don't you want to take the first swing?" Nick asked sardonically.

She grinned, hoping the excitement that sizzled was attributed to the festivity of the morning. "No, thank you. That honor is all yours."

He nodded, swung the pick over his head and slammed it down onto the ground. A small wedge of dirt broke apart.

Everyone cheered. The project was officially launched.

Within a few short minutes only Ellie, Nick and Jed remained.

"Looks like we're the work crew for today," Ellie said.

"Everyone gets a turn," Nick said, hefting the pick again. "The others are scheduled for the evenings or on the weekend."

Ellie watched, enjoying the soothing rhythm as Nick raised the pick over his head, then swung it down smashing it into the hard earth, loosening clods of dirt. The ground broke up, spread, until there was a layer of dirt ready for the shovel. His muscles rippled beneath his skin, straining with effort to break up the hard ground. She watched, fascinated, as his body moved rhythmically, easily.

Jed stepped in and scooped up the dirt on his shovel, dumping it into a wheelbarrow. Once it was full, he headed for the corrals. Nick planned for the dirt to be spread there.

Around ten, Ellie went inside to get cold drinks. As soon as she left, Nick leaned on the pick, resting. He'd been trying to ignore Ellie's presence all morning, but during the last few minutes, he had lost that ability, had been intensely conscious of her eyes on him. He stretched and tried to loosen his muscles. He could feel the exertion already, and knew he'd be sore tomorrow. Last week it had been from riding. Now from this. He began to wonder if his body would ever feel normal again.

But it felt good to be doing something physical, it helped work off his anger and let him forget. Of course being around Ellie sometimes had him forgetting in a totally different way. And that was dangerous.

The sun shone hot overhead and the skimpy top and shorts she wore weren't making Nick cooler. He pulled his shirt over his head and mopped his forehead. Tossing the shirt aside, he grabbed the pick and started again. Maybe he could work until he was exhausted and sleep the night without fantasizing about the woman.

Ellie interrupted a few moments later with a large glass of icy lemonade.

"How're you doing?" she asked, her gaze running over his shoulders, down his chest. From the look in her eyes, Nick felt ten feet tall. She looked as if she could eat him up.

Heady sensations rushed through him as he reached for the glass. What would it be like to have her hands touch him? To have her fingers brush along his skin, teasing, tormenting?

He drank the cold beverage quickly, averting his eyes from the hungry look in hers. Dammit, she was driving him crazy!

"The ground's harder than I thought." Nick said, mopping the sweat from his face. Taking a final swallow of the lemonade, he looked at her. "Want a turn?"

She wrinkled her nose. "Now that I see how hard it is, I don't think so."

"Smart lady." He handed her his glass. Their fingers brushed lightly and Ellie felt a tingle where he'd touched her. Nick didn't appear to notice.

Ellie stepped back, watching him as he worked. He talked softly with Jed, explaining what he thought about the pond, about the hole they were digging.

The play of muscles under his skin as his arms rose and fell was enticing. Ellie ignored his quiet voice as she feasted her eyes on him. She longed to run her fingers along his shoulders, against his chest, to feel the play of muscles beneath her fingertips, to run her hands all over his trim, hard body.

Licking suddenly dry lips, Ellie wondered how it would feel to have his lips against hers in a deep kiss, with his hot skin beneath her hands, against her body as he drew her to him? Her hands ached to feel the muscles of his back move beneath them, her breasts tingled in yearning and desire.

Nick had shown no interest in her, only a brief caress against her cheek when his friends had left. For heaven's sake, she chided herself, he'd been without a woman for over three years, if he had the slightest interest, he'd have made some move by now.

The next time Jed took a wheelbarrow full of dirt toward the barn, Nick ran his eyes down Ellie's lithe body. Why was she hanging around? Didn't she have a clue how hard she made things? He grimaced at his pun and slammed the pick back into the dirt. His lips drew into a line of strong disapproval, and he turned slightly away from her lest she see the evidence of his body's growing reaction to her proximity.

"I don't want to dig in this heat, but I want to contribute something. Is there anything I can do?" Ellie asked.

"The only thing you'll contribute is a distraction in those indecent shorts," he remarked.

"It's hot today. I want to be cool," she replied, startled at first, then unexpectedly excited by the look on his face. So her attire disturbed him?

"I want to be cool, too, but I won't be, watching you in those shorts."

Ellie gave a soft gurgle of laughter. "Then don't look," she said provocatively.

He ignored her, lifting the pick to slam it into the hard ground, loosening soil, raising it again. His muscles strained to the work, his rhythm smooth and steady.

He lifted the pick again. Maybe he could exhaust himself and forget about Ellie and her trim little body—her trim *sexy* body. He slammed the pick into the ground again and swallowed as he shifted slightly so he couldn't see her from the corner of his eye. Not that he needed her there to see her. His mind had captured every aspect of the woman, and delighted in recalling each detail.

Within the confines of his own personal goals he would try to make this program work. But she was playing with fire. If she didn't watch out, he'd throw her on the hot ground and show her what wearing sexy skimpy clothes did to a man. She was bright, endearing and sexy as hell—and either was the most innocent woman he'd ever met or one who played a deep, dangerous flirtatious game.

"Ellie, where's Jed? It's his turn to help with shopping and I'm almost ready to go," Alberta called.

Jed appeared from behind the barn. Slowly he brought the wheelbarrow back to the pond site. "Guess I have to do that, huh?"

Ellie smiled. "Sure do, buster. Shop fast so you can get back to this."

"At least it'll be air-conditioned in the store," he mumbled as he picked up his shirt. "I'll have to change before we leave." He waved to Nick and headed for the bunkhouse, calling to Alberta that he'd be ready in just a few minutes.

"How about if I put the dirt in the wheelbarrow and move it?" Ellie asked. "We just can't leave it here to pile up for Jed's return."

"If you think you're up to it." The last thing he wanted was her hanging around. Why couldn't she have gone with Alberta to shop and left Jed with him?

She moved the empty wheelbarrow close to the loosened dirt and pushed the shovel into it.

He stepped back. She was too close. He could smell her light scent, almost feel the warmth from her body.

Ellie lifted a shovelful of dirt and dumped it into the wheelbarrow. Nick watched her arms strain beneath the weight. Watched as she swiveled around to drop it in the wheelbarrow. Leaning over to get another scoopful, her rounded derriere pressed against her shorts. He could almost feel the softness against his hands. He tightened his grip on the pick. He was going to go crazy standing here watching her flaunt her sexy body around him.

He wiped the sweat from his forehead and looked away,

then back when he heard a soft sound. She tried to move the wheelbarrow, but it was too heavy.

"I'll do it." Careful not to touch her, he took the weight and tilted the cart, pushing it up the slight incline.

"You'd never manage it this full. Next time don't put so much in at once," he instructed.

"Right." She didn't mind watching him as he walked away. The expanse of muscles in his back was just as enticing as the front view.

As the day grew warmer, Ellie's enthusiasm waned. She stopped for a rest, watching Nick take over the dirt removal as if the temperature had not climbed to such a high degree.

Nick's skin took on a shimmery bronze tint. Every once in a while when he leaned over, she caught a glimpse of a startling strip of white flesh just below the edge of his jeans. Each time, Ellie had to take a deep breath, force her thoughts elsewhere, force herself to keep her fingers from reaching out and touching that tantalizing strip of skin.

They ate lunch alone in the cool kitchen. Alberta and Jed had not returned and the rest of the crew was scattered.

"We need to take a break after lunch," Ellie said as she placed their sandwiches and drinks on the table. "It's too hot out there for such hard work."

Nick glanced up at her, then looked back at the food. "Good idea. I've got some things to do."

"Not another walk."

"No, I'm getting more than enough exercise working around this place."

"So no more walks? Tam will be disappointed."

He hesitated and looked at her. "I still like walking—it gives me time to think."

"About what?"

"This and that," he said vaguely, taking the iced tea and tipping the glass, pouring the cool beverage down his throat.

Ellie watched the muscles of his throat work as he swallowed the drink. She looked away, her hands held tightly in her lap.

To think, he'd said. About what? What the future must hold? When his friends had visited, he'd told her to ask if she wanted to know anything. Dare she?

Tracing patterns on the glass's condensation, she glanced up at him from beneath her lashes. ''Accessory doesn't seem to fit what you did. You didn't participate in the embezzlement. You didn't take any of the money. Why did you get time in prison?'' she asked quickly before she lost her nerve.

He looked startled, then wary. ''The original charge was accessory because Sheila embezzled money after the time I discovered it. Since I did nothing to stop her once I discovered the crime, I was charged with being an accessory. It was reduced to 'after-fact' when I pleaded guilty and repaid the difference in the money from what she took and what they recovered from her. The judge in the case was very much against white collar crime, convinced most perpetrators got off with only a slap on the wrist. He made an example out of us. I received a thirty-month sentence after already spending six months in jail pending trial. Sheila got ten.''

Ellie blinked, trying to imagine how it would be to know you were being locked up for a decade. Wryly she felt almost a hint of sympathy. She'd felt like a prisoner for much longer. All the long lonely years she'd had to care for her father had been like prison. Only her art classes and work with Margot gave her a glimpse of how a normal life could be.

She wished she had been strong enough to leave her father when she'd been younger. Regrets and rage had flooded when she'd first discovered her father's perfidy about the ranch. But the past could not be changed, she had learned from it and moved on. Today she was her own woman, independence hard-won, but cherished because of the past.

Nick helped with the dishes without a word. Once finished, he headed for his room.

''I'll start up again around four,'' he said before closing the door firmly behind him, shutting Ellie out.

She refilled her glass with iced tea and went to sit in the swing on the shady porch. There was no denying she was attracted to Nick Tanner. She liked to watch him, listen to him talk. Wished she knew more about him. She sighed and took a sip, starting the swing moving. Even though he didn't think so, the next three months would pass swiftly. He had most of his life ahead of him. How he'd laugh if he thought she entertained fantasies of figuring in that life. She'd treat him as the others, then wave farewell with a smile on her face.

Her heart constricted at the thought. She didn't want to wave goodbye, she wanted him to stay. Suddenly a thought struck her. She couldn't be falling in love with Nick Tanner!

She closed her eyes briefly and took another long sip of the cold tea.

It was absurd. He was a guest, just like Jed or Brad or the others that had stayed at the ranch. Besides, he didn't see her in any romantic light. There were too many obstacles to overcome to make any relationship between them possible. Their separate life-styles were vastly different. She had lived a cloistered existence with her ailing father. Once on her own, instead of remaining in the city and making friends, she'd moved to the country and surrounded herself with society's misfits. She didn't feel like a crusader, but she was determined to make a difference—because of Bobby. In memory of her brother.

She didn't know how long she sat, but her tea was long gone when she finally moved. Bored with sitting, wanting to get away from her thoughts, Ellie wandered behind the barn. Eyeing the pile of dirt dumped by endless wheelbarrow trips, she grabbed a rake and began spreading the piles across the corral, glad for the activity.

The horses dozing in the afternoon sun watched her. One chestnut ambled over to be petted, interfering with her work, but she didn't mind. He wanted attention, like she did. She was glad to give it to him, wishing Nick would give her some attention.

As she pushed the dirt around, she wondered again what would it be like to be loved so strongly that a man would lie for you, cover a crime, give you a second chance when you didn't deserve it. Ellie was jealous of Sheila. Jealous and angry. How could the woman throw all that away?

After dinner, Ellie excused herself early to soak in a hot bath. She was bone weary and longed for bed. Through the open window she heard the others still working on the pond. It was a good project, one that had her small group working together, pulling together just like a family should do. It gave them experience in cooperation and teamwork. In sharing a common goal, and working together to achieve it.

She climbed into bed too tired to even read. But not too tired to think. Again she wondered what Nick did holed up in his room. He spent a lot of time there, yet she never heard the radio. Did he read? Or brood?

She awoke sometime later with a crick in her neck and a raging thirst. Focusing on her clock, she saw it was one-thirty. It felt closer to dawn. Sighing, she threw off the sheet, grabbed her robe and padded softly down the stairs moving quietly into the kitchen. The house was silent. Everyone slept. The light from the moon spilled in through the window, illuminating the room sufficiently for Ellie to find a glass and draw water.

Greedily she drank, quenching her thirst. She placed the

glass quietly on the sink, trying to keep from making noise. She didn't want to wake Nick.

She heard a scrape outside. Before she could investigate, the back door flew open.

Nick clicked on the overhead light and stared in startled surprise at Ellie standing in the middle of the kitchen wearing a short pale-peach cotton robe, her hair tousled around her face.

"Wow, you scared me half to death," she said, hand over her pounding heart. "I thought you were in bed. I didn't know you were still out. Didn't Gus lock up?"

"Guess he thought you would. You went to bed early."

"Digging is tiring. Why are you still up?"

"I went for a walk." Nick shut the door and let his gaze wander slowly down Ellie's slim frame. The pale-peach color of the robe enhanced her soft skin tone, his look raised a flush to her cheeks, making her eyes seem bluer. The robe hid most of her curves, but he remembered from her skimpy attire that afternoon. Her legs were shapely beneath the short hem. She looked soft and warm and sleepy. And sexy enough to entice half the male population in California.

Nick's gaze moved back to her face.

"I came for water." She motioned to the glass on the counter, anxious to break the silence, afraid he'd hear her frantic heartbeats, know what havoc his look caused.

He was so tall, she had to tilt her head back when he stepped closer. His eyes softened to silver and his mouth lifted into the lopsided half smile he wore when he was relaxed. Why didn't he say something?

He took another step closer and gently reached out a finger, slowly tracing her cheek, her jaw, down her throat to the neck of her robe. His finger left a trail of fire beneath her skin, dragging the breath from her, causing her to desperately draw air in through parted lips.

Ellie swayed toward Nick, drawn to him as she'd been

ever since they first met. She forgot the reason he was here, forgot his distrust of women. She knew only the longing and desire a woman had for one particular man. Her body yearned for his touch, for the feel of him against her, her mouth longed for his taste, for the passion that would waken dormant needs.

He moved to meet her, slowly, lowering his head until his warm lips touched Ellie's, touched and captured. Before she could take a breath, he reached around her to draw her up against him, his mouth hot, tantalizing. His lips moved, exerting a compelling pressure and opened her, tasting the sweetness within, testing her resistance as he moved against her lips, delving into the moist warmth she made available.

His body was hard and hot against the delicate caress of her gown, contrasting with the softness of hers as he molded her along his length, pressing her hips into his, her breasts against the strong muscles of his chest. Her temperature soared where they touched, building a fiery intensity.

Ellie forgot where she was, what she had been doing. She could only feel: Nick's mouth against hers, his hands on her back, the solid sensation of his body.

Her fingers threaded into the thickness of his hair, tracked the strong column of his neck, the wide expanse of his strong shoulders even as his hands held her so tightly against him she could scarcely breathe. Greedily she reveled in the feel of him. The warmth of his body seemed to melt through her robe and gown, warming her, matching the heat building within. His muscles felt iron hard, pressed against her as if to impress their image permanently against her skin, hot and strong.

She tightened her arms, her fingers restlessly searching to discover more, feeling the slight rasp of his beard against her hand, the thick hair he wore too long, the strong pulse at the side of his neck, the contours and shape of his shoulder muscles, his biceps.

The world spun and tilted, a kaleidoscope of colors exploded behind her closed lids. Nick's scent filled her nostrils as she gulped in air, trying to breathe. If time stopped at this instant, she would only regret the ending of this kiss.

After an endless, wonderful, timeless moment, Nick stiffened, slowly withdrawing, pulling her arms from around his neck, stepping back.

Ellie didn't want the kiss to end, but he drew away. She opened her eyes to focus on his face. His expression was remote. She shivered slightly as the cool night air swirled around her heated body.

"I'm sorry, Ellie. I shouldn't have done that. Blame it on the fact I haven't had a woman in years. It won't happen again."

The moment of bright delight, of glorious happiness and fleeting dreams shattered.

Scared her voice might tremble and give her away, she shook her head. With tremendous effort, she turned the corners of her mouth into a travesty of a smile and turned to leave, blinded by the tears that suddenly filled her eyes. "Good night," she managed to murmur.

With head held high, she made it to the stairs. Once beyond his sight, her control slipped. Her knees gave beneath her and she sank onto the steps, tears spilling down her cheeks. The ache in her breast felt as fierce as the delight she'd experienced only moments ago. She caught her lower lip between her teeth, refusing to make a sound until she reached the privacy of her own room. She dare not make any noise lest she wake up one of the girls.

Dragging herself up the stairs, she longed for oblivion. Once in her room, she carefully closed the door before throwing herself on the bed, burying her face in her pillows to muffle her weeping.

He'd only kissed her because he hadn't had a woman in years. Not because she was anyone special. Not because he liked her haircut or her new clothes. Not for herself. For one fleeting, wonderful, magical moment, Ellie had imagined he wanted to kiss her. That he had not been able to help himself!

But he'd shattered that fleeting dream. She was female, available, and he hadn't had a woman in years.

The hot flush of embarrassment burned through her. How would she face him in the morning? What if he said something to the others? What if everyone in the place soon knew she had thrown herself at him and lured him into kissing her? And that he'd complied not because he wanted her, but because he'd been without a woman for so long anyone would have done in a pinch.

Tears spent, she slipped beneath the covers and tried to sleep. Staring into the darkness, she had a few short hours to decide how she would handle things in the morning. It wasn't the worst thing that had ever happened to her. But for a few seconds, it sure felt like it. Slowly she drifted to sleep, deep down reliving the glorious kiss, the delight and enchantment it had brought, for however brief a moment.

Nick Tanner was undoubtably the sexiest, most desirable man she'd ever known. And for one wonderful moment, he had made her feel special.

Nick lay on his bed in the dark calling himself every name in the book. Clenching and unclenching his teeth until his jaw ached, he tried to forget the armful of sweet femininity he'd just held. God, he ached. Ellie was so pretty in a fresh wholesome way that he hadn't seen when he was living in the city. She displayed no artifice, no silly games to offer what really wasn't there.

With her hair tousled around her face and her eyes drowsy with sleep, she'd been as pretty as the dawn. Her cheeks had been flushed, rosy and sweet. He longed to see that soft spill of hair on his pillow, her eyes filled with yearning for him alone.

Dammit, thinking about her wasn't helping. He should be taking a cold shower, or another walk.

He clenched his fists. He had nothing to offer a woman. He wasn't even a free man for another three months.

And he'd learned his lesson well—never trust a woman.

But it didn't stop the wanting.

And he wanted Ellie. Wanted to strip the soft lacy nightgown from her body and see her naked on his bed, waiting for his touch. He wanted more kisses that seared his soul. Wanted to find something to hold on to in the dark of midnight. He wanted her to ache for him as he ached for her, to reach for him—

He had to stop or he'd go crazy. He didn't need any complications. He'd set his course and he'd stick to it. Alone.

Chapter Eight

Ellie did her best to act in a normal manner the next morning despite the fact Nick's kiss remained in the forefront of her mind. She greeted him calmly and with her usual amiable manner, drawing on the strength she'd developed when dealing with a cranky old man who found fault with everything. If she couldn't quite meet his eyes, at least no one commented on anything out of the ordinary.

Grateful for the presence of the others at the breakfast table, she quickly asked what each person's plans were for the day, ignoring Nick for the most part.

Jed and Brad volunteered to take turns on the pond. Kat watched Nick. "I could help tonight, after dinner. If you'll show me what to do, Nick."

He looked at her and nodded, but didn't say anything.

Normally quiet, no one commented on his silence. Kat smiled and seemed happier than she had before.

By the time breakfast was over, Ellie felt she could go on. Nothing had really changed. It had just been a kiss.

Men and women did it all the time, casually, without any lasting meaning. She'd provide the assistance Nick needed to move on as originally planned. Then he'd leave for the rest of his life.

And Ellie would take in other guests to make a difference in their lives. To help them avoid the senseless waste spiraling out of control could cause. She took her coffee and went to sit on the porch. For a long moment she thought about Bobby. She'd loved him devotedly. When she'd been a shy, scared young girl leaving behind everything she'd known, he'd been the bright spot in her life—welcoming her to their father's home, trying to ease her pangs of homesickness.

He could relate, he'd often told her. His mother had been their father's first wife, whom he divorced when Bobby was a baby to marry Ellie's mother. Bobby hadn't known their father until his mother had abandoned him abruptly one day. With no place else to go, he'd been sent to his father.

They had that in common.

But Bobby was five years older and already rebelling against fate by joining a gang, looking for a feeling of belonging and sense of accomplishment with young hoodlums rather than in more acceptable forms. Unfortunately in trying to prove himself for the gang, he'd been caught attempting to rob a store and spent two years in jail.

She'd loved him despite his faults. And still felt the anguish of his death. If he had had a place to go when he got out of jail, if he could have lived on the ranch instead of rejoining the same gang that caused the trouble in the first place, he might be alive today. Instead, a drive-by shooting ended his life at nineteen.

Helping Brad and Jed also helped her heal from the knowledge she had been powerless to save her own brother after all he'd done for her. Too young at fourteen to be able to do anything, she still felt the rage she'd experienced when she realized their father could have helped, and hadn't.

Finishing her coffee, Ellie looked up as Nick headed around the side of the house toward the pond site. She shook off her pensive mood. She had work to do—and it did not include wallowing in the past.

The day passed swiftly. Ellie worked at her painting, glancing from time to time to the yard where Brad worked with Nick. The pool was taking shape. The hard-baked clay soil made it slow going, but they continued through the morning. Lunch was a hasty affair. Gus had assignments for Nick and Brad in the afternoon and Ellie breathed a sigh of relief. Out of sight, out of mind. At least she hoped so.

Gradually the spell of the kiss began to fade. He'd attributed nothing to it. There were no sly looks, no insinuations, no provocative comments. She began to relax. Nothing had changed.

That evening, Ellie joined the others after dinner around the pond site. Kat flirted with Nick, Ariel and Jed bickered as was their habit. Brad worked the hardest. Ellie liked watching the dynamics of the group. Seeing how they learned and how they each gradually lost their earlier negative behavior patterns.

Once again she was struck by Nick's patience. He ignored Kat's flirting, showing her over and over how to wield a shovel using leverage to get the maximum amount of dirt in the wheelbarrow. He and the boys had established a kind of connection and they talked easily.

The pond had been a good idea, she thought, her eyes drawn again and again to Nick as he worked. The group of guests were pulling together on a project. It demonstrated teamwork, the value of setting goals and working to achieve them.

She should be pleased. Why did she feel left out?

* * *

The next morning, Ellie woke earlier than usual. She might as well start breakfast for Alberta. It wasn't often she felt in the mood, but liked to indulge when it hit her. While Alberta loved her job, she didn't mind others pitching in from time to time.

Ellie was in the midst of preparing biscuits for breakfast, setting the bowl in the sink to soak once the dough had been rolled and cut, when she caught sight of Nick coming from the barn. She hadn't known he was up. No one else stirred around the place. Glancing at the clock, she knew why. It wasn't even six yet. What was he doing up and dressed? Or had he gone to bed?

"Ellie!" Nick's voice held surprise when he entered the kitchen. "I thought Alberta had come early."

"How long have you been up?" she asked.

His eyes narrowed and his defenses rose. Intrigued, Ellie watched. It was as if she could see the barriers erect themselves.

"For a while."

He hesitated a moment, then shrugged and placed the basket of eggs on the counter. "I couldn't sleep, so thought I'd get the eggs. Want to come and see what one of your fool chickens has done now?" he asked.

"What?"

"Come and see." He stepped back, held the screen door open.

Walking beside Nick as she dried her hands, she wondered if he would make any mention of their kiss now that they were alone. He remained silent until they entered the cavernous barn. Once a few feet inside, Nick stood and pointed up. Balanced on a narrow cross beam beneath the rafters sat a large brown egg.

"How did she lay it up there?" Ellie asked, gazing in amazement at the egg. "Why didn't it fall?"

"I don't know." Nick said, shaking his head. "I don't know how she balanced herself long enough to lay it."

"I wish I could have seen it," Ellie said with a wide grin, trying to envision a hen on the narrow stretch of wood. She'd have to tell Margot; it would make a good scene in a book.

"Can you get it down?" Even as tall as Nick was, the beam was beyond his reach.

Nick nodded, glancing around. Spotting a pail nearby he brought it beneath the beam, turned it upside down and stepped on it. Just as his fingers reached the egg, the pail began to crumple on one side.

"Watch out!" Ellie cried, startled. She didn't want him to fall.

Off balance, startled by her cry, Nick's fingers brushed the egg, knocking it off its perch just as he jumped to his feet. Slowly the egg fell, landing on his head above his left eyebrow.

Ellie burst out laughing.

He glared at her.

"Are you all right?" She asked, gasping between waves of laughter. "Here, use the towel to get it off." She stepped up to blot some of the runny egg goo from his face, brushing ineffectively against his shirt, trying to pick large chunks of shell from his head and shaking them from her fingers onto the dirt floor.

"At least egg shampoos are supposed to be good for your hair," she said, giggling softly, smearing some of the mess into his hair.

"Thanks. Next time, do yours." He rubbed some of the gooey egg white on her.

"Yuck!" She stepped back and threw the towel at him.

He caught the towel with one hand, but with the other, wiped more of the egg from his face. "I'll share," he offered, holding up his fingers. Egg yolk dripped between his fingers as he menacingly followed her out of the barn.

"No, you don't!" Ellie turned and ran back toward the kitchen, Nick inches behind her. "No, no, don't put that

yucky stuff on me!'' she shrieked as she ran. Reaching the
screen door, she tried to open it, only to have Nick reach
around her and push the door against the jamb, trapping
her between him and the door.

She turned to face him. "Don't you dare!"

"Oh, I dare." Deliberately Nick washed her face with
the egg still dripping from his fingers, laughing down at
her as she squirmed away.

"You're right, it is funny," he said innocently, his left
hand still firm against the screen door.

"Just you wait," she threatened as she moved out of
reach. "I don't know how yet, but I'll get you back.
Ooohhh, this stuff is gross."

"You sound like a kid. It's your chicken, your egg. Only
fair to share."

"If you weren't so klutzy, it wouldn't have fallen."

"I like that. It was your pail that collapsed."

"Only because you're too heavy for it."

"Oh, so now I'm too fat." He moved toward her again
threateningly.

"Nick, no. No more!" She tried to fend him off between
giggles.

Ellie couldn't evade him. He imprisoned her between his
arms, his body pressing her against the screen door as he
threatened her again with the gooey mess.

"I'm not fat, just strong," he said.

"Yes, you are." The laughter died. Her body ignited.
She didn't realize how sensitive her skin was, even beneath
the layer of clothing she wore. Aware of every inch of the
man, from his warm hard arms to his strong solid chest to
the long length of his legs, every one of her nerve endings
clamored for his touch, for his heat. She was caught, yet
strangely reluctant to be released.

She looked up into his eyes. It seemed the most natural
thing in the world to give him a slow, seductive smile.

Never mind that her heart raced, that the images that flashed in her mind were X-rated. She wouldn't change a thing.

"I don't think you're fat," she said softly. "I think you're very strong. Espccially to do all that digging on the pond." Daringly, she reached out to touch his hard biceps.

Nick's smile faded as he gazed down into her pretty blue eyes. When had she taken off her glasses? Her eyes stared up into his, bright and shining—a deep-blue, fringed with sooty dark lashes. He wanted to lose himself in her eyes, in the innocence that beckoned. Heat swept through him as he grew hard just being near her. He remembered every second of their kiss as if every inch of her body had been permanently imprinted on his brain. Would he ever forget that night?

She remained quiet. Silence stretched out.

Slowly he lowered his head. If she didn't want this, she could tell him. Push him away.

Instead, she didn't move. Seemed to hold her breath. Only the rapid beat of her pulse at the base of her throat gave him hope.

His lips firmed as he reached for her. His arms drew her against him as his mouth sought, found and delivered a searing kiss.

Ellie was lost. She could only feel Nick, think Nick, breathe Nick. The sticky egg drying on her face forgotten as the warmth of his embrace engulfed her. Time stood still, spun out of control. Was it day, or night, or endless eternity? Eyes closed to shut out the world, she let herself slip into the moment, relishing every spark of exquisite excitement.

There was only Nick and his mouth to bind her to the earth, his lips hot and erotic against hers, his tongue delighting her, enchanting her as he deepened the kiss. His arms held her against him, pressing her softness into the strength of his own body. His legs spread to support them, letting Ellie savor the feminine heat that threatened to consume her. Her fingers threaded in his thick hair, reveling in the sensations that washed through her like a tidal wave.

Light-years later he slowly drew back, staring down at her, a puzzled expression on his face.

Ellie was afraid to speak. She hadn't a clue what to say that wouldn't shatter the moment. She licked her lips, still tasting him. Taking a deep breath, she could smell him, the warmth of him, the tangy male scent. She studied his expression and wondered where they went from here. What would he expect now? What did *she* expect now?

Swallowing hard she tried a shaky smile. Her heart raced, as if she'd been running. Her entire body tingled from touching him.

"You're a beautiful woman, Ellie. A man can only stand so much temptation before giving in," he said, brushing the dry patch of egg on her cheek. He stepped back, leaving at least a foot of space between them.

Ellie felt cold, hot, mixed-up.

No one had ever told her she was beautiful. The compliment swept through her like fine champagne, bubbling up and exploding in sensations of pure delight.

"Time for breakfast?" Alberta asked from behind them.

Nick turned instantly, as if protecting the woman behind him.

Ellie peeked around him at her cook. "We were gathering eggs."

"Gathering or wearing?" Alberta asked, looking suspiciously from one to the other.

"One fell. The rest are in on the counter." Ellie tried to smile, knowing the effort was wasted.

"Great. How do you want your eggs this morning?" Alberta asked as she waited for them to move so she could enter the kitchen.

"Not on my face," Nick joked, but the smile didn't reach his eyes. They were smoky, smoldering, watching

Ellie with a hunger she could plainly see. As could anyone who looked at him.

"I'd like mine scrambled this morning, Alberta." Taking the towel, Ellie moved to open the door and step inside, her emotions spinning. Without waiting for the others to enter, she fled upstairs. She washed her face and made sure all traces of the egg were gone before venturing back to the kitchen.

"Thanks for starting the biscuits," Alberta said when she entered.

"No problem, I woke up early." Ellie darted glances at Nick's door as she leaned against the counter, talking with Alberta while the cook prepared breakfast. He didn't appear until everyone was seated at the table. Slipping into his normal place, he ignored Ellie.

"I'm going into town tomorrow, after lunch," Ellie said. "Anyone need anything?"

"Yes," Nick said, meeting her eyes for the first time. "I need to go to the post office. Might as well get my driver's license renewed, as well."

By the time Ellie and Nick left for town after lunch the next afternoon, Ellie had her emotions firmly under control. Proximity had caused their kiss. She refused to read anything further into it.

She stopped at the Department of Motor Vehicles first and waited in the truck while Nick took care of getting his license reinstated. He'd brought a large brown envelope for posting, leaving it on the seat when he went inside, address side down. She was curious as to what he was mailing and to whom. But she didn't look. Nick deserved privacy, as did all her guests. But she couldn't help wonder to whom he was sending a thick envelope.

When he left the building, she drove quickly to the covered parking lot.

"The post office is a couple of blocks down that way."

Ellie watched as Nick nodded and then began to amble

down the street, heading for the brick building. He didn't seem out of place today in his faded jeans and cotton shirt, but Ellie knew his stay was temporary, no matter how much he seemed to fit in.

Where would he go when he left? Would he keep in touch like some of her guests did? Probably not. Once gone, Nick would be gone for good.

She hated to admit it, but she was becoming too wrapped up in her latest guest. After the morning's fun with the egg, she recognized the attraction two people could have for each other, the desire to share a life of happy times, as well as hard times. To just be there for each other. Like Margot and Philip, or Alberta and Gus.

No one person had to dominate her as her father had. Was that one of the contributions to her parents' divorce? She wished she could have had her mother longer, had someone to answer her questions.

She planned to be independent for life, which meant being alone. Now she fantasized about what could never be.

The phone was ringing as they pulled into the driveway and Ellie jumped from the truck to run into the house to answer it. Obviously no one else was around or it wouldn't keep ringing.

It was Margot.

"When do you want to get together to finalize the book? How about dinner tomorrow? Bring Nick. While you and I do business, Philip will have someone to talk to."

"I'll see." Turning to Nick as he came in, Ellie smiled at him. "It's Margot. She's invited me to dinner tomorrow. Want to go?" she asked.

He paused for a moment, then shook his head slowly. "No. I don't. We aren't going to start doing things together. A kiss means nothing, Ellie. Don't get stars in your eyes because of a couple of kisses. I'm not part of a couple. I don't ever plan to be." The hard edge was back in his voice. The bleakness filled his eyes.

Ellie was surprised at the shaft of pain that hit at his words. Did he think she was trying to match them up? Trying to force them into a couple's role? So starved for affection, for a man's attention that she'd read something into a few kisses?

There was no reason for Nick to think that; she knew better than anyone how impossible that would be. Hiding her hurt and embarrassment, she turned back to the phone, trying to keep her voice light, though her throat ached with unshed tears.

"Margot, I'll come around six. Philip will have to be content with his own company, Nick won't make it."

"*Eh bien.* Bring the drawings and we'll have a final check to see how soon we can mark this one *fini.*"

Ellie hung up and reached for her parcels. Without looking in Nick's direction, she started for the stairs.

Nick leaned against the counter and watched her go. He felt like a jerk who had kicked a puppy. He could have gone. He'd liked Philip and Margot when he'd met them.

But he didn't think he could have stood the ride there and back alone with Ellie. Especially the ride back in the darkness, with her sweet body so close to his in the truck. The soft scent that emanated from her, like sunshine and wildflowers, drove him crazy in the daylight. It was growing harder and harder to keep his hands off her as it was. He didn't need any other temptation.

Margot was delighted with Ellie's haircut.

"Ah, *chérie,* it is perfect! So chic. Do you like it?"

Ellie nodded, still feeling a little self-conscious.

"And Nick, how does he like it?" Margot asked in a sly tone.

"All right, I guess," Ellie answered casually, shrugging her shoulders.

"I was hoping for more, *vraiment.*"

"I know. Honestly, Margot, there's nothing there. He's

simply one of my guests from Helping Hands. As soon as
his sentence is up, he'll be moving on.''

"When his time is *fini,* he doesn't have to leave.''

"I wish I shared your belief. But I don't." Settling in
her chair, sipping the wine Margot had poured, Ellie explained what she'd learned about Nick and Sheila and the
reason for his prison term.

"So the other woman made a fool of him. *Pauvre
homme.* But, *chérie,* what is important is how you and Nick
feel about each other."

"Well, Nick doesn't feel anything for me. I'm just someone who's helping him get a start on his road back." And
how she felt for him was not open for discussion. She
didn't want to examine those emotions too deeply herself.
Everyone she'd loved had abandoned her. If she allowed
herself to fall in love with Nick, to fall all the way in love
with him, he'd still leave her as everyone else had.

"Whatever you say, *chérie.*" Margot fell silent.

After dinner, the business discussion of their book began
in earnest. Margot had finished with the final draft, Ellie
had most of the illustrations completed—just two illustrations to touch up. They would then put the combined prod-
uct together and send it to their agent.

Agreeing to meet in two days, they also agreed to spend
time then blocking out the next book.

It was late when Ellie pulled into her driveway. Tam rose
from the front porch and pranced out to the car, tail wagging. The house was dark behind him except for the light
in the hallway. Everyone had already retired for the night.

"Hello, old boy, how are you?" She fussed over her dog,
glad to see him. He always welcomed her. Here was one
creature that didn't care if she was half of a couple, didn't
even know about society's expectations, wouldn't be leaving her.

She heard the creak of wood from the porch. Walking

slowly forward, she could make out Nick on the swing, slowly swaying back and forth.

"Hi," he said, watching her walk through the starry night. "Sit a spell."

"Okay." She sat gingerly on the end of the swing, letting Nick set it in motion again.

The heavens were full of bright stars clearly shining against the velvet darkness of the night, unmarred by streetlights, lights from other houses or a bright moon. The air was cool, but still. In the silence Ellie could hear the soft clucking of roosting chickens, the stomp of a horse's hoof in the paddock. It was peaceful.

"Get everything finished?" Nick asked.

"Just about. We've scheduled another meeting in a couple of days. After that we can mail the complete book to our agent. Dinner was great. Margot is as good a cook as Alberta. They said they hoped you could come another time," she finished lightly.

"I was a damn fool not to go tonight," Nick said unexpectedly.

"Why didn't you, then?" Ellie's heart began beating a little faster. She wished could see him, but it was too dark to make out more than his silhouette against the star-splashed sky.

"Dumb reasons," he said, but didn't elaborate.

"They want to be friends. I want to be a friend," she said gently.

"Sometimes, Ellie," he said reaching out his hand and trailing his fingers down her cheek, resting his palm against her neck. "Sometimes I want you for more than a friend."

She didn't say a word. It would have been impossible. She could scarcely breathe. His touch wreaked havoc with her senses. She felt tingling to her toes and yearned to have his mouth cover hers and demand a response. But she was afraid to move.

Nick gently placed his hands on her arms, drawing her

slowly across the swing to bump against his hard thigh. He was giving her plenty of time to draw back if she wanted.

Ellie tried desperately to see his expression in the faint starlight, but she couldn't. What was he thinking, feeling, wanting? Did he experience the same pull of attraction and desire as she? Did he long to be with her, touch her, hold her? Listen to her voice speak softly in the darkness?

Her eyes stared up at him, wanting to know what he wanted, what he felt about her. Wanting more than just a brief passing in the night.

With a muffled groan, Nick scooped her up and nestled her in his lap, his arms cradling her. His mouth found hers in the darkness.

To keep her balance, Ellie encircled his neck with her arm, raising her face expectantly, a soft sigh escaping her lips. This was exactly what she wanted. He must want the same thing, she thought.

This was not a gentle kiss. There was nothing gentle about his embrace. He held her in rock-hard arms so tightly against him she could feel a button from his shirt press against her left breast. His mouth was hot and wet and demanding as he ravaged the softness of her own, forcing apart her trembling lips and plundering the dark moistness of her mouth. His tongue traced her velvety inner lip, rasped against her teeth, and mated with her own in a sensual dance as old as time.

She felt a primitive raw hunger for him as she pushed closer, her tongue tasting him, moving against his, pushing into his mouth. The passion of the kiss drove out all other thoughts. She absorbed Nick's body, yearned for his touch, moved against him searching for fulfillment.

His hand roamed across her back, pressing her against his hard chest, feeling the soft contours of her spine. Moving to the front, he eased her back until he could softly caress one breast, feeling it swell to his touch. He slipped his hand beneath her soft cotton top, tracing the hardening nipple through her sensible cotton bra.

Releasing the clasp, his hand came back to slide beneath the cup and hold her warm flesh in the calloused palm of his hand. His thumb tormented, driving her wild with longing, wild with desire.

Ellie shifted to give him better access, to relish all the delightful sensations that exploded beneath his hand, the sensations that drove her to the edge of reckless abandonment.

"You feel good. You're so soft and satiny, sweet and hot." Nick tipped her head back, trailed fiery kisses along her neck, down to the frantically beating pulse at the base of her throat.

Ellie felt as if she floated on a cloud of happiness and sensuality. His hand was hot as he learned her curves, contours. His mouth followed the line of her collarbone, as she began to suspect its final destination. Beneath her fingertips, she learned him, the smooth skin of his shoulders, the hair-roughened skin on his chest.

"It's been so long since I've had a woman," Nick said as his mouth moved across the soft swell of her breast.

It was like a dash of cold water. Ellie struggled and over-balanced them. The swing moved wildly, threatening to topple them off.

"What…?" Nick stopped. Desperately seeking balance, he stopped the swing's wild gyration.

"You don't want *me*." She pushed against him, her hands clenched into fists. "You would take any woman who happened along. Let me go." Ellie pushed again, falling back off onto the porch when he let her go.

"Ellie…"

"Shut up!" She stood and pulled down her blouse, her bra still unfastened, her breasts throbbing. Spinning around, she ran inside the house, feeling rotten. How could she have let herself be beguiled and drawn into such a fantasy? Men were out for themselves, no one else. Hadn't living with her father proven that? Even Bobby, whom she'd adored, had been out for his own thrills, his own way in the world. Why would Nick be any different?

He'd wanted a woman because he'd been without for so long. Any woman would have done. Biting down on her lip, she was determined not to cry, at least before she reached her bedroom. Dashing up the stairs as if the devil himself were behind her, Ellie reached her room and slammed the door behind her. Slammed the door on her dreams, hopes and longings. Was this to become a habit? She gritted her teeth. She would not cry!

"Well, hell!" Nick said, staring out on the black night. The very reason he'd declined the offer of going to dinner was because he didn't want to be with Ellie in the truck on the drive home. Now he'd really blown it.

He closed his eyes in disgust. He could still smell her, taste her, feel her. Want her! She was so soft, so sweet, so trusting.

And he was a bastard using that softness to ease his own needs.

He heard her door slam and winced. She was going to wake the entire house. He held his breath, waiting for the lights to come on. But the house remained in darkness. Could Kat and Ariel have slept through that?

Frowning, he heard her words echo in the silence. She thought he just wanted a woman, that any female would do. And he'd done nothing to change her mind. He could have told her no one else would do—just her. Not some nameless woman's body.

He could have said something about how he could forget the past for a while when he was with her. How he liked looking at her, listening to her talk. Watched for the glow in her eyes when she spoke of her paintings, or her ranch.

How he loved the laughter that rang out when she was happy.

Sighing, he rubbed his face. He never thought he'd want a woman again, except for a physical release. The desire that had flared with her in his arms hadn't abated. He ached so much, he hurt. He had to wait until his body calmed down, until he could forget how desirable she was, how her skin had felt like soft velvet, how her hair seemed like silk when the curls tangled around his fingers. How even now his blood raced through him thinking about her.

How could he have been so callous? He'd given her time to object, if she'd wanted. Yet sometimes he felt she was new at this. She gave such mixed signals.

She was old enough to know the score. Yet he often thought of her as a naive young girl. Probably because of her size, and that soft, sultry, sexy southern drawl. Or the way her eyes widened sometimes in startled surprise.

He wanted to hear her voice deep into the night, pillow talk after he'd made love to her, after she was sweaty with pleasure, sated with satisfaction and drowsy with sleep. He wanted to hear his name on her lips as he brought her to climax. Hear her tell him she loved what he did to her, loved the feelings he could bring her. He alone could bring.

Damn, he was still aroused and wasn't getting better.

Chapter Nine

As Ellie dried herself off from her shower the next morning, she took stock of herself in the mirror. Her short hair was already curling after being only towel-dried. It made her look younger. Peering at close range, she was vaguely pleased to notice there were only a few lines around her eyes. Smiling, she realized they were all laugh lines. Better than lines of discontent, she thought, remembering her father.

Her figure was still slender, her breasts firm, her stomach taut, her hips nicely rounded. She could feel Nick's hands on her body as they had touched her last night. His thumb and fingers caressing her breasts, stroking and fondling until she thought she would die with desire. Merely remembering caused her to become breathless with longing.

"Stop it!" she commanded herself.

After three years without a woman, was it any wonder he wanted one? It meant nothing. *Nothing*. And the sooner she recognized that, acknowledged that, believed that, the sooner she could put it behind her.

She repeated it to herself as she dressed in cotton shorts and a loose cotton shirt. She tucked her glasses into her pocket. Distant things would be a little blurry, so maybe she wouldn't have to see Nick's gaze or meet his scorn. He probably thought she acted like a scared rabbit. She was an adult, as was Nick. She should have handled the situation differently, better.

Maybe she should have continued.

The thought tantalized. Would they have ended up in his bed? Would that be so awful? Only when he left at the end of his time. Then she would be devastated. But she was well on her way to being devastated whether or not they made love. Maybe she should build some memories to last her the rest of her life.

Descending the stairs, Ellie wondered how she should greet Nick. Politely, it went without saying. But with friendliness? Or a distinct coolness? Maybe distant reserve. She wiped her damp palms against her shorts. Taking a deep breath, she stepped into the kitchen.

Ariel was just coming in from the yard, holding a basket of eggs. Her eyes met Ellie's. "Are you all right?" she asked.

"Sure, how about you?"

"I didn't slam my door in the middle of the night last night," Ariel said as she placed the basket of eggs on the counter near Alberta. The older woman turned and studied Ellie after hearing Ariel's comment.

She felt her cheeks grow warm. Hoping she wasn't blushing beet-red, she tried a smile. It felt awkward, but she ignored that.

Nick entered from his bedroom just as Jed and Brad banged open the screen door. "It's going to be cooler today," Brad said, swiping a piece of toast and starting to munch it even as Alberta slapped his hand.

He grinned at the woman and hurried to the dining room table. Jed followed suit, a bit more devious in his toast snatching.

"If it stays cool, we can get the cement and start pouring by the end of the week," Nick said, striding to the table. He sat, his eyes on Ellie as she followed Alberta, each carrying a platter piled high with food.

"We'll need everyone to help. Can Gus schedule ranch work around it?"

"Of course," she said, not meeting his gaze.

He nodded, his eyes drawn to that mouth, hungry for her mouth.

Ellie stopped in midstep, glancing at him, seeing the naked hunger in his face as he gazed at her mouth, flicking out her tongue to wet suddenly dry lips. Nick closed his eyes briefly and then turned away.

Kat made an entrance. "Good morning, all." Sashaying over to the table, she pulled out the chair next to Nick and gave him a sultry smile. At his slight nod, she seemed satisfied and looked around the table. Suddenly her expression changed when she met Ellie's eyes. "What got you all in a tizzy last night? I heard your door slam in the middle of the night."

"A breeze yanked it right out of my hand," Ellie said brazenly, refusing to look at Nick.

"It was windy last night?" Jed asked.

"Freak wind," Nick murmured, his eyes dancing in amusement. "Listen up. If the weather holds, we can pour concrete Friday."

Ellie walked to the pond site, watching Nick and Brad and Jed as she approached. Nick wore cutoff jeans, riding low on his hips, and no shirt. The two young men were similarly attired.

It was cooler than other days but still hot in the sun. Nick was smoothing the dirt, sculpturing the bottom. The other two pounded the ground smooth in preparation for the concrete.

"Will you want Philip over to help?" Ellie asked.

Nick looked up, his eyes squinting against the sun. "We could use his expertise. He knows more about this than I do," Nick said, never pausing.

"I'll call and see if he can make Friday," she said.

He nodded.

Kat came out of the house and sauntered over to the work site. The shorts she wore made Ellie's look dowdy. Her abbreviated top displayed a smooth stretch of tanned abdomen.

"Looking good, Nick," Kat called.

The work, or the man? Ellie wondered.

Jed looked up. "We're all working on it, Kat. When are you going to take a turn?"

"I worked the other night, remember? And I'm here to help today as well."

"And Friday," Nick said. "We'll all be home to work on the cement."

Kat examined her hands. Her nails were long and red. "I don't want to ruin my nails," she said slowly, waving them so Nick could see.

"Then wear gloves," Nick said shortly. He flicked a glance at Ellie. "Did you want something else?"

She shook her head, avoiding his eyes. What she wanted and what she was prepared to deal with were two different things. "Just watching."

He pounded a square foot of dirt and glanced up at her again. "Thought you were going to call Philip."

"I can do that later. It would be better to call around noon."

"You boys want something cold to drink?" Kat asked, her eyes on Nick.

"Yeah," Jed answered. "A really big glass of cold water."

"Me, too," Brad said, not stopping work.

Nick nodded.

"I'll bring it right out. That's helping, isn't it, Nick?"

"It would be a huge help," he said, smiling at Kat.

Ellie simmered. She would not feel jealous of a nineteen-year-old girl! She didn't care that Nick smiled at Kat and didn't smile at her. She didn't need his smiles to make her day.

But one wouldn't hurt, a small voice whispered.

"Then I'll go call Philip, now. That'll be a help, won't it Nick?" she mimicked, then immediately felt ashamed of herself. She was acting no better than Kat.

He looked at her for a long moment, then stepped out of the depression, dropped the shovel and strode over to her. Taking her arm he pulled her away from the pool, away from the house and away from everyone who could listen.

"Last night wasn't about me wanting some woman to ease an itch," he said in a low, hard voice. "It was about being enticed by your sassy, sexy little body beyond what I can resist. You are a beautiful, tantalizing woman, Ellie. You know that and I know that. You can take my kisses however you want, and respond however you wish, but don't you *ever* think I wanted just anyone. I'm sure I could find a good-time girl in Jackson if I looked hard enough. Or take Kat up on her blatant invitations if I just wanted to ease an itch. You got that?"

Ellie swallowed hard and nodded. He called her beautiful again! She almost missed the rest of his tirade as her heart caught on the word. Nick Tanner thought she was beautiful!

He started to say something else, but Kat called to him and he turned toward her. "I'll be right there."

Kat hesitated at the edge of the depression that would soon be a pond and watched Ellie and Nick suspiciously.

"There's no damn privacy around here," he muttered.

"That's one of the tenets of Helping Hands—make sure

the guests have privacy," Ellie murmured, perversely wishing to annoy him.

"Well, you're falling down on the job. I could use a hell of a lot more privacy right now." He glared at her for a long moment before releasing her arm and heading back toward the others.

Ellie remained where she stood, watching him until he was too blurry for her to clearly see. *He thought she was beautiful.* If he never said another word, or touched her ever again, her heart would always remember this morning and the sincerity of his tone.

Ellie left them to their work and went inside to call Philip.

Friday dawned cool and overcast. High clouds drifted by, and a slight breeze rustled the grass and the leaves. The entire ranch turned out early to eat breakfast and discuss the plans for the day. Rusty, Tomas, Jed and Brad rushed through chores so they'd be ready to go to work on the pond when the cement pouring began.

Philip and Margot arrived before eight. By eight-thirty everyone was lined up beside the huge hole that had been dug for the pond. Nick was delegating instructions, Philip and Gus each heading up teams with different assignments.

Margot stood a bit apart beside Ellie.

"Interesting, *n'est-ce pas?*" she asked watching the activity avidly.

"What?"

"Your Nick acting like a general. Rallying the troops. Every one of your guests is lined up ready to plunge into the fray."

"Brad would rather be riding, but is joining in. Kat is worried about her nails, and I feel like a fifth wheel. With so many people milling around, how will anything get done?" Ellie said, deliberately ignoring Margot's comments.

"Watch and see, *chérie*. I suspect your Nick will manage."

"He's not *my* Nick," Ellie protested.

Nick and Philip started to prepare the concrete, mixing the bags of cement with water in two wheelbarrows. The others gathered around, watching. Ellie stood near Nick, fascinated as he stirred the gooey mixture, mesmerized as the rock and sand began to assume a slurry consistency.

Nick glanced over at her. "Hold the hose and add water when I say," he ordered.

She picked up the hose and held it in anticipation of his next command. When he nodded, she squeezed the handle and sprayed water into the mix.

"Enough." Slowly he stirred some more. When she glanced up at him, he stared at her, his eyes unreadable. "Don't you want to put something else on?" he murmured softly. None of the others appeared to hear him as they bantered back and forth.

"Why would I?"

"It's those indecent shorts again. Philip is a married man, he shouldn't be tempted like that."

Ellie glanced around, afraid someone heard. No one paid any attention.

"Shhh," she whispered.

He kept stirring, but the amusement was obvious in his eyes. "Don't look at me like that. Your timing is lousy. The cement will set up in the wheelbarrow if we don't begin pouring. And the privacy issue is one we need to discuss."

Ellie stared back at him, her eyes widening, a slow smile filling her face even as her heart began its rapid beat. "You think so, huh?"

"Yes, I do." He leaned over and kissed her hard on her smiling mouth. Then he stepped back to stir the concrete as if nothing had happened.

Ellie felt as if her world had been turned upside down.

The sky was spinning, the sun seemed brighter than ever before. Her heart began to slow. To stop? She stared at his dark hair, watching the play of muscles as he stirred the thick mixture, the strength in his shoulders, his arms, his hands. She licked her lips. Not a word passed his lips. She glanced around.

Kat glared at her.

No one else had seen. It had been too brief. Far too brief. Trying to pass it off, Ellie winked at Kat. But the girl turned away, furious.

"Ready to pour," Philip called.

Everyone quickly fell to work, and before the afternoon was over it was done. Cement covered the ground, liberally sprinkled the helpers, and splattered on the grass nearby. But the pond had a definite shape, and a rock-solid base.

"It looks so nice," Ellie said, proudly surveying the work. The sun was low in the sky. Everyone was tired, dirty and more than ready to quit. But the pond was finished, except for the waterfall.

"When can we put the water in?" she asked.

"It needs to set up first, to cure," Philip said, cleaning his hands on a rag. "Probably a few days. You don't want to rush it. You'll have it for years—no need to take a chance by filling it too early."

"We need to get the stone-work finished first. And the waterfall," Nick added, rinsing the last of the cement from his wheelbarrow.

"I can hardly wait. Do you think the ducks will like it?"

"If they don't, we can have roast duck for dinner one night," Philip remarked, laughing and starting to pick up the shovels. Ariel and Margot gathered the empty cement bags. Kat moved to stand near Nick, offering to help clean off the last traces of sand and grit.

"I'm starving," Jed said, lying down on the ground and groaning. Brad and Tomas sat beside him, looking beat.

"What's for dinner?"

Alberta started to reply when Nick stopped her.

"Wait a minute. We're not quite finished."

Everyone looked at him.

"Everyone signs their name around the perimeter. For all time, everyone will know who helped build Ellie's pond. Ariel, you go first, then Brad and so on in alphabetical order." Looking around for a solid stick, he handed one to the girl. Glancing at Ellie, he noted her pleased expression. It seemed to take so little to have her light up like a kid at Christmas.

Ariel proudly stepped forward and began to trace her name in the still-soft concrete. Brad stood beside her, watching carefully.

"Dinner? I didn't start anything. Too busy here," Alberta said, sinking on an overturned wheelbarrow. "I'm as tired as Brad. What do you want that's fast?"

Ellie smiled. "I have the perfect solution. My treat to pizza. Everyone can pitch in for the evening chores, then with a quick wash and we'll be ready."

"All right!" Jed yelled, punching the air with a fist.

The pizza place was crowded and they had to stand in line to order. Ellie scanned the large menu on the wall, unconsciously rotating her shoulders to try to loosen up her stiff muscles.

Warm hands closed over her and began kneading gently. She looked over her shoulder at Nick. His eyes stared down into hers for a long moment, then he shifted his gaze to the back of her neck, to his hands soothing the strain of the day's work away.

Ellie felt deliciously cared for. She had not had anyone concerned for her since her mother died. She'd been the one to worry about her brother, and her father. This made her feel...cherished. It was unexpected. And so very nice.

They commandeered a huge round table near the back wall and sat with a pitcher of beer for the adults and several pitchers of soda for the younger ones. Ellie was pleased to notice how relaxed Nick seemed. The reserve that seemed so much a part of him was missing tonight. All her guests were out to have a good time, and Nick fit right in.

Slowly the different interests in the group sorted themselves out. Ellie leaned back against the wall and let the wave of noise wash over her. She was happy. Truly content in this moment. The satisfaction she received from watching these young men and women turn their lives around made life worthwhile. She wished Bobby had had this kind of chance. Wished she could talk to him once more, tell him how much she missed him. How she hoped he was pleased with what she was doing with her life—as a memorial to him.

When pizza arrived the conversation became general. As the evening progressed, Nick told a couple of stories from his life in San Francisco. Not to be outdone, Jed bragged about some of his exploits, and before long everyone was trying to outdo the other with outrageous tales.

After starting the ball rolling, Nick was content to listen as the others exchanged stories. He caught a look from Ellie and suddenly wished dinner had just been the two of them, without the others. What was it about Ellie that made him curious to find out everything about her? To discover what life had been like for her, to ease away any hurts and disappointments. To learn what made her happy, and what made her mad.

Nick pulled up and leaned back in his chair, trying to distance himself from the others. After Sheila, he didn't want to get involved with anyone. Ellie had a sexy little body. He was interested, there was no question about that. But that was the extent of it. It had to be. When his time was up, he was moving on.

"I'm feeling muscles I didn't even know I had," Philip said after a moment. "I think we should be heading for home, darling."

"I am more than ready," Margot said as she gathered her things. "*Merci, chérie,* for including us in your back-breaking work. Next time do not call!"

Ellie laughed. She thanked her friends, hugging Margot and bidding Philip a warm farewell. She and the others followed them from the restaurant. Everyone was tired. But the beaming smiles on each face warmed Ellie's heart. These kids needed success stories behind them. They could feel proud of the work they'd done today, and add it to their list of accomplishments. Enough good ones to out-weigh the bad ones, Ellie hoped.

Everyone piled into the two ranch trucks and Gus and Alberta's old car. Ellie drove one truck, Rusty the other. She noted Kat made sure she sat next to Nick in Rusty's vehicle. She sighed, hoping Nick wasn't encouraging her. And that Kat didn't do anything outrageous.

"Ellie," Ariel said. The girl sat next to her as she drove, Tomas on the far side. He appeared to be dozing.

"What?"

"Do you think I'll ever get married?"

"I expect so," Ellie said.

"I wasn't sure I wanted to, but now that I see Margot and Philip, maybe," Ariel said softly. "He doesn't hit her, does he?"

Ellie blinked and threw a quick look at her young charge. "No, Philip would never hit Margot, any more than she would hit him."

"That's nice."

"They love each other," Ellie said.

"You're not married," Ariel said.

"Marriage isn't for everyone. But if you meet the right man, you want to share your life with him, build one to-gether. Like Margot and Philip. And if you're lucky, you can have children to enrich that life. Like Gus and Alberta. They have four sons."

For a heart-stopping moment, Ellie thought about Nick.

She could almost envision a life together, sharing the ranch, having him teach each of her guests about accounting and project management and how to fill out forms, get cost estimates, pay bills. Would their children have light hair, or dark like his?

"I guess it's better to be on your own," Ariel said slowly.

"It's not better or worse, just one way to live," Ellie said.

"Lonely, sometimes," Tomas added.

"Thought you were asleep."

"Who can sleep with two women yakking?" he teased.

"How can you be lonely when you date half the women in town?" Ellie retorted.

"Because there is no one special person who cares about me," he said, his eyes still closed.

"Being married is like being in a family, isn't it?" Ariel asked.

"Yes, it is a family. A family of two. That could grow, or be enlarged by relatives or very close friends," Ellie explained. She knew Ariel came from an abusive home, that she'd run away and been caught stealing to stay alive. For a moment Ellie's heart threatened to break thinking of the hardships the teenager had faced at so young an age.

All the more reason for Ellie to work in Helping Hands. She reached out and squeezed Ariel's hand. "Plenty of time for you to decide if you want to get married or not. Don't rush into anything."

"Do you like being alone?" she asked.

"I'm not alone. I have you and the others staying with me, Tomas and Rusty, Gus and Alberta."

"But no one all yours."

"No." She had chosen that way, deliberately. Was she having second thoughts? She valued her independence more than most. But just lately she'd realized with that independence came loneliness.

They pulled into the ranch yard and got out. Surprisingly Ariel reached out to hug Ellie. "Thanks for pizza. And for letting me sign my name on your pond."

"Thank you, Ariel. You can come to visit any time you want after you leave, and always see your name there."

"And if I ever do marry and have kids, can I bring them to see it, too?"

"Of course." Ellie was touched. She brushed back Ariel's short-cropped hair, ignored the five earrings in the girl's ear and looked into her eyes. "This is your home, honey. And when you leave, you'll still be welcome to come visit whenever you want."

Good-nights were said, and the boys headed for the bunkhouse. Gus and Alberta held hands as they walked toward their cottage. Ellie watched for a moment with a pang of envy. Alberta didn't seem to be lacking in anything she wanted. Did she feel the loss of independence? Or was there a kind of independence in an interdependent relationship?

Ellie followed the girls toward the house, slowed and glanced around. She spotted Nick leaning against the corral fence, his hand running along the neck of one of the horses.

Taking a deep breath, she veered in his direction.

"Aren't you tired?" she asked when she approached.

He turned and leaned against the fence with one shoulder, crossing his arms across his chest.

"I think if I went to bed now, you couldn't wake me before the end of next week."

"Then why are you up?"

"Just enjoying things."

"Like aching muscles?"

"Like remembering dinner. First beer I've had in a while."

"Well, if you'd gone with me to Margot and Philip's the other night you could have had all you could drink."

"Tonight was enough. Are you happy with your pond?"

"I am. Thank you, Nick. And your idea of having everyone sign the cement was brilliant. I think it made it all the more special."

He shrugged.

"Once the waterfall is working, we might be able to hear it out here," she said inanely, knowing she should get into the house before she made a fool of herself.

"Tell me about your dad, Ellie," Nick said.

Surprised by his question, she tried to see his expression in the night. "What brought that on?"

"Curiosity."

"You'll be disappointed, there's not much to tell. He was a crotchety old man when I first met him. He was twenty years older than my mother. I don't know why she ever married him. She was his second wife. He had a son by the first, but my Aunt Caroline only told me about him when I was leaving for California. Bobby lived with his mother until she abandoned him one day and he ended up with our father, who never had any use for either of us, except for what we could do for him. He was not a man who should have had children."

"Was it hard coming to California?" he asked gently.

"What do you think? It's so different from Georgia. I lived in a small town, knew everyone. It was safe and quiet and friendly. My mother's sister lived nearby. We had a lot of love and laughter in our home. Until my mom got sick and died. My aunt couldn't afford to keep me. She thought she was doing the right thing by sending me to live with my father.

"San Francisco's a big city, dangerous at night, and impersonal. Perfect place for my father."

"I liked San Francisco. It can be an exciting place to live."

"I had to be home to cook and clean and fetch things for him. He never appreciated anything. Or tried—"

She stopped. The familiar ached spread from her heart.

"Tried?" Nick prompted.

"He never tried to help Bobby. By the time my brother needed him most, my father had developed early stages of Alzheimer's. He picked a fight every chance he got."

"So you nursed him."

"It wasn't so bad in high school. But then he got worse. He was my father. I was all he had. At first I could leave long enough for art classes, but toward the end he needed constant supervision. I was still young, and had no place else to go."

Nick studied her, thinking of what she'd just told him. While other girls were out dating and having fun and falling in love, Ellie was at home taking care of a cranky old man. From the time she was eleven until just five years ago. How had she stood it all those years?

"What happened to Bobby?" he asked.

She looked up at the sky, at the millions of stars that shone so brightly in the dark expanse. "Bobby was five years older than I. He ran with a wild crowd—a gang, really. His way of rebelling, I think. He got caught stealing and was sent to juvenile detention for a couple of years. When he got out—"

The old hurt resurfaced, the desperate need for her brother to be with her, the frustration with her inability to do anything to help.

"When he got out, our father was worse than before. Hostile. Baiting. He refused to have anything to do with Bobby. A nineteen-year-old has an abundance of pride. Bobby went back to his old friends, and in three weeks was dead of a gang-related shooting." Ellie blinked back tears. Even after all the time that had passed, she still felt the loss of the one person who had made life joyful.

"The worst part," she continued a moment later, "was that my father owned this place all the time and we never knew it. Bobby would have been fine if he'd come here. Gus and Alberta have worked here for decades. They held the ranch together after my grandparents died. Can you see Gus letting a punk kid get away with anything? He'd have taught Bobby useful skills, given him a place to live away from the gangs and—''

Tears threatened. She never spoke of her brother, or her father.

Turning, Ellie started for the house. Nick's hands on her shoulders stopped her.

"I'm sorry, Ellie." Slowly he turned her around and drew her into his arms.

"It was so senseless. Being killed because he belonged to a gang. He was only nineteen—same age as Jed and Brad."

Tears started, quiet ones, hopeless ones.

Resting his cheek against the top of her head, he held her. Now he knew what drove Ellie Winslow to volunteer for Helping Hands. And her reasons were as far from something Sheila would have done as the earth was from the sun.

"My life was different, before I screwed it up," Nick said slowly, staring out into the black night. He couldn't let her go just yet. If ever anyone needed something, it was this woman.

"My folks are still happily married, still living in the house I grew up in. It's a big white house in Salisbury, on Maryland's eastern shore. My dad's in banking and my mom teaches third grade. I have two sisters and an older brother. Loads of cousins, aunts, uncles. I even have one grandfather still going strong."

"You're lucky, Nick, to have such a big family! My aunt Caroline never wrote me after I left. Do you see them often?" She closed her eyes, envisioning his family gathering for holidays or for a day at the beach. She had so often longed for a normal family, for outings that she could have shared with Bobby. Slowly she wiped the tears from her cheeks, took a breath.

"Not lately, of course. They don't know I've been in prison."

"What?" Ellie pulled back and looked up at him.

"I never told them."

"Not your parents?"

"They have high expectations."

"But how could you hide it?"

"Steve helped. I transferred the phone to his apartment and hooked up an answering machine. If they called, Steve let me know and I called them back from prison. We were allowed one phone call a week. Steve took the letters I wrote and mailed them from San Francisco."

"They never came to visit?"

"I put them off the one time they suggested it. Trumped up an excuse." He looked up at the dark sky. "I couldn't tell them."

"Wow." Ellie thought about what he said. If she had a family, she would want to feel she could go to them with anything, even if she made a mistake.

"Surely your family wouldn't turn their backs on you just because you made a mistake. You gave Sheila a chance, and she wasn't even family. You must have gotten that from somewhere. I'd think they'd want to know. I think they would have stood by you."

"They'd just be upset and disappointed. I'd feel like hell telling them."

"But they're a part of your life. They would want to share all facets of your life, not just the good things. They'd understand."

"I don't know," Nick said bitterly. "I'm not sure I understand myself. Hell, I don't even know why I told you." Without another word, he let her go, and headed into the dark house.

Slamming the door behind him, he stood in the dark for a long time, trying to control the frustration and anger that built in him. Damn Sheila and her pretty lies. And damn him for believing her. Believing in any woman.

And damn Ellie for getting under his skin, for sharing parts of herself that were so personal he suspected she rarely spoke of them. She had no business giving him reasons to open up to her and tell her things he didn't tell anyone else. She was another woman and he'd better watch his step around her.

He had work to do. Flipping on his light, he picked up the package that arrived that afternoon. With all the work on the pond, he hadn't even opened it. This was important. This was the key to his future. Not getting involved with a woman, no matter how much he wanted her. He'd done without for the past three years, he could do without forever if he needed to. He'd learned his lesson—learned it well.

Chapter Ten

"Well, that went well, Ellie," she said softly. Two steps forward, two steps back. They were right where they started. He had a chip on his shoulder and she was as unsure around him as she had been on day one.

Entering the house and locking up, she paused in the kitchen. Should she knock on his door and make sure—

Make sure what? That he wasn't interested in a goodnight kiss? That he truly wanted to be alone. She was aching and tired. Time to go to bed. Tomorrow was Saturday. She had the weekend ahead with Jed and Brad arguing about the proper way to breed horses, Ariel flitting around complaining about her job, and Kat throwing sultry glances at Nick. Life would resume its normal beat.

Monday morning Ellie received a call from Alan Peters, the coordinator for Helping Hands. She had a responsibility to report on all her charges once a month. After scheduling a meeting for Tuesday, Ellie hung up the phone feeling a twinge of guilt. So caught up in the day-to-day living, with the emotions she felt around Nick, she had almost forgotten why he was there. Reviewing her progress with each of her guests, she feared she was shortchanging them. Especially Nick. She dreaded the meeting. What if Alan suspected her feelings for Nick? What if he reassigned him?

She would have to mention the appointment at dinner. Ask if any of the guests had any concerns, or wished to speak with Alan individually. So far no one ever had, but she always asked.

Fretting did no good, except to make the day seem endless. She took her paints and rode to one of the tallest hills on the ranch. Trying to capture the view soothed her, but in the back of her mind hovered the worry about Nick's reaction to her reporting in.

Bottom line he could handle it. He was a grown man.

Ellie felt awkward for the first time discussing her appointment at dinner. Nick handled it all right, he shut down and refused to look at her, nor say another word. The others shrugged off the announcement; it was not the first time they'd heard it. None of them wished to speak to Alan Peters. No one had any topics to discuss.

Alberta had made chocolate cream pie and they were more interested in that than Ellie's appointment.

Immediately after dinner, Nick left without a word and shut himself in his bedroom.

Later, Ellie lay awake long into the night. She should have told everyone individually. That way she could have explained things better to Nick. Darn it, she wished he was more the type to talk things through. Though what man was?

Tossing and turning wasn't getting her sleepy. She did not want to show up at the office the next morning looking haggard and worried. Tossing off the sheet, she pulled on her robe. She'd see if some milk would help her sleep.

Quietly Ellie entered the kitchen, her bare feet making

no sound. Nick's door was slightly ajar. His light still on. Couldn't he sleep, either? Flicking on the overhead light, she quickly poured herself a large glass.

She heard nothing from Nick's room. Slowly she walked over and pushed it farther open with one finger.

Nick had pushed off his shoes, but otherwise lay fully clothed against his pillows, sound asleep. A pen and stack of papers rested against his chest.

Ellie remembered the night he'd caught her asleep with the light on. She'd been reading—what had he been doing?

Curious, Ellie slipped inside, quietly tiptoeing across the room. There were papers scattered all over his bed, a small stack on the table beside the lamp. Neatly typed sheets of paper. She drew closer, her eyes on Nick. His chest rose and fell gently with his breathing. The dark lashes were long and thick, curling slightly against his cheek as he slept. He looked younger asleep, almost vulnerable. Ellie's heart lurched in her chest and she stared down at him for a long moment. She wanted to brush back his hair, watch him sleep, then watch him waken slowly and smile at her as if she were the pot of gold at the end of the rainbow.

You've been hanging out with Margot too long, she admonished.

Looking at the papers on his bed, she was puzzled. What were they? She leaned over to try to read the top sheet and lost her balance, splashing a few drops of cold milk on Nick's hand.

He came instantly awake. His hand shot out and grabbed her wrist, pouring half the glass of milk onto the bed.

"Oh, watch it!"

"What are you doing here?" He glared at her, noticing the thin cotton robe over her nightie, noticing how her nipples peaked, clearly visible beneath the soft cotton. He felt the silky softness of her wrist where his hand gripped.

Ellie swallowed and tried to pull her hand away, but he didn't release her.

"I came down for a glass of milk and saw your light. Your door was opened so I peeked in to see if you were awake. When I saw you were asleep, I was going to turn off the light."

He sat up, looked down at the work in his lap, the pages scattered across his bed, the small puddle of milk, then back to Ellie. His eyes narrowed as he released her wrist and took the glass of milk from her. He put it on the table and looked back at her. Ellie's eyes were wide as she stared at Nick.

"I'll get a towel." She whirled and started for the kitchen.

"I thought you told me this room was off-limits to you," he said through gritted teeth, conscious of the sweet spring scent that was hers alone. Despite the surge of desire that seemed to come from nowhere, he knew he had to resist. He knew he couldn't trust a woman, and she'd just proved it. So much for her glorious talk about his privacy.

"I was just going to turn off your light. I wasn't prying," she said evenly a moment later, blotting the damp spot on the spread. "Don't get paranoid."

Sighing heavily, Nick leaned back against the pillows and closed his eyes. He wanted her. His body clamored for her. His senses filled with her. Her skin had been warm and silky beneath his fingers. Her scent reminded him of sunshine and flowers, spring and laughter.

Dammit, he had to hold on to his sanity or he'd be lost.

He snapped open his eyes, steely in his determination.

"So now you know. Your curiosity is satisfied."

"Know what? That you sleep with the light on?"

"This." He motioned to the papers.

"Writing?" she guessed studying the pages.

He nodded, looking directly at her, anger glinting in his eyes.

"That explains a lot, doesn't it?" she said, almost as if to herself. "The long solitary walks, the hours you spend silently in your room. You're working all the time, aren't you?''

He nodded.

''I never heard a typewriter.''

''I write longhand, have it typed by someone else.''

''The package in today's mail?'' she guessed again.

He nodded. ''I'm proofing the pages, then will mail it in.''

She stared at him. ''You're writing a book? Why didn't you tell me? I've wondered what you did in here for hours on end. What kind of book?''

''It's a mystery novel. I didn't tell you because it's none of your damn business.'' He began to gather up the scattered pages.

''Based on your experiences?'' Ellie asked, moving away slightly from the bed, suddenly conscious of her scanty attire.

''The first one was, to a degree, only it was a murder mystery.''

''The first one?'' Her curiosity rose.

He flicked her a dark look. ''I was almost six months in jail awaiting trial, another two weeks during the trial, then prison. I almost went stir crazy at the beginning. Steve suggested I develop some activity that would take my mind off my incarceration.''

He rose, putting the pages on the table.

''If there's nothing else, I'd like to go to bed,'' he said.

Ellie shook her head, backing toward the door. ''Nothing else. But I'm curious about the book. Did you sell it?''

He nodded curtly.

''And?''

''And what, Ellie? It's late.''

''If I wrote a book, I'd shout it from the rooftops. Aren't you excited? Has it been published? Can I buy a copy?''

He hesitated a moment, then leaned against the wall with one shoulder, crossing his arms over his chest. ''I was lucky first time out. A publisher bought it, revised the hell out of it. It'll be on sale soon."

"What did you call it?" Ellie was fascinated by this revelation. She had never suspected.

"*Trust No One.* Appropriate, don't you think?"

"Why didn't you mention this when you first came? Why pretend you wanted to learn more about the ranching or get experience in construction? Why not just up and say you had something else lined up? For that matter, why did you even go in the Helping Hands program? You really don't need it. From what I gather, you have a house, investments, and a future as a writer. You have no reason to commit another crime. You're not exactly high risk."

"For starters, I got out of prison three months early by joining. That's worth anything I have to put up with. For another thing, I'm not going back to San Francisco. I've instructed Matt to sell the condo. And nothing is assured. I wanted to finish this book to see if it sells. If it does, maybe I have a career choice. Not that there's a lot of money in a single book. There are no guarantees. If this one doesn't sell, I'll have to find something else. In the meantime, Helping Hands is buying me time." He fell silent, his face closed, as if he resented telling her. He was shutting her out again.

"If it's a secret, I won't tell anyone," she said softly.

"Right—trust a woman? Ha. It's not possible."

She tightened her lips. She was trustworthy. If he didn't want to believe that, it was his problem.

"I'll say good-night," she replied primly and shivered a little in the cool night air. "And I won't mention this to anyone if you don't want me to. But I think the others would be thrilled to know this. Think how much that would show them there is a lot to expect in life."

Nick reached out and took her upper arms in his warm hands. He wanted more, but stopped. "I'm not some saint.

I'm not a role model for your kids. I'm in the same boat as they are. And I don't want anyone looking up to me.''

"You could be an outstanding role model.''

"Yeah, right. Some model, an embezzler.''

"Nick, you were never an embezzler. You tried to help someone who convinced you she was sorry for committing a crime. Because it backfired doesn't mean your intentions were wrong. Just…misplaced.''

"Misplaced? Try explaining that to Harold Roberts.''

"Who?''

"My boss.'' His grip tightened slightly.

"Maybe you should explain it to him.''

"Like I could.''

"Why not?''

"In the first place, he wouldn't even let me in the building. In the second, there is no excuse.''

"No excuse, maybe, but an explanation.''

Nick stared into her eyes, his bleak and barren. "You don't understand, Ellie. Harold gave me a break. He pushed a promotion that happened years before I might have expected it. I was in that position of trust that I violated because of him. I sometimes think that was the worst part of the whole damn mess—letting him down.''

"So tell him. It might make him feel better to know everything.''

"Everything came out in the trial.''

"Not how you felt, I bet. Not that you regret losing his trust. Maybe you need to do that for yourself, too, Nick. Forgive yourself. You made a mistake. It is unfortunate, but not life threatening. Forgive yourself for being human, for trying to do the right thing for someone you loved. Then move on. You can't change the past, don't live in it.''

"I'm doing all right.'' He refused to look at her.

"Doing all right means having done all you could to make amends, explain. Then plan for a bright future.''

"Pollyanna.''

She smiled and shook her head. "I don't think so. But I'm doing the best I can to make things better for others. And for myself. I have my work, my ranch and am doing some good for these kids."

"I'm not one of your kids."

She shook her head, very aware of the difference. "I want to know more about your book. Can I read it?"

"Get real."

"Is that a yes or a no?" she asked, smiling shyly up at him. Fascinating as the conversation was, she couldn't ignore the sensations sweeping through her while he held her arms, while she felt the radiant heat from his body counter the cooling air. His hair was in disarray from sleeping, his jaw looked rough with his beard. To her he looked dangerous and dramatic and as enticing as a hot-fudge sundae.

Suddenly the bleakness faded from his gaze. His eyes focused on her mouth and grew silvery.

His hand reached out for and flipped off the lamp and they were plunged into darkness.

"Don't go back to your bed, Ellie. Stay in mine, and I'll let you read the book," he said in the velvet night.

She laughed softly, nervously. "Bribing me to stay?"

"Why not? Don't you feel something between us?"

"Nick, you're a guest in my ranch. I can't—"

"Stay," he interrupted. "I'll let you read the book either way, if you want. But stay."

"I can't," she whispered, her breasts longing for his touch, her body moving to lean against his, reveling in the feel of his hard chest against her softness. She could feel his warm breath fan her cheek as he exhaled slowly.

"Stay," he said before his mouth came down on hers. His lips were persuasive as he moved them gently across hers, firming slightly as the kiss deepened. His tongue touched the corner of her mouth and Ellie parted her lips to meet him and find the delight and pleasure she'd found before.

He tilted her head and kissed her jaw, the soft sensitiv
skin beneath her jaw, trailing hot kisses down her throa
licking the fluttering pulse at its base.

One hand left her arm to capture one breast. As it too
the soft weight, Ellie thought she'd explode with wild ex
citement. Feeling herself respond to his touch, she wante
more. More than he was giving her. Until he trailed hi
mouth down the swelling mounds, covering a pert nipple
sucking through the cotton nightie and robe, feeding he
wanton out-of-control craving for Nick and his embrace.

Ellie whimpered slightly as the intoxicating feeling
spread. She threaded her fingers through his thick hair a
she held his head in place, never wanting him to stop. Th
sensations churning through her, spreading heat through he
body were new and exciting and exhilarating. How had sh
lived so long without this man's touch? Without the passio
he evoked in her?

Gone were inhibitions. Gone were the restraints of a lif
time. She could only splash through the waves of ecstas
that built, and offer herself to his every touch.

His hand slipped down her hip, back up, tracing the ir
dentation of her waist, spreading out across her flat bell
His palm was hot, but the heat rising in her matched hi
Ellie could scarcely breath with the fiery blaze buildin
within. Every inch of her skin tingled with delight. S
craved his touch. The mixed sensations confused, delighte
engulfed her.

His hand cupped her bottom and pulled her closer, h
mouth never leaving its sweet caress against her breas
Ellie held him with one hand while the other one trace
his shoulder muscles, the strong muscles of his arm, wan
ing to feel his smooth skin beneath her, not the material
his shirt. Wanting to learn his secrets, assuage the buildin
desire that threatened to topple her.

When his hand slipped beneath her nightie, she caug
her breath. He raised his head and stared down at her, h

breathing as erratic as her own. He should have left the light on. She wanted to see him, see his chest muscles ripple and move beneath her hand. See his eyes turn molten silver with emotion. Wanted to see caring and desire when he kissed her.

"You are so soft, so incredibly soft," he whispered as his fingers traced her skin, over the gentle swell of her hips, learning her.

"And you feel like iron sheathed in hot velvet," she said against his neck, shyly kissing him there. "Hot iron," she whispered as her fingers touched his heated skin.

His hand moved up her body, beneath her nightie, capturing one breast and caressing it, his thumb teasing the taut nipple beneath the damp cotton. His mouth found hers again and he kissed her over and over as his hand roamed freely over her heated flesh.

Ellie fumbled, then found his buttons. She tore them from the holes, opening the shirt so she could touch him, tangle her fingertips in the hair that grew on his chest, stroke his nipples, startled and delighted when his reaction mirrored hers.

"I'm only human, Ellie, and you're driving me crazy," he muttered against her throat as he jerked again when she touched him.

"You have on too many clothes," she whispered, pushing the shirt from his shoulders.

In only a moment, Nick helped by whipping off his jeans. Again Ellie wished he hadn't turned off the light. She was missing so much.

"You're the one now who's overdressed," he murmured, reaching for the hem of her nightie and pulling it up over her head, and tossing it and her robe across the room.

In one motion, he swept her into his arms, molding her fevered body against the length of his. Ellie almost cried in her pleasure. She'd never been so close to another person before and it was exhilarating, miraculous. He was so different from her, so wonderfully different.

Gently he placed her on the bed, the fever building between them as they touched and kissed and nibbled, learning what pleased the other, learning the contours and valleys of each body by touch, by taste.

When Nick parted her legs she gasped.

"Wait," she said, suddenly fully aware of what they were doing. For a moment the desire and longings faded and she was scared. She had no business being here. No business kissing and caressing this man.

"For?" He raised up on his arms and looked at her. The light from the outside made it possible to see his silhouette nothing more.

"Are you sure we should be doing this?" she asked feeling lonely with his attention diverted. Why had she opened her mouth?

"Not at all. You having regrets? Second thoughts?"

Ellie took a deep breath. She couldn't afford to make a mistake. Yet nothing about this felt like a mistake. She loved being with Nick. Yearned for his touch. Wanted more with him than anyone else.

"No regrets, no second thoughts," she said firmly. Let the future take care of itself. For once she was going to do something purely for herself. Selfish, self-centered and all. Just for herself.

Slowly he leaned over her and teased her with soft kisses until she became so caught up with the pleasure that spread she couldn't think anymore, only feel.

Nick covered her, pressed against her, and entered.

She jerked against him at the unexpected pain.

Nick stopped dead. He broke his kiss and raised up on his elbow, his hand gripping Ellie's jaw. "What the hell" Ellie, dammit, why didn't you tell me?"

She cleared her throat. The pain had been fleeting. It was already gone. Instead, the most delicious, delightful languor filled her. She liked being this close to Nick. Liked being linked.

"It sort of never came up. This was rather fast, don't you think?" she asked, tracing random patterns on his back. "Are we finished?"

Shaking his head, he moved against her, gently, in and out, his hands caressing her, his mouth finding hers again and kissing her deeply. In only seconds Ellie forgot the interruption, caught up in the flaming gratification that built and expanded with each stroke.

The spiraling sensations returned, stronger than ever. Ellie clutched his shoulders, returning each kiss as her hips began rocking against him, reveling in the sensations coursing through her, reveling in his touch, his body, his loving.

Suddenly Ellie felt as if she were exploding. Waves of pleasure washed through her again and again, as if her body had splintered into a thousand fragments of shimmering ecstasy. She thought she was falling in love with Nick , but after this enchantment she knew for sure. She loved him. Would forever.

She felt his own pulse deep within her and knew for certain she'd attained heaven. If life held no more than this, she could be satisfied. No, ecstatic. She'd been created for this moment. And for the moment, it was enough.

Ellie awoke just past dawn. For a second she didn't know where she was. Then memories flooded. She lay snuggled against Nick. She'd stayed the night with him. Made love with him!

For a long moment, the wonder of the event superseded every thought. She wanted to always remember. Imprinting every feeling on her mind, she tried to see how her arm felt lying across his chest, her leg warm between his legs. She could feel his heart beating beneath her ear and drew in a deep breath, inhaling his scent. It was so special. So perfect. It had been worth waiting her whole life for Nick.

Slowly, so as not to awaken him, she slipped from the bed and found her nightie and robe. Slipping them on, she gazed at the man once more before creeping from the room. No second thoughts. No regrets. But she had to leave. She could never let the others know she'd stayed the night. That she'd been in his bed.

Her entire future with Helping Hands could be in jeopardy.

But she had no regrets. How could anyone regret perfection?

Ellie slipped up to her room, grateful she met none of the others. Quickly showering, she lingered beneath the warm water, her hands tracing her skin where he'd kissed her, caressed her, tasted her. No wonder people got married if they could make love with their partner every night.

Dressing quickly, she knew she had to push the memory from her thoughts before she saw the others. One look at her, would everyone instantly know? She sincerely hoped not. What kind of mentor would she be to the teenagers if they discovered her violations of the rules? She should not have stayed.

Ellie waited until she heard Kat and Ariel descend before leaving her room. The usual rambunctious commotion filled the large kitchen when she walked in. That made it easier to avoid a direct confrontation with Nick.

Helping serve the meal, Ellie kept her distance and gratefully sank into her seat when everyone was served. Her knees felt like jelly. She had never considered how to face him once daylight came. She wasn't sure if she wanted to repeat the event, or just savor the memory. Reminding herself nothing could come of it, she tried to focus on what everyone was saying. Was it always so hectic in the morning?

"I'm working today," Kat said. "Yvonne asked me if I could help out because the other girl couldn't come in today."

The pride in her voice warmed Ellie's heart. This young girl would never go back to life on the street—she was building her own pride and assurance. With her natural fashion instinct and sales ability, she'd have something to build a life on. One with a much better chance of succeeding because of her stay at the ranch.

Gus was assigning tasks for the day when the phone rang. Alberta hurried to answer it, calling Nick. The level of noise diminished a little while he was on the phone. Everyone stared at him when he returned to the table. While each one was entitled to make and receive calls, the younger guests had never done so.

He looked around the table, ending with Ellie.

"I need to go to the city one day this week to take care of some business with the sale of my place. Will you go with me?"

"San Francisco?" Kat asked, her frown quickly replacing the pride that had so recently shown itself.

Nick nodded, his gaze still on Ellie.

"If I weren't working, I'd like to go to the city," Kat muttered, darting a dark look at Ellie.

"Not me," Jed said. "I like it here better."

"Yeah, man, there ain't no horses in the city," Brad added.

"Aren't," Ellie corrected automatically. A dozen excuses hovered. She should refuse. He could go on his own. She'd trust him. Prove she trusted him. She didn't need to spend the day with Nick.

But how could she refuse?

She nodded. "Sure, I'll go."

On Thursday Nick drove the ranch truck to San Francisco. Ellie kept quiet during most of the trip. She had argued with herself all week about coming with him. About keeping her distance. And about telling him how much she'd loved his book.

Nick had given her a copy of his manuscript Tuesday night after dinner. He said nothing to her about their night together, merely placed it beside her when she'd been watching TV with Ariel and the boys.

She'd read it Wednesday, spending hours engrossed when she should have met with Margot. The book was gripping, exciting. And cynical. But that last bit wouldn't matter. It gave the book an edge that she felt would rocket it to the top of the bestseller lists.

Did Nick realize how compelling his characters were, how their ultimate faith saved them from giving up, and allowed them to triumph? Somehow that was a surprise to find in the cynical theme.

"You never said why Matt needed you to come in today. Is there a problem?" Ellie asked as she settled herself beside him.

"He called to tell me my tenants are moving out. I wanted to sell the place and thought they were interested. But apparently they're having a baby and want a house. I need to list it and get the sale going."

"Don't you want to hold on to it in case you decide to move back?"

"No. I didn't want to hold it this long, but Matt insisted. I don't want to even see it again. I certainly have no intentions of living in it."

"I loved your book," she said shyly. She should have told him last night. Or first thing this morning. But they hadn't been alone before and she wasn't sure he truly wanted the rest to know he was writing.

He slanted her a glance. "Thanks."

"I mean it, I'm not just being nice. I did nothing yesterday but read it. Which puts me behind on my schedule."

"Which going with me today doesn't help."

She shrugged and said, "Doesn't matter. Schedules aren't set in concrete. Have you been writing long?"

"I told you it was something to do to while away the tedious hours in prison."

"I think you're talented."

He made a muffled noise, but said nothing.

"I'd like to read the first book. I bet your editor will snap this one right up."

"Time will tell, won't it?" The cool tone ended the discussion. Ellie gave up and began gazing out the window. The closer they drove toward San Francisco, the more the scenery changed. It had been years since she'd been to the city. Would it look very different?

Nick stopped at a real estate office that had handled the rental and listed the condo with the woman on duty. They discussed prices, how soon he'd want to close, and financing. Ellie thought it took surprisingly little time to put his home on the market.

"Could we drive by?" she asked when they left. She was curious about where Nick had lived before, and this was likely her only chance to see it.

He hesitated, gazing out the front window. Then he started the truck.

"Why not?" he said.

He turned to the right and before long slowed his speed while they passed a modern two-story condo complex. The neat, postage stamp yards all looked the same, every window had the same color curtain. The uniformity depressed Ellie and she studied the complex in bewilderment. Why did people live in a home that was identical to seventy-five adjacent ones?

There were few trees, and those that had been planted were young, with scrawny branches and sparse leaves. The pristine grass, dainty flower gardens with regimented rows of flowers did little to improve the setting in Ellie's eyes. She remembered how she first felt when she'd seen the ranch. The wide-open spaces, the quirky old farmhouse, the gravel driveway had felt like home.

Glad she no longer lived in the city, she glanced at Nick. "Which one is yours?"

"Third in from the left."

She looked at it, but it had no distinguishable features. Nothing to show his personality. Of course, Nick hadn't lived there for the last three years. She looked away, around the neighborhood and then back at Nick.

"Matt doesn't think you should sell it?"

"No, but I've made up my mind. We can stop by Matt's place and give him the bad news. He has a few other papers for me to sign. I can get that taken care of while we're here. I'm glad you came with me, Ellie. I wasn't sure if I could come by myself."

She nodded but remained silent as he drove. He would not have been allowed so far from the ranch without supervision. But she didn't need to tell him that, unless he particularly asked.

After Nick finished signing the necessary papers at Matt's law office, he told Matt he was going to stop by Steve and Sally's place before he and Ellie headed back. Ellie hadn't known Nick planned to stop by to see them. She was surprised to learn Matt was also a friend of the Davises when he said he'd join Nick and Ellie. Slowly she tried to relax. So far Nick had said nothing about the other night. The night they'd spent together. A few hours with his friends would ensure he couldn't bring it up.

At least she hoped he didn't plan to bring it up. That would put her in a very awkward situation. She still wasn't sure how she felt about things. The last thing she wanted was a discussion on the topic!

Chapter Eleven

When they arrived at Steve's apartment, both he and Sally greeted Ellie as if she were an old friend. When Matt joined them a short time later, he was also welcomed. Ellie listened avidly as the others discussed old times, other friends. She found them an odd assortment to be such good friends.

During the course of the conversation it became known that Ellie was privy to the secret of Nick's writing. Steve said nothing, but looked sharply at Nick in surprise, an assessing look to his eye.

"Come with me, Ellie. I have something to show you," Sally said, standing up and moving down the hall in the small apartment.

She smiled at Ellie as she entered the spacious bedroom. "I thought the guys might want to talk without having to entertain us. They go back to Stanford days together."

"I didn't realize Matt was a personal friend as well as Nick's attorney," Ellie said as she gazed around the room.

"He handled Nick's personal affairs while he was in

prison. He wasn't the trial attorney. Said he couldn't have mounted a strong defense. Not that the one Nick's attorney used did that much good according to Steve. Tough break on the guy, I thought. Especially since all the money was repaid. Want to see a dream of a dress I got for our honeymoon? We took a cruise to Mexico, so there was dancing every night. I loved it!'' Sally said as she drew a lovely confection of lace from her closet.

"I've never been on a cruise. What did you do all day, stare at the ocean?''

Sally laughed and began to tell Ellie about their honeymoon. Soon their conversation moved to other topics.

Ellie examined the dress as they spoke. Sally was right, it was a dream. For a long moment Ellie imagined herself dressed in something similar, with Nick bending over her, dancing with her. Except for the cotton dress she'd worn to church one Sunday, Nick had never seen her out of pants or shorts. Would he like her in something so feminine?

There was a curious strained silence when the women returned to the living room. No one spoke.

"Did we miss something?'' Sally asked looking around at the expressions on the men's faces.

"No. Let's get some Italian food for dinner. Then we've got to head back.'' Nick stood abruptly, avoiding Ellie's eyes.

Falling in with Nick's suggestion, they went to a small Italian restaurant off Columbus Street in San Francisco's Little Italy. The service was quick, the food excellent. The talk was as lively as the wine that flowed with the meal. Ellie was quiet for the most part, listening to the sports banter between the men, the discussion of who would win the pennant, who had the best chance for the Super Bowl next year. She was quiet by nature and easily entertained by listening to the others.

"Come again, Nick, and bring Ellie,'' Steve said as they

said their farewells on the sidewalk in front of the restaurant.

"We'll see." Nick was weaving slightly as he and Ellie headed toward the truck. He'd been drinking steadily during dinner.

"I'll drive," she said firmly, climbing behind the wheel. Nick acquiesced without a word and climbed in next to her.

Steve leaned in through the window looking at Nick. "Remember our conversation. Don't make another mistake."

"Mind your own damned business," Nick said, settling back in the seat, a frown on his face.

Ellie waved goodbye. Throwing a curious glance at Nick, she shifted into gear and settled down for the long drive home.

From time to time she glanced over to her passenger. His face remained tight, drawn, set. His silence hadn't seemed important until she realized he was angry. Seething. Why?

Twice she tried to start a conversation, but he abruptly cut her off with his curt responses. When they reached the ranch, Nick slammed out of the truck and strode down the driveway, off on one of his walks.

Ellie watched as his long stride swiftly carried him away. Was he already regretting his hasty action with his condo? Had being in the city raked up memories of Sheila? Did he still love her? Still miss her?

Ellie turned toward the house, recognizing her jealousy. Nick had loved the woman. Loved her enough to cover for her in a crime. He'd never hinted he loved Ellie. Even the other night, wonderful though it had been, he'd never said anything of love.

Ellie fixed herself a cup of tea and walked slowly out to the swing. She was too wide awake after that drive to go to bed immediately, though it was well after midnight. She refused to consider that she was waiting for Nick.

It was much later when Nick returned. He saw her on

the swing and swerved to head that way. Hesitating, he stepped up on the porch and leaned against the railing, crossing his arms across his chest.

"Want something to drink?" she asked gently.

"No, I don't," he growled.

Obviously his temper had not cooled.

Searching for something to say, Ellie remembered her appointment on Tuesday.

"When I saw Alan Peters at Helping Hands on Tuesday, I didn't mention your writing. But I think I should," she said.

"Why?" His voice was cold, harsh.

"He needs a progress report on each guest staying here. It would certainly put a different slant on the career part of the program."

"And is this whole damn setup a part of the program, too? The old maid so anxious to please that she lets the ex-con paw her whenever he wants? Catering to his whims, his moods, even sleeping with him? What do you get out of it, Ellie? A saintly sense of doing good, helping those less fortunate than you?"

Ellie was shocked at his words, at the anger lashing out toward her.

"What is it you get out of this? I've never figured that out. At first I thought it was for the money. But I've seen your accounts. The state doesn't pay you enough to cover food, much less to make you rich. So is it a little free work around the ranch? As I remember you wanted to play a mother role. Is that from frustrated motherhood on your part? Do you see these kids as kids you should have had? Or is it something more? Lady Bountiful? What am I, your latest pet, like Penelope?"

Each word pierced her like an arrow, each an angry attack on her self-esteem, her sense of worth. Why was he saying such vitriolic things? What was wrong?

"No," she replied in her soft drawl, her voice shaky,

pain spreading through her soul. "Nick, that's hateful. What's wrong?"

He remained silent, but she felt the tension roll off him like waves.

"I only wanted to help. And the other night was special." At least for me, she thought, watching him.

She loved him. Swallowing hard, she blinked, trying to understand. She could never tell him that. Never admit it aloud.

"I don't need you telling me what I should or shouldn't do. Nor do I need the Helping Hands' program. I just wanted to escape prison as early as I could. I sure as hell don't need Matt and Steve matchmaking between you and me. Telling me how trusting and trustworthy you are. I know about women. I learned hard and fast from Sheila. I'm not going that route again."

"Nick…" What had Matt and Steve said? *Matchmaking?* Something was wrong with this picture.

"'Don't let her get away,' they said tonight. Dammit, I might want to bed you, but I sure as hell don't want to *marry* you! You or anyone else. Never trust a woman!" he snarled.

She rose slowly, heartsick, hurt, confused. Raising her head, she turned toward the house. Tears threatened. Her throat grew tight holding them back.

"Good night." There was nothing else she could say. Holding on to her tenuous control, she walked stiffly, as if the slightest jarring motion would shatter her into a thousand pieces.

The screen closed quietly behind her and Nick muttered an expletive. He pushed away from the railing and followed her into the house. It was dark. He stopped, listening for a moment. He heard nothing. The place was quiet, everyone in their rooms. No slamming door tonight. Nothing.

He turned and strode to his room. Leaning against his

wall, he gazed out over the barnyard. Nothing moved. Everyone slept.

Had Ellie fallen immediately asleep? Or was she upstairs now wondering why he'd blasted her?

He was a bastard! She'd done nothing to incur his anger. It should have been directed to Matt and Steve. Or to himself. He'd made some comment that they took as an interest on his part in Ellie. And while he might want her, he knew there was no future there. He still hadn't figured her out, but once he did, it would cool any ardor he might imagine.

Until then, he'd stay the hell away from her. Away from her wide eyes, and silky skin. Her laughter which was so contagious, and her compassion that misled and enticed. She had an angle. Everyone did. He just needed to dig a little deeper to find hers.

Damn, he was drunk. He shouldn't have said those things to her. He felt like hell.

Tomorrow he'd have to apologize. There was no help for it. Damn!

Ellie spent the next day by herself. She rose early, grabbed some fruit and saddled her horse. Taking her painting supplies, she headed for the high country, determined to forget the aching pain she'd felt since Nick had spoken the hateful words. Tam ran beside her, sharing her delight in the cool morning air. For the moment, it was enough. She'd think about it later. Right now she just wanted to enjoy her ranch, enjoy the freedom of riding, of exploring.

But it was not enough to drive away Nick's words. They echoed in her mind as she kicked her mount into a gallop. Tam streaked beside her. She couldn't face Nick. She felt battered, bruised, humiliated.

So much of what he'd said was true. The way he'd said it had hurt, but the words were true. She would have liked to have children, would have loved to be a mother. She had not, however, planned to substitute that by working at Helping Hands. She believed in what she was doing. And it was in memory of her brother—who had not had the help when he could have used it.

That he'd misinterpreted her actions in his room could be rectified. It was apparently all right for him to sleep with her, but he saw her as expecting a lifelong commitment if she slept with him. Ha! Showed how much he knew. She refused to be at the beck and call of another man. She'd had a surfeit of that with her father. Maybe she could remind Nick of that.

Or maybe she could ignore him the rest of the time he was on the ranch.

Her body ached as she remembered the delight and pleasure she'd found with Nick. It hadn't all been about that night. She remembered every word they'd exchanged— from the time he'd first met her until last night. How patiently he taught Brad about accounting. How he cajoled Ariel and Kat into doing their share in the planning of the pond. How he treated the ranch hands with deference and respect.

And the time they found the egg on the rafter. Each time a cherished memory surfaced, she'd ruthlessly push it aside. She would not let something like that happen again. She'd had her night of splendor. Now reality returned.

He was her guest. He had weeks remaining before he left. If she were to survive that time, she had to build some defenses.

She found a sheltered cove near a small stream and dismounted. Hobbling her horse, she let the mare roam for forage. Setting up a portable easel and withdrawing her paint she found the joy in the day was dimmed, the inclination to paint gone. Lying in the sun, Ellie dozed, and tried to forget Nick Tanner.

Waking near noon, she called for her dog and took a walk along the creek. Gradually the land soothed her. The hills calmed her. The fresh air and balmy breezes comforted her. The sky was a deep-blue, without a single cloud. The dark green of the ponderosa pines made a beautiful contrast to the sky. The soft breeze mingled the scents of dry pine needles, grasses and cattle.

She'd tried to do what she thought was right. She wasn't looking for gratitude, but she wasn't looking for slurs and insults, either. She couldn't change because of it. She would get over the hurt, not dwell on it. She'd been happy before Nick came. Life would right itself again and she would go on.

But it hurt right now.

Nick woke late. His head throbbed, and his stomach churned. His first thought was of the words he'd hurled at Ellie last night. The angry things he'd said. He closed his eyes in anguish. She had been nothing but kind to him since he met her. She'd opened her house to him when he truly didn't fit the profile of her other guests. She'd discussed her hopes and dreams, told him of her past and shared her body with him. And he'd repaid her by cruel words derived because of his own anger at a woman she'd never even met.

He had to make amends.

He sat up and clutched his head, thinking it would split open. After a moment, he realized it wasn't going to. He stood and went to take a shower.

Standing in the tub, letting the cool water run over his head, he leaned his hands against the tile and concentrated on keeping upright. How could he apologize? How could he make amends? His behavior had been inexcusable, but she had to excuse him. Had to know it was the wine talking.

That and fear.

He couldn't afford to get close to her. She'd rip him apart if she turned on him like Sheila had. Damn Steve and Matt for asking if he was going to marry her. He had nothing to offer Ellie. Nothing but distrust, anger, bitterness and a prison record. Fine thing for a sweet woman like Ellie Winslow.

He took a deep breath, letting himself remember the feel of her body against his as they made love. The shock he'd felt when he realized she'd been a virgin. She'd trusted him enough to give him that, and he'd repaid her with slashing insults.

Dressed and shaved, he slowly opened his door, not yet ready to face the music, but knowing he couldn't put it off.

The house was silent. Checking his watch, he saw it was approaching noon. Alberta would be coming soon to prepare lunch. He walked through the quiet house to the porch. No one was there. Retracing his steps to the kitchen, he pushed open the screen and stepped out into the yard. The day was hot. The sun blazed from a cloudless blue sky, slashing into his brain. He winced. The heat reflected from the brown hills was dry, parching. He didn't see Ellie or anyone else.

A reprieve of a kind, he thought, heading toward the barn. If nothing else, he might be feeling better by the time he saw her. But he still didn't have a clue how to make things right.

It was late afternoon by the time Ellie rode into the barn. The return ride had been slow, for her dog's benefit. Tam had been run ragged. Ellie shared the feeling. She dreaded returning, but it was her home and she would not be driven from it by anyone. She would see Nick's assignment through, though right now she wasn't sure just how. What she'd like to do is call Alan Peters and request a transfer. But she'd never shirked hard work before.

There were only eight weeks remaining before Nick left. A person could stand anything, if she knew that the end was in sight.

The boys were joking and tossing fresh straw into the stalls. She greeted everyone and unsaddled her horse. So far, so good. No sign of Nick. The key was to never be alone with him. If she could do that, she could make it.

"Want help with your painting stuff?" Jed asked.

"I'll take care of the horse for you, Ellie," Brad said, reaching for the reins.

"Thanks." Smiling at the boys, she let Jed take the easel and wooden paint box. She gathered the canvas and fell into step with him. Just as they reached the huge double doors of the barn, Nick joined them.

He stopped and looked at Ellie. "I need to talk to you."

"I need to get cleaned up for dinner," she said, continuing to walk beside Jed. She knew she was using the boy as a shield, but she needed that right now.

Nick glanced at Jed, frustration evident. He reached out and stopped Ellie with a hand on her arm. "Take her things inside, Jed. We'll only be a minute."

The boy nodded and continued.

Fuming, Ellie shook loose his hand.

"I'm sorry for last night," he said. "I was drunk and mad and took it out on you. You've been nothing but kind and I repaid you by being a bastard. I'm sorry."

"Apology accepted," she said curtly and turned toward the house. She really didn't think she could bear it; he brought the entire scene back. She pressed a fist against her heart, trying to ease the ache. She might accept his apology, but it would be a long time before she forgot the words.

Ellie avoided Nick for the next week, spending most of the days in her studio. Each mealtime, she made sure everyone else was in the dining room before joining them. After dinner, she sat with the younger guests watching TV or playing some of the board games she had.

Nick avoided her as assiduously as she avoided him. Ellie noticed he kept to his room after dinner. Probably working on his book. Or he asked Gus for assignments that required working away from the house. He spent a few afternoons with Brad in the office reviewing the accounts, posting expenses to keep them in order. When time permitted, he and Jed worked on the stone waterfall for the pond.

Kat hung around him when she wasn't working. Ellie glanced out her window once or twice, worried about the girl. She obviously had a huge crush on Nick. But besides keeping an eye on them, Ellie refused to interfere. Kat had to grow up on her own. And Ellie didn't feel she could offer any kind of advice to the young woman. Her own situation was not a stellar example of how to develop a relationship.

When Ellie mentioned her concern about Kat to Alberta, the older woman just smiled and continued working. "Not to worry, Ellie. I've taken them drinks while they're working on that pond. Nick knows what he's doing with her."

"That's what I'm afraid of," Ellie murmured, worried. What if he took what Kat so blatantly offered?

"He talks to her as if she's thirty," Alberta explained.

"What?"

"I think she's finding him just a bit old for her. A bit—stuffy maybe?"

"Nick?" Try as she might, Ellie could not imagine anyone finding Nick stuffy.

"It'll work out. And without any hurt feelings this time," Alberta said kindly.

"Maybe." Afraid of where the conversation might lead, Ellie left the kitchen and returned to her studio. She'd give anything to sit on her porch and let the view soothe her. Swing back and forth and enjoy her home. But not while Nick was out there.

Two days later Alberta climbed the stairs to Ellie's studio.

"Time Ariel and I headed into Jackson for grocery shopping. Want anything special?"

Ellie looked up and smiled. "Nope. Anyone else around?"

"Tomas and Brad are out by the south bore, cleaning the water hole and checking on the cattle there. Gus had the others spread out along the northern boundary to give the fencing one last check. If everything looks good, I think he's going to pull back on that chore for a while. They all have their lunch with them. So you'll be on your own."

"I think I can manage a sandwich."

"Good, because I'm treating Ariel at that new ice-cream place in town. She loves hot-fudge sundaes. Can't believe the child never had one before coming here."

Ellie nodded and said, "That's what's so good about the program. It gives them a chance to see something more than what they had growing up."

"I reckon. See you later." Ellie heard her call for Ariel a few minutes later and then the sound of the truck engine.

There were many things her guests had been denied growing up. As had her brother. For a moment a deep satisfaction spread through her. She was making a difference. And it wasn't frustrated motherhood. She was doing it for her brother. If she made a difference in young lives because of Bobby, it was fitting enough tribute to the brother she'd so loved.

When Ellie went down to the kitchen sometime later for lunch, she was startled to find Nick.

"What are you doing here?" she asked before thinking. She thought she'd be alone.

"I live here. Temporarily at least," he replied. He turned and stared at her defiantly, his hip leaning casually against the counter, his stance arrogant and cocky.

"I thought you were out," she said, hesitating in the doorway. The last thing she wanted was to be alone with the man. Yet she refused to turn and run. She wouldn't give him that satisfaction. Tilting her chin, she stared right back.

"My horse threw a shoe and Rusty said I had to bring him back. Rusty will reshoe him when he gets in. Alberta gone?"

Ellie nodded. "Shopping."

"Lunch on our own?"

Slowly she walked into the room feeling almost like the first night when she'd fixed dinner for the two of them. "I thought Alberta said you had your lunch."

"Gus has a sack for everyone. I didn't stay to eat."

Ellie hesitated, then nodded. "Okay, I'll fix you a sandwich."

"I can do it myself, if you prefer."

"I was planning to fix one for me. Making two isn't any harder."

Nick remained where he stood as she drew meat and cheese from the refrigerator. She had not forgiven him—that he could see. Maybe she'd accepted his apology, but she had neither forgiven nor forgotten. Watching her, he wondered what he could do to change things. These past few days he'd missed Ellie's attention. He wanted her to ask him questions, to explain things to him, to talk to him.

He wanted to recapture the friendship she'd extended when he arrived. Before he'd blown it to smithereens. Even if she never came to him again in the dark of night, he could handle it. But he wanted her to smile at him again. He wanted to see the shining happiness in her eyes. To hear her laughter, to enjoy that soft Southern drawl when she spoke.

His body began to harden as he thought of how hot she'd been the night she'd come to his room, how sexy. How innocent!

He closed his eyes for an instant. He'd taken her innocence and then blasted her with cruel words. How could he make amends, get the warm and giving woman back in his life again?

Ellie placed two plates at the table, sitting opposite Nick.

She'd lost her appetite, but wouldn't give Nick the satisfaction of knowing that. She never lifted her eyes from her food and as soon as she was finished, cleared her plate.

"Ellie—"

"I have to go." Coward or not, she fled.

Taking advantage of the empty yard, Ellie sought her swing.

She thought about the angry words he'd flung at her after their dinner in the city. She knew he'd been drinking, and that he still had a lot of resentment. The words had spilled out in anger and frustration. It had to have been stressful being with his friends, knowing he'd missed three years of his life because of shielding Sheila. Was he resentful of his friends and the fact they'd gone on without him?

He didn't owe her anything, not love, nor loyalty, not even kindness. That night with Nick had been special. She'd wanted him to touch her, make love to her. She could have stopped it, as she would stop any future involvement. It wasn't fair to either of them. But he owed her nothing.

Slowly she felt better. Life was never perfect. She had the memory of one perfect night. It would have to be enough.

Curious, she wandered over to the cement and studied her pond. It looked as if it were almost finished. Nick had been patient in lining up the rocks, showing Jed how to take care in a job well done. She had watched him work with both boys when laying the power and the water lines. How much longer before she'd have water in it? Before the ducks could swim, and she'd enjoy the soothing melody of the waterfall each evening when she sat on the porch?

Looking at the pond, she knew she'd always remember Nick. She'd have a tangible reminder of his stay. And in time, the memories would soften. The waterfall would be cherished and the hurt would fade.

Nick stepped out on the porch, walked to the railing and

leaned against it, looking at the pond, at the woman studying it.

"We're almost finished," he called.

"You and the others have done a fine job."

He wanted to step closer to talk to her, but this was the
first time she hadn't fled when he came near. Holding still,
he gazed over the hills. "Was there more to your meeting
with the coordinator of Helping Hands than you told me?"

"No."

"Did you call him back and tell him about my writing?"
His hands clenched the railing. He wanted her to look at
him in the worst way. Wanted to see the expression on her
face, the short wavy hair that looked like an angel's cloud
around her face. He felt a tangible yearning to see her
bright-blue eyes and her expressions as she talked.

"I didn't tell him."

That surprised him. "What did you tell him?"

"That you wanted to learn about ranching like the other
two boys. That you were instructing me and them in accounting basics."

"Did he give you a hard time about it?"

She shrugged.

"Better he know about my writing than think you're not
doing your job," Nick said slowly. For the first time he
began to understand Ellie's position in this program. He'd
put her in an awkward situation.

"It's your secret. If you want him to know, you tell him.
You did say you wanted to learn more about ranching. I
just passed that along."

He stared at her, his emotions confused. She could have
told Mr. Peters. In fact, she should have told him. Should
have told him Nick didn't really need Helping Hands. That
he should have been left in prison for another three months
and released without this program. But she hadn't. Why?
And especially after his verbal attack the other night. He'd
have thought she would pull strings to get rid of him.

And he didn't want to leave.

But he knew why she hadn't arranged to return him to prison. Because she was a nice woman. A kind, gentle, loving woman. One who even when she was hurt wouldn't lash out and take revenge. An honorable woman who stood by her word. And that, perversely, made him almost as angry as if she had betrayed his confidence.

"Ellie."

"What?"

"What's next?"

She turned and looked at him. What did he mean? What was the next project? What else did she have planned for him before he left? Or what was next for them? Could she forget and go on? Try to recapture the tentative friendship they'd started? See if the next few weeks went as swiftly as the past ones had?

"What do you mean?" Her voice was hushed, soft, southern.

"When the pond is finished. Shall I make the next project to paint the house? It looks as if it could use it."

The next project? And she'd thought he'd meant them. She felt like a fool.

"That would be fine." She walked away, around the side of the house and out of sight. She couldn't stay another minute.

Gradually things resumed an even keel. Ellie became more comfortable around Nick, yet made sure they were never alone. She would not open herself up to foolish dreams or expectations. He was a guest, just as Jed and Brad and the two girls were. Only in Nick's case, he didn't need as much attention or guidance as the others. No one-on-one sessions every few days to check in. No time alone with him at all. Not if she wanted to keep her sanity.

She visited the optometrist and started wearing contacts, enjoying the freedom from glasses. She and Margot blocked out the next story. And she painted a new view of a favorite vista.

Once the last stone for the waterfall was set in place, Nick turned to the house-painting project. It would be several days before they could add water to the pond; the mortar holding the stones had to cure first.

Nick approached the house painting in the same manner as the pond, assigning tasks to the others, getting cost estimates, renting scaffolding, buying paint, scheduling painting times. The others weren't as enthusiastic about painting, but everyone pitched in and pulled their weight with minimal grumbling.

Nick himself took on the arduous task of scraping the old paint off where it was blistered and peeling, sanding edges, patching gouges. He and Rusty and Tomas set up the scaffold and he was able to work his way up the sides of the house.

He worked hard during the morning hours and early evening. In the afternoons he rode out on assignments Gus gave. At night he stayed shut away in his room.

Ellie tried to ignore him, but found it harder and harder as the days slipped by. His shoulders seemed to be growing more muscular the longer he worked around the place. Clearly visible when he pulled off his shirt in the heat, she'd find herself gazing at him for long moments before realizing what she was doing. She'd remember the night they'd shared, and her body would tingle, tighten. Her hands yearned to touch his hot skin. Her mouth longed for another kiss, deep and passionate.

She put in long hours with her paintings, trying to fill the time, to forget the tantalizing man she was so conscious of. She wished for the contentment she'd known before he arrived, yearned for its return once he'd gone. Yet dreaded his departure. To never see him again, never hear his quiet voice explain business practices to the boys, to watch him as he mounted a horse and rode with almost as much assurance and ease as her regular hands. She would miss him. God, how she would miss him!

On Saturday, Ellie was alone. Or practically alone. The cowboys had gone off for the day. Gus and Alberta had left to visit friends. Kat and Ariel were working. And Jed and Brad had taken horses for a long ride. She wondered what either of them would do if they didn't get a job at a ranch when they left. They were so horse crazy it was pathetic. And delightful. She knew that of all the guests who had passed through her ranch, these two boys had benefited most.

Nick was in his room. She could live with that. Sitting on the swing, she closed her eyes. It was a lazy day. Maybe she'd go upstairs and take a nap. Or finish that book she'd started. Or not even move until supper time.

When she heard a footstep, she looked around. Nick walked from the back of the house to the pond. He squatted by the rocks, running his hands over the stones. Looking over at her, he rose.

"I think we can fill it, if you like," he called.

"Really?" Ellie's heart skipped a beat. "Let's do it then."

They connected all the hoses she had, one to another, and drew the end out to the pond. The pump would recycle the water once it was filled.

At her signal, Nick turned on the faucet. In only seconds water began gushing from the hose into the concrete pool. Slowly the water level rose, seeking the nooks and crannies at the bottom, slowly rising, starting up the sloping sides.

Nick wandered to the opposite side of the pond and hunkered down to watch Ellie spray the water. The mist caught the sunlight, formed rainbows. She was happy and he liked looking at her. She hadn't been smiling all that much lately.

The pond gradually filled while he filled his senses watching her.

Growing bored at the long time it was taking to fill the

pond, Ellie tossed down the hose, spraying Nick in the process.

"Hey!" He stood up, brushing water from his jeans and shirt. "That's cold."

"Poor baby. It's only water," she mocked him.

"Only water, eh?" he murmured. Reaching down into the pond, he splashed a handful of water right at Ellie, soaking her shorts and bare tanned legs.

"You rat."

"Hey, it's only water."

Eyes narrowed, she stepped in the pond and slapped a spray of water toward him, only getting a few drops on him as he jumped back out of range, grinning smugly at her.

Rising to the bait, she scooped both hands and delivered a cascade of water, soaking him from head to foot.

The battle ensued. Splashing and sloshing back and forth they battled until both were soaked and laughing so hard they could barely stand on the pond's slippery sides.

In a last-ditch effort to win, Ellie grabbed the hose, squirting it directly at Nick.

"Hey, no fair." He jumped from the pool and circled behind her, crimping the hose to stop the water.

Ellie tried futilely to tug the hose from his hands. Nick's laughter sounded in the afternoon as he slowly, steadily pulled her toward him.

Snatching the hose from her hand, he released the crimp and let the water pour down her body, his free hand grasping her arm and holding her for his merciless assault.

She shrieked and laughed, pushing the nozzle away, trying to avoid the deluge of icy water. "Stop, you horrible man! It's freezing. Stop!"

Laughing, he relented, tossing the hose into the pond. "I win," he said, a broad self-satisfied smile on his lips.

"You rat, I'm soaked!" Ellie said, looking down at her wet clothes. They clung to her body like a second skin. The coldness of the water peaked her nipples and they pressed against the damp cotton of her shirt, clearly outlined for all the world to see.

Nick stared at her, his laughter fading as hunger took its place. His body tightened in response. He wanted her! Despite his angry words, her coolness over the past weeks, he wanted her in a primal gut-wrenching way. Did she have any idea of what she was doing to him just standing there looking like a man's dream?

With a muffled groan, he pulled her into his arms.

Chapter Twelve

The chill was instantly banished as his heated body melded with hers. His mouth demanded a response as he claimed her lips in a crushing embrace.

Ellie could scarcely breathe. Flames leaped within her in answer to his touch; warmth washed through her body and limbs. His hunger was matched within her, her body ached for his touch, yearned for fulfillment, for love.

She lost track of time and place. She was anchored by Nick's embrace, his mouth wreaking havoc with her senses, his hands drawing responses she didn't know herself capable of. If he hadn't banded her to him, her rubbery knees would have given way.

His clever fingers found, released the buttons on her shirt. Spreading it open, he exposed her bare damp breasts to the warmth of his gaze and the heat of the sun. Lightly, reverently, he traced the swell of first one then the other, drawing smaller and smaller circles against her heated skin until his fingertips reached the thrusting peaks of her rosy nipples.

Ellie began to tremble, mesmerized by his touch, longing for more, much more. His eyes flared when he met hers, his look frankly passionate, hungry and full of arousal.

Slowly he lowered his mouth to capture one peak, drawing the nipple within, laving it with his hot raspy tongue, pressing into her as he gently suckled the hot nub.

Ellie moaned deeply as a shaft of pure pleasure pierced her. Holding his head against her, glad of his support, she gave herself up to the unexpected delight his mouth induced. His free hand moved against her waist, around her bottom, caressing her, learning her again.

Nick stepped back, yanking his shirt over his head and tossing it on the grass. He drew her against him until her bare breasts pressed against his chest, pulled her to him until she could feel the hard core of his desire. His mouth moved from her lips to trail hot kisses across her cheeks, to nibble softly on the small lobe of her ear.

"I want you, Ellie, most damnably. You drive me wild! Don't be mad any longer. Forgive me."

He slipped his hand beneath the skimpy material of her shorts, caressing the smooth skin on her rounded derriere, his fingers brushing the warmth of her.

She caught her breath, trembling with desire.

"Nick, stop. We're outside in the wide-open. Anyone could come. We're in plain sight of the road," she said as she rubbed her breasts back and forth against his chest. Her arms tightened against his neck; her mouth sought his again. She knew they had to stop, but she didn't seem to be able to make herself step away.

With one smooth motion he picked her up and strode for the house. Pausing only to tell Tam to stay outside, he headed directly for his bedroom. Laying her down, he impatiently pushed aside the papers he'd been working on, scattering them all over the floor.

After slipping out of his jeans, he reached out to ease the damp shirt from her shoulders.

Ellie feasted her eyes on him. He was gorgeous. Dark where he was tan, startlingly pale where his jeans had been. The evidence of his desire was plain to see. She caught her breath at the beauty of his male form.

What was she doing here? In his room? Getting naked with Nick Tanner? Hadn't she been hurt enough after the last time?

She rose, intending to leave, but he leaned over her and kissed her. Softly, hesitantly, tentatively. It was the sweetest kiss she'd ever received and it melted her resistance like a blowtorch.

Slowly Nick trailed his hand down her side, all the way down her legs, slowly back up again, caressing her, touching her, inflaming every inch of skin he passed. Again. This time he slowly traced patterns along her calves, caressing the sensitive skin behind her knee, the soft silken inner thigh.

Ellie began trembling again as he moved to the apex of her thighs. She could scarcely breathe. Her heart was pounding, pounding, sending the blood rushing through her, singing in her veins. She knew what to expect now, this time. And her body was on fire. She couldn't get enough of Nick's touch, of his scent. His tantalizing love play drove her to the edge again and again.

Her eyes never left Nick even as her body began to move with his in the age-old rhythm, even when she could scarcely see him because of the myriad sensations sweeping through her. He watched her as his fingers found the softness he was seeking, lightly caressed, then moved on. Up across her abdomen, to the soft swollen mounds awaiting his exploration.

Ellie almost cried aloud when his hand covered her breast. She ached with desire, ached with longing and wanton unassuaged craving.

"Nick!" The word was full of need as she reached out for him with frantic fingers, wanting him like she'd never wanted anything before. Forgotten for the moment were the hurtful words. Remembered was only the memory of their first time, and the delight and pleasure they'd shared.

He smiled slowly and put his lips where his fingers had been, the rosy peak engulfed by his hot mouth, his rough tongue teasing, tantalizing, tormenting.

Ellie writhed beneath him, reaching out to encompass him, to draw him to her so he could assuage the burning longing building, building deep within.

"Easy sweetheart, it's so good. We don't want to rush."

"Yes, we do," she panted, moving her hand to encircle him, caress him, love him.

He gasped at her touch.

"Maybe you're right." He kissed her hard, his hands urgent now, urging her on.

Ellie moved to meet him, receive him, the wonder of it filling her again, expanding in her, exciting her. He moved, bringing her with him to the edge of delight and beyond into ecstasy. The world exploded and Ellie rode the rapture to its full height before slowly drifting back to earth and sanity. The world was still there, but she was forever changed.

He kissed her neck, moved to kiss her cheek and as she turned to see him, he kissed her mouth, long and hot and hard. His hand slowly moved along her side, from the soft swell of her breast to the top of her thigh, slowly back up.

"Ellie, forgive me. You have to," he said. "I didn't mean a single word."

Slowly her eyes opened; uncertainty filled her face. "You already apologized."

"Forgiveness is different. You need to grant me that."

Taking a deep breath, Ellie nodded. How could she advocate forgiveness if she wasn't willing to show him the way?

Closing his eyes, Nick rested his head next to hers, breathing in her unique scent. Something had been lifted. He wasn't sure what happened, but he felt lighter—almost purged.

It was late afternoon when Ellie awoke. The sun rode low in the sky, the soft air still. She stretched, slowly turning her head to survey the room. She was alone. Where was Nick?

She rose, gathered her shirt and shorts and went to the door, peeking out. The house was silent, still. She hadn't a clue where Nick had gone, but at least the others hadn't returned, either.

With a burst of speed, she ran to the stairs and flew up them. Taking a quick shower, she dressed in jeans and a pullover top. Drying her hair, she put on a light trace of makeup and went to find Nick.

He wasn't around. She checked the barn, the toolshed, scanned the scaffolding, the pond. She didn't see him. Tam was also missing. Had they gone for another of their long walks?

She wandered over to the pond. It was full, the pump working, making a pleasing, splashing, gurgling noise as water cascaded down the rocks. Smiling in delight, she went to the porch and sank into the swing. She could hear the soft murmur of the waterfall, just as she'd imagined. Even as she watched, her two ducks waddled over, suspiciously eyeing the waterfall, the pond. Then, with the joy of recognition, they scurried into the water, paddling round, tucking their heads beneath the surface, coming up with a shake to shed the water.

Ellie smiled at their antics, elated to have the pond finished. For a moment an ache in her heart stopped her breathing. Each time she'd look at it, she'd be reminded of Nick, of all the work he'd done on the pond, of their water fight, of the afternoon in bed.

She shifted position slightly on the swing, setting it to

moving. What would become of them? In a few weeks
Nick would be moving on. Helping Hands prepared the
hosts for that. It was essential that the offenders return to
the outside world, no matter how much they wanted to stay
with their hosts.

Nick had to leave, too. No matter how hard it would be
to say goodbye.

How would she stand it when the time came? She'd
never felt for any of her guests what she felt for Nick. She'd
never felt like this with any man.

Tears glistened in her eyes when she heard him crunch-
ing up the driveway, Tam as always gamboling at his side.
When Nick saw her, he changed directions for the porch.

Dashing the tears away, hoping he hadn't noticed, she
put on a bright smile. She didn't regret what they had done
and never wanted him to suspect she did. Life was too short
to waste time on vain regrets. It was as it was.

"Out walking? Don't you get enough exercise?" she
called as he drew nearer. "I can ask Gus to find other things
for you to do."

He laughed, looking younger than ever, and almost
happy. "Some muscles are out of shape due to lack of use.
We ought to remedy that." He sank beside her on the
swing, took one of her hands in his, lacing his fingers
through hers and resting their linked hands on his strong
thigh.

His jeans were snug, worn, soft beneath her hand. The
cotton checked shirt fit snugly across his broad shoulders.
Ellie thought he looked great, but she couldn't tell him.
She felt tongue-tied, looking away in confusion.

"The pond's super. Thank you."

"I had to get up. We'd left the hose on. It was close to
flooding the yard by the time I came out. I don't think
you'll have to add water for quite a while. You were still
sleeping, so I went for a walk. Are you feeling all right?"

"Yes." She squeezed his fingers and leaned over to rest

her head against his shoulder. For a long time they were silent, gently swinging back and forth. Ellie smiled through the moisture in her eyes. She'd treasure this bittersweet moment long after Nick had gone.

"It's nice here," Nick said.

"I love it. It's peaceful, quiet and safe. And the waterfall sounds just like I thought it would when you first suggested it. For me, this is as perfect as it gets on earth. I don't really like cities."

"Not at all?" he asked.

"Maybe to visit once in a while. The ranch is my home."

"Salisbury is a small town, but I wanted out. I wanted to hit the big town, make my mark on things." He was silent for a long moment. "I guess I did that."

"Put it behind you, Nick," she said softly. "Forgive yourself. You made a mistake. We all make mistakes. But if we learn from them, don't repeat them, we can let them go and move on."

"That's what I'm doing—starting with selling the condo. Material things were so important at one time. The more I had, the more successful I was. Didn't I have the status symbols to prove it? Now it seems so superficial."

"Greed can distort things. Even just trying to outshine your neighbor can be harmful. Perhaps if Sheila had had a more balanced view of things, she wouldn't have stolen the money, wouldn't have involved you. But it is in the past, and you'll have to forget it, forgive yourself for the lapse and go on."

"I won't ever forget it, Ellie. It's something I have to come to terms with before I can go on. But I won't ever forget."

"Was being in prison awful?" she asked after a bit.

He nodded, silent for a few moments. "I think the worst of the whole experience was Mr. Roberts."

"Your boss." She remembered what he'd said before.

"He trusted me to do my job, to be an honest man. I let him down. I can still see his face when he realized what I'd done. ████, I hated that the most."

"You need to tell him," she asked after a moment.

"What?"

"Go see him. Explain. Apologize." That would be cathartic for Nick, would help him along the road to recovery. She suspected he was too honorable to ever sleep well at night knowing what he'd done. Maybe it was time to find redemption by telling his old boss about Sheila, make him see how he'd been caught up in believing in a woman he loved. Surely anyone could understand. Not condone, but understand.

"Hell, Ellie, I told you, he'd never see me."

"You don't know if you don't try. He might. He probably wants to understand why you abused his trust, might relish an explanation."

"We've had this discussion before."

"So we can have it again."

"He heard everything at the trial."

"Well, he heard what the lawyers said. But does he know how you felt? Why you stalled for time? What you thought was going to happen, that Sheila was going to replace the money? You could explain how you were trying to give Sheila a chance, to justify the trust you had in her. The love."

"My trust wasn't justified."

"You know that now. But tell Mr. Roberts how it was then. It might make you feel better. And maybe him as well. Anyway, it can't hurt, right?"

Nick stared ahead, but didn't see the grassy hillside. Instead he saw the face of his boss, the man who had believed in him, trusted him. The man he'd let down. Then he thought about this afternoon. He'd wanted Ellie. They'd made love, brought intense pleasure to both of them. But what he remembered most was the peace that flowed through him when she forgave him.

Could he ask Harold Roberts for that?

"Trust is a very fragile thing. Once it's gone, you can't just get it back," he said slowly. He had learned something from the experience; too bad it came too late.

"He doesn't have to trust you again, just understand what happened. You aren't planning to go back to him to apply for a job."

"Trusting a woman is similar," he said slowly. Yet he was beginning to trust Ellie.

Ellie grew still. The discussion had veered into another direction entirely. She swallowed and said, "Trusting Sheila isn't likely to come up again."

"Or any woman," he said. "If one woman would betray a man's love, why wouldn't they all?"

She laughed softly. "Nick, be serious. That's no more true than if one man betrays another man's trust that means all men will. That same man may not ever do it again. I trust you."

"Even if I don't trust you?" he asked.

She shook her head. "It's not tit for tat. I'll trust you whether you ever trust me or not. But you can. Maybe you'll have time to find that out before you leave."

"Where am I going?"

"Your time's up in a few more weeks. Don't tell me you don't have the days marked."

"Maybe I'll stay."

She blinked. She'd not expected that. "No, you can't. You have to move on. Get on with your life. This is a halfway house. But you have to go out into the world all by yourself." She knew she sounded patronizing, but she believed in the program.

"I told you once before I have a mother, I don't need you mothering me." His voice was hard, and his grip on her hand tightened in anger.

"Nick, this is all artificial. You've been without a woman for more than three years. I'm available, I'm attracted to you, it was inevitable."

"What a foul thing to say. It wasn't just sex with me, Ellie. I'm...fond of you."

If ever she'd thought some miracle would make things come right, his words dashed that hope. He was fond of her. *Fond!* It was not a word of passion, desire, lifelong love and fidelity. *Fond!* She was fond of her ducks, for heaven's sake.

"Please, I don't want to discuss it further. It's pointless. When your time is up, you'll leave. A few days after that another guest will join us. That's the way the program works. When Jed and Kat's and the other's terms are finished, they'll move on." Saying goodbye was always hard. But she'd done it before and would continue to do so. Success with these kids made all the difference.

He looked at her in exasperation. "I'm damned if I understand you. I'd have thought after this afternoon the idea of my staying longer wouldn't be so unappealing."

"What we shared was special." How special, he'd never know. "But making love does not constitute a lifelong commitment to another person. Unless I've misread something here."

She couldn't believe she was saying those words, because that's how she felt. One way or another she'd made a lifelong commitment to Nick Tanner. There'd not be another man in her life. For one brief span of time she shared her home and thoughts with a man. And it was wonderful. She couldn't do it with anyone else. Never in this lifetime.

"I think we should give it a try," he said.

"There's too much against it," she said, pulling back and sitting up in the swing. "You haven't done anything in more than three years but mark time. You need to see new people, write your books, find someone you want to spend your life with. Not hang around a woman who values her own independence. You're young, you need to get on with life and not hide from it here.''

''And you,'' he snapped back. ''What about you? You're not old. You're the same age as I am. What have you done with your life? First tied to an old man while other women were out falling in love, having babies and seeing the world. Once you were free, you cloister yourself out here in the back of beyond caring for disadvantaged kids on whom you lavish your attention and then let go. I think you're scared. Too scared to make any kind of commitment.''

''I'm doing just what I want, Nick. This is not some passing fancy. I've been involved in Helping Hands for almost five years. Please, don't spoil what we have, Nick. It's special.''

''And that's supposed to be enough. A few more weeks together, then goodbye?''

She nodded, turning her face so he couldn't see the tears in her eyes, hoping he wouldn't demand she speak now when her throat ached with unshed tears and her breathing was shallow and faint.

''A few weeks,'' Nick repeated. He could get her to change her mind. He would bide his time, make himself indispensable. He'd help with the others, learn more about ranching so he would become invaluable. She wouldn't want him to leave when his time was up. The pretty jailer would release him from his bonds, but keep him shackled to her side through her own sweetness.

He turned and scooped her up off the swing. ''Time's fleeing, we need to make the most of it.'' He kissed her and headed for his room.

Ellie awoke the next morning wishing she were in bed with Nick. They'd inhabited a world of two most of yesterday—until the others in the household returned. But even though there were a half dozen other people in the dining room at dinner, she felt only Nick's gaze, heard only his voice.

She wished she could have spent the night with him, snuggling against his warm body, waking this morning with his arm heavy across her stomach, his hand curving around her waist. She remembered watching him while he napped after they'd made love a second time yesterday. He'd slept on his stomach with his face turned toward her. His breath fanned across her cheek.

Her heart blooming in love and joy, she hugged the memories. She'd never been in love before and wanted to treasure every moment. Yesterday his face had looked so relaxed, almost boyish as he slept. His brows were dark, his skin deeply tanned from working in the yard. His lips were soft and sensual. She remembered the feel of them against her skin, against her own mouth and her heart began beating faster.

It was hard to carry on an affair with a houseful of people. Would they ever find time to themselves again?

"Want to take a shower with me?" he had asked her when they moved to get up late in the afternoon.

She'd refused. And he had laughed softly. "Shy?" When she floundered for an answer, he'd brushed back her hair and gazed into her eyes, his warm and smoky gray.

"Shy! Honey, I've touched you everywhere, tasted you everywhere, watched you as we've made love. What's the difference if we shower together?"

"I don't know." She had tucked her head in beneath his chin, her cheek resting just over his heart where she could feel its steady beat. She'd closed her eyes, breathing in his special tangy scent, and the scent of love. She hadn't wanted to move.

"Maybe another time, then?" he'd asked softly.

Now she wondered if she'd blown her one chance. When would the house be empty for hours on end? When would they be assured no one would burst in and discover them?

Wistfully she wished she'd joined him.

Once showered and dressed, Ellie headed for the kitchen. She noticed the wall calendar as soon as she entered. Greeting Alberta absently, she headed toward it, calculating. Thirty-seven more days until Nick left. It didn't seem possible. That was all the time she'd have? Her heart stopped for a second, then surged. Only thirty-seven more days and he'd be gone. It would come too soon.

Ellie was resolved to let him go when his time was up. She soaked up every word Nick said, storing memories for the future. She watched him when she hoped he didn't know. Careful to be prudent around the others, she spent every moment in his company she could without causing undue comment.

But she held some of herself back. Holding back against the hurt she knew would come because she loved him. He was fond of her. And she could see it as they shared tasks together. It was in his eyes, in the way he watched out for her. But she wouldn't embarrass him nor herself by assuming there was more.

The week flew by. One afternoon, she took cold drinks out to the men. Nick and Rusty were replacing some of the railing on the corral fence. The day was hot and dry.

"Iced tea?" she asked holding up two frosty glasses.

"A lifesaver, Ellie," Rusty said, tucking his gloves into his side pocket and reaching gratefully for the glass.

"Sounds great," Nick said, reaching for his glass. His fingers caressed hers as he took it.

"Who was the guy here earlier?" he asked as he leaned against the fence and studied Ellie. He liked her hair, liked the way the soft curls twined around his fingers when they were alone and he could touch her as he wanted.

"Alan Peters from Helping Hands. He makes unannounced inspections from time to time."

Nick hated being reminded why he was here. For a moment the memories of the past few weeks disappeared. Anger flared, anger at Sheila, at the situation, even at Ellie.

"He reported on how well Kat and Ariel are doing at their jobs in town. He'd talked to their supervisors. Then he wanted to see everyone's room. We didn't enter any of them, just peeked in the door. He has a theory if people take care of their home, they'll take care of themselves. Yours was the neatest room."

Nick said nothing, but his lips tightened. Another reminder he was not a free man.

"He also wanted to know how you were doing in ranching. He has some names of possible employers for you," she said evenly, glancing over at Rusty. He had moved into the shade by the barn. She didn't think he could hear them.

"So why didn't you just tell him I already had something lined up? If this second book sells, maybe I can consider a career in writing."

"First of all, it's not my place telling him your business. If you want him to know that, you tell him. In the second, you came up with this proposal for working on a ranch. This organization is trying to help you. He's just doing his job, to the best of his ability."

"Unlike I did mine, is that it?" Nick said, anger and shame mixed in his expression.

"I never said anything like that. Why are you looking for slights that aren't there? The whole purpose of this program is to help people."

"Help them, or control them? For all intents and purposes, I'm still in jail. If I decided to get in your truck and drive away, you'd call the cops. Right?"

"You signed up for this program. You knew what it was about going in. Don't stay if you don't want to. Go!"

It all meant nothing! She'd done her best and he still had the same chip on his shoulder as when he'd arrived. He still saw her as a jailer. For a moment Ellie's knees threatened to collapse. She couldn't breathe. How dare he, after kissing her and making love, how dare he consider her nothing more than a jailer!

"And by night be back in prison."

"No way, Nick. You can't go back to something you never left!" she said, staring straight back at him.

"What are you talking about?"

"You carry that prison around with you. You left the walls behind, but not the bars. You made a mistake. A big one, actually. But the State of California deemed three years of your life suitable reparation. You've paid for that mistake. Put it behind you and move on!"

He thrust the empty glass at her and let go. She caught it before it fell.

"Leave me the hell alone." Turning, he yanked on his leather gloves and picked up the next rail. "You ready, Rusty?" he called.

Ellie gathered Rusty's glass and headed back to the kitchen, uncertainty building. Would he try to leave? Would she have to call and report him gone? God, not that. She'd had confrontations from time to time with her other guests, but her own emotions hadn't been so entangled. She'd been able to handle their blowups better. But with Nick, it was much more personal.

When Ellie came for dinner, she looked at Nick's place. His empty place.

"Where's Nick?"

"Went out to check on one of the wells after we finished the corral," Rusty said, reaching for the huge bowl of stew Alberta had started around.

"Shouldn't he be back by now?" She couldn't help remember his words about leaving. He hadn't, had he? If he pushed her, she'd fight back. Much as she cared for him, she also cared for the program. It was her way of remembering her brother. Of dealing with his youthful death.

She'd give Nick every benefit, but at some things she drew the line. Escaping before his time was up was one of them.

"He'll be along," Gus said, looking at Ellie. "Problem?"

She shrugged and shook her head. Forcing a smile, she glanced around the table at the others. She would not raise any suspicions. At least not now.

But by bedtime she was really worried. Everyone knew something was wrong. Nick should have returned long ago. Ellie couldn't concentrate on the comedy playing on the television. She kept listening for the sound of his footsteps, the sound of a horse being ridden.

"Do you suppose he got lost?" Jed asked, picking up on her unease.

"Or hurt?" Ariel asked. She was lying on the floor. Looking up at Ellie, she rolled over to see her better. "Maybe we should all saddle up and go out like a posse."

"Posses are for chasing bad guys," Brad said.

Smiling wryly, Ariel nodded. "Aren't we all?"

"No!" Ellie said firmly. "You are not bad guys. And you might be right, Ariel, he could be hurt." She hoped it was that. Not that she wanted him injured, but it beat having him leave.

"So, we go look for him?"

"Where would we start? How would we see? It's pitch-black outside." Jed said. "Would lanterns or flashlights be enough?"

"Do you know where he went?" Kat asked. "This is a huge ranch, and I don't see how we could even begin if we didn't have a good idea of where to look."

"Good point, Kat. But if we do decide to mount a search for him tonight, I want you all to stay here. I'll have Rusty and Tomas and Gus go. No sense in all of us going out there and running the risk of getting hurt."

"I can help," Brad said quietly.

"I'd want to go, Ellie," Jed added.

"Me, too. Didn't you say we're like a family?" Ariel said, sitting up. "Nick can be a pain in the butt when he's passing out assignments. And he's such a stickler for doing the best we can. But he's part of the group."

Kat looked at her hands and sighed. "If I break a nail because of this, heads will roll!"

Ellie almost laughed. But she was touched more than she could say. Even Kat wanted to join in the search. What if it were all for nought? What if Nick had just left, just cut out early to be away from all reminders? How would that affect these kids who were trying so hard to turn around their lives?

If he had pulled out, she'd never forgive him.

Chapter Thirteen

Ellie wondered if she should call to let Alan Peters know Nick had been missing since midafternoon. But she couldn't. Not yet. If he really had gone, she'd have to let the authorities know. She'd agreed to the rules of the program when she signed up. But she wouldn't do anything just yet. He might return. She'd give him time to do so.

"What's that?" Jed asked, jumping up and hurrying to the back of the house. Everyone in the room immediately followed.

Flipping on the outside light, Jed ran out the back door. The slow gait of a horse could clearly be heard.

"Nick, are you all right?" Brad asked, running outside to the horse that was ambling into the yard with Nick slumped in the saddle.

As soon as Nick became aware of the others, he made an attempt to sit up straight. Seeking Ellie, he smiled wanly.

"Got knocked down by one of your damned steers

Think I sprained my wrist,'' he said, cradling his arm against his chest.

"We were so worried about you. Can you dismount? We'll go into the hospital and get them to look at your arm. Brad, take the horse. Jed, go tell Gus and Alberta. Ariel, look in the first-aid kit in the kitchen and see if we have something we can use as a sling.''

"I have a scarf that'll work,'' Kat said, turning to run into the house. Ariel hovered with Ellie as Nick gingerly dismounted. His left arm and hand were swollen. Lines of pain radiated from his mouth, around his eyes. But his gaze was steadfast as he stared at Ellie.

"Sorry I worried you.''

"We were all worried,'' she said, afraid to touch him. Afraid to give way to the emotions that threatened to choke her. He was here. Safe if not sound. He hadn't left.

Gus and Alberta hurried from their cottage. Rusty and Tomas, hearing the commotion, joined them.

Ariel looked around and then looked at Ellie. "A family rallies round,'' she said wonderingly.

Ellie nodded, already working with Alberta to tie Kat's scarf around Nick's neck and slipping his arm carefully into the makeshift sling.

"Cool fashion statement,'' Jed murmured at the bright, colorful scarf.

"That's enough. I need someone to go with me to the hospital. Just in case Nick passes out in the truck or something. Jed?''

"Why does he get to go? Girls make better nurses,'' Ariel said.

"I need a man. Nick's no lightweight.''

"I'm not going to pass out. Let the boy get his rest. In fact, I appreciate the show of support, but you all can relax, I'm doing all right. We could wait until morning, to get this checked out,'' Nick said.

"Nope, not then. Now. I'll get my purse. If you really

feel you'll make it, we won't take a third. It would be crowded in the truck and I suspect the rough ride will be hard enough on your arm without knocking it against someone else.''

Two hours later Ellie turned the truck into the ranch driveway. Nick had broken his wrist in two places. Cast on, pain medication given, the doctor released him with the instructions to take it easy for a few days.

Ellie felt almost euphoric with relief. He was going to be all right. And he had not been trying to leave. She wanted to tell him how afraid she'd been. How awful she felt thinking he might. But she kept silent. There was no point in revealing her lack of faith.

It was after midnight by the time Ellie stopped the truck and shut off the engine. The house was dark except for the back porch and the kitchen lights. The other buildings were dark as well. Everyone had gone to bed.

''Sorry to keep you up so late,'' Nick said.

''And I'm sorry you got hurt.'' Ellie said, moving closer, her arm going around his neck, her head resting against his shoulder. She could take this bit of comfort. Just this little bit.

''If you keep that up, I'll be responsible for what happens next.'' Nick's low voice sounded above her head, amusement lacing his tone.

She tilted her face up. His eyes were closed. She could still see the pain in his face. Wasn't the medication working?

''What did you say?'' she whispered. Had she imagined he spoke?

''Usually people say they won't be responsible for their actions, but I wanted you to know that I would be.'' He pulled her a bit closer and leaned over to kiss her. His free hand brushed across her cheek.

''Tired?'' he asked.

"Aren't you?"

"Yeah. It's been a long day."

They walked into the house together, quietly, so not to waken anyone.

"Do you need anything?" Ellie asked. He had the pain pills even though he wasn't to take any more until morning.

"Just you."

"Me?"

"Stay tonight, Ellie. Will you?" He watched her, his eyes smoky-gray, filled with hunger. For her.

Ellie hesitated. She wanted to stay. He was only going to be here a few more weeks. And he'd been hurt. What if he needed something in the night?

Throwing caution to the winds, she nodded. It would hurt no one and mean so much to her. "Okay, but I'll have to get up really early so no one else knows."

"Can't have anyone knowing, can we?" he asked bitterly, turning for his room.

Ellie locked up, turned off the light and followed him, already questioning if she should be doing this.

The soft light from the bedside table illuminated the room. Shutting the bedroom door, Ellie sat on the chair and pulled off her boots. "Need help with yours?" She would not give in to the nervous tension that gripped her. She wanted to stay, he wanted her to stay.

"Why did you agree?"

"Because I want to." Rising, she crossed to Nick. Holding his gaze with hers, she slowly raised her arms and encircled his neck. Tugging slightly, she pulled his head toward hers until she could kiss him. Gratified when his arms came around her, she knew she'd made the right decision.

A few moments later she pushed him gently until he sat on the side of the bed. She pulled off his boots and sat beside him, efficiently unbuttoning his shirt.

"You have on too many clothes," she murmured, brushing her lips against his muscular chest.

"I could say the same thing about you, sweetheart." Using his free hand he slipped her shirt over her head, reached around to unfasten her bra. Slowly his fingers traced the faint veins of her breasts, lightly circled the hard tips that yearned for his touch. His caress was unhurried and deliberate. It was all Ellie could do to remain still beneath his touch. Inside she was a boiling cauldron of craving.

She longed to press herself against him, feel the hard strength of his muscles, the contours of his body beneath her, above her, around her, but reveled in the sensations that built, that swept through her like a brushfire.

Nick raised his hand to thread his fingers through her hair, drawing her against him, settling her as his lips captured hers. In only moments they were lost to place and time, dwelling only in the heat and desire that detonated when they touched. With passion shared, their world contained only the two of them, caught up in the pleasure and bliss each could only give the other.

Ellie exploded beneath his touch, nerve endings sensitized by his hands, his mouth, his body. Each time she knew she could do no more he brought her to newer heights, newer levels of ecstasy. She gloried in the pleasure he built and the rapture that together they experienced.

Lying still in the quiet aftermath, Ellie lightly trailed her hands up and down his back. Feeling the heat of his body gradually cool, feeling the breathlessness gradually fade, she was utterly content. If time would freeze into one moment, she'd want it to be this one.

When Ellie walked into the kitchen the next morning, her eyes involuntarily flew to the calendar. She hated it hanging there. It reminded her constantly of the limited time she and Nick had together. She couldn't take it down, it would cause too much comment. And it would change nothing. She had to accept the fleeting time and make the most of it.

But every time she looked at it, she was reminded and felt herself die a little.

She had yet to decide what she was going to do to protect herself from the inevitable hole in her life his leaving would cause. She couldn't continue to be involved with him. She smiled to herself. How could she stop? It was a craving— to spend time with him. To hear him talk, to touch him when they were alone.

To make love when the chance presented itself.

She couldn't stop, but she had to protect herself. She had to keep a part of herself safe. Separate, isolated against the inevitable departure day. She had to keep part of herself safe from loving him.

Naturally at breakfast, everyone wanted to hear Nick's account of the accident. Several suggestions were made on how he could have prevented it, on how to watch out for steers. Which led to a general discussion of what to do when injured. Whether on the ranch or in town.

Nick smiled as he watched Ellie lead the discussion. If he wasn't careful, he'd be smiling a lot more. But today he figured he was entitled. She hadn't stayed all night. Sometime during the early morning hours, she'd risen and left. He didn't know the exact time, but he knew when she'd left.

Now she was in her element. Teaching these disadvantaged kids the basics of life. Giving them each a boost in the right direction to enable them to turn their lives around and achieve the kind of lives most people took for granted.

As he had.

Reminded once more, he thought of their discussion about forgiveness. He had been thinking about it a lot. Would it make a difference?

"So, does this mean we're putting the painting project on hold?" Kat asked.

Nick looked at her. She no longer flirted with him. His tactics of demonstrating their age difference, the differences in interest and common ground had worked. But he had a warm spot in his heart for the young girl.

"Nope. Just means I don't have to paint. I can still supervise."

"It's your left wrist that got broken, not your right one," Jed pointed out with a cheeky grin. "Seems to me you could still hold a brush."

"Thanks, pal," Nick drawled.

"Nick's teasing you, boy," Tomas said, looking up at Nick. "He ain't a man to let a little thing like a broken wrist slow him down. Expect he'll be on his horse sometime today out doing regular chores. Maybe not stringing fence 'cause that needs two hands, but most of the other work can be handled with one. Right, Nick?"

A wave of pride washed through Nick as he nodded. He hadn't expected to receive such a vote of confidence from one of the ranch hands. He'd been a bit wary around them, knowing they probably didn't appreciate working with prisoners. But the accolade touched something deep inside.

"Don't see why not," he said slowly.

"I think you should rest your arm," Ellie said firmly.

Nick grinned around the table. "Well, maybe I do feel a bit under the weather. Maybe I should have you wait on me today."

Gus and Tomas laughed. Even Rusty smiled broadly. "Milk it for all you can, man. She usually kicks us out to work even if we're dying."

"I do not!" Ellie said.

"Take it easy today, son," Gus said. "You get all the paint and stuff you need for the job, we'll all pitch in next week and get this house looking like a showplace. And no riding until tomorrow. Expect you'll need help saddling a mount for a few days anyway."

Getting everything lined up for the painting project didn't take long. While in the office, Nick double-checked the accounts. Brad was doing a good job keeping them straight and current. The kid had a true affinity for ranching. Nick hoped he got a great job at a place that would let him use his newfound skills.

Hunting for Ellie when he finished, he couldn't find her. Probably just as well. He had other work to do.

Shutting himself in his bedroom, he pulled out the last draft of the book and started reading. With any luck, he'd finish it and get it off by the end of the week.

Ellie stayed away all day. Nick and Alberta ate lunch alone. Then she left for errands and he had the house to himself. Was Ellie's absence deliberate? Was she avoiding him? It seemed as if she were, but he could come up with no reason for her to do so. Maybe she just rode out to cover his chores today.

Not knowing where she was drove him crazy. He couldn't remember feeling like this about other women. Not even Sheila, for whom he'd ruined his own life. He was shaken at the intensity of his feelings, with the obvious need he felt. Walking out to the porch, he sank into the swing and gazed over the hills.

Suddenly Nick realized he didn't want to leave when his time was up. It was so clear and simple. He could stay on and help out around the ranch. His accounting should be worth his keep alone. And he liked learning from Gus and Rusty and Tomas. There was so much he didn't know, yet his knowledge of ranching increased every day.

Ellie remained stubborn. From her side, when his term was up, he left. Damn, he'd made no headway in changing her mind. She was as stubborn as hell! He'd find her and make her change her mind. He had to. He was beginning to think he would not like a life without Ellie in it.

But nothing he did over the next three weeks changed her mind.

The house was painted. The pond a huge success. The boys learned more and more about the business end of

ranching. Ariel decided to try for college in the fall—with
a view to major in psychology. She wanted to do what Ellie
was doing, helping people in need. Kat already spoke of
finding an apartment in Jackson, of continuing to work in
the clothing store. Maybe one day having a store of her
own.

Ellie mothered them all. Stood by them all. But she
would not change her mind about Nick, and she knew it
was driving him crazy.

Tomorrow was his last day.

Their lovemaking was particularly sweet that last night.
But after Nick fell asleep, Ellie rose and slipped out to her
own room. For the last three weeks she'd thrown caution
to the winds to spend most of each night in his arms. From
now on she would be sleeping alone. Might as well start
getting used to it. She felt as if the iron bars of a prison
were closing in behind her, closing off life, love, happiness.
She was a long time falling asleep.

Ellie went into the barn the next morning to feed the
animals, wondering how she would make it through all the
rest of the mornings in her life. One day at a time, she
thought. Just as she had when Bobby had died. And again
when she'd found out her father owned this ranch and had
never made it available to his only son.

Nick rose from the darkened interior, a shadowy figure
looming over her.

"Nick! You startled me." She caught her breath at the
sight of him.

"I want to talk with you. Why did you leave last night?
I almost came upstairs after you. This issue is not resolved."

"It is resolved. Today you are a free man. Free to go
where you wish, do whatever you wish, as long as it's legal.
I have the papers in the office. I'll give them to you after
breakfast. I've already talked with Gus and he'll take you

to Stockton so you can catch a bus to San Francisco, or wherever you wish to go.''

"And what if my wish is not to go, but to stay here?"

She took a deep breath, hoping her pain wouldn't show in her expression or voice. "Well, that's not an option."

She turned to get the feed for Penelope. The pig squealed and paced in her pen. Ellie was flooded with reminders of that first day with Nick, how surprised he'd been to see Penelope. Other memories crowded in. His feeding the chickens and ducks, how seriously he'd done it those first few times. His long rambles with Tam. Finding the egg on the rafter, their water fight by the pond. God, she was going to miss him so much!

Hard hands grasped her arms, turning her to face him.

"I'm not leaving. We'll get married, if that's what you want."

Ellie blinked in surprise, her heart beating heavily. *If that's what you want.* Her chin tilted up as she faced him. He'd never know what she wanted.

"Nick, being here has been a safety zone for you. I'm the first woman in your life since Sheila. You don't know what you want yet. You've not done any dating since Sheila, haven't had the opportunity to meet other women, find someone you could fall in love with, make a life with."

"There's no comparison between you and Sheila."

"Oh, for heaven's sake, you loved her enough to commit a crime for her. Now you're trying to say you've forgotten all about her and want to marry me?" Because he was *fond* of her? Ellie thought she would choke with the rage that flared. She wanted the kind of love Sheila had carelessly thrown away. She wanted to be desired and loved and cherished. And she vowed she would not settle for anything less.

"Sheila used me. All feelings I had for her are gone. Except bitterness at being used, maybe," Nick said.

"You need to get out on your own," she repeated stubbornly. She stepped back and his hands reluctantly let her go. "Get a new place to live. Meet other people. If writing is going to be your source of income, you need to set up an office for that. Work at it regularly."

"I like ranching. I've learned a lot, Ellie. I know the accounting side, can pick up whatever else I need. And now I can do almost every chore around the place that Tomas or Rusty do. Except shoeing."

"There's more to life than a ranch. If you really like the work, find a job on another spread. The West if full of them."

"I like this ranch."

"Mr. Peters said…"

"What—now I'm fighting Mr. Peters, too?"

"He says guests get comfortable. You made the transition from prison to here, but you need to be challenged, get back into the mainstream."

"Hell's bells, Ellie, I'm challenged right now. This is not easy. There's a lot about ranching I don't know. May never learn what people born to the way of life know. But I can make a go of it. Can make it work. Let me stay."

"No! Haven't you heard a word I've said? You can't stay here. Go find your place in the world. Be a writer, or try something else. Find a ranch and hire on. Go home and visit your folks. Make something of your life. You deserve the best, Nick, don't settle for less." She struggled to keep the tears from her voice, from her eyes. It was so hard. Why did he keep arguing with her? Why wouldn't he go and let her die in peace?

"What if I don't go?"

Ellie wasn't getting through to him. The final reason would. She couldn't keep on with this. It wouldn't grow easier by prolonging it.

"I don't want to marry you. I don't want you on my ranch. Your time is up. Go away, Nick, just go."

With an oath, he turned and left the barn.

Ellie watched him go with an ache in her chest that rivaled the feelings when Bobby died. If only Nick had loved her. It didn't even have to be as much as he'd loved Sheila. But she wanted some love. Blinking frantically, she tried to stop the tears. But they welled up faster than she could blink. Brushing her hands against her damp cheeks, she turned and walked deeper in the barn.

She would not let him know how she felt, or any of the others. Nick had been a guest. He'd changed since he first came. Now it was time for him to go on. The program had succeeded again. Only this time she couldn't rejoice.

Two days later, Ellie sat alone on the porch swing, listless, lethargic. Slowly one foot pushed the swing back and forth, a cool glass of iced tea forgotten in her left hand. She gazed out at the duck pond, her mind seeing Nick when he worked in the hot sun; the water fight; the afternoon that followed.

Her eyes filled with tears at the memory of the happy times, forever gone.

The crunch on the gravel alerted her to a visitor. Turning slightly, Ellie watched Kat walk around the house, step up on the porch.

"Want company?" she asked.

"Sure." Making an effort, Ellie tried to smile. From the look on Kat's face, she'd not been successful.

Kat's expression was sober as she took in Ellie's listlessness, the tear-swollen, blotchy eyes behind the glasses. She shook her head in sympathy to Ellie's misery, hesitating, unsure.

"I guess you miss Nick, huh?"

Ellie nodded, turning back to gaze out over the hills.

Kat joined her on the swing.

"Is he ever coming back?" she asked.

Ellie shook her head. "I told him not to."

She thought of those last few hours before Nick had left.

They had been awful. Nick had railed at her for her stubborn attitude, for denying the chance he wanted. She remained steadfast in her position, though it had become harder and harder. Finally, in anger and frustration, he had stormed out.

She wished he had not left in anger. That was her one regret. No, that wasn't true. She had lots of regrets, and knew she'd have handled things differently if only—

"This is not the end," he'd yelled at her when Gus drove him down the driveway to catch the bus to San Francisco.

"Please don't come back," she'd said stoically, all the time screaming in her heart for him not to leave. Unlike the other guests, she could not extend the invitation to return whenever he wished. She could not subject herself to this a second time. With Nick, she had to make a clean break.

"I think he likes you," Kat said after a minute.

"I like him," Ellie said. "I like all my guests."

"I wanted him to like me, love me, really. But he didn't. Guess that was a dumb idea, huh?"

"No, it wasn't. But it just would never have worked, honey. He's years older, and was burned badly by a woman. He can't trust any of us. And that's not good for a lasting relationship."

"At least you didn't say I was too young."

"Did he?"

"No. For a few days I thought we were becoming close. He never kissed me or anything, but he talked to me."

Ellie wondered what Kat thought about Nick now. "And?"

"And he's still a nice guy. And gorgeous to look at. But he's old. Too old for me. He doesn't listen to the same music I like, didn't want to do crazy things," Kat said, looking at Ellie. "Don't take this wrong, but I like Jed a lot better."

"Jed and you have interests in common. You'll find oth

ers who do, too. And one day you'll find a special man who will want to share his life with you. I want to be invited to the wedding!''

''One of the sheriff's deputies asked me to coffee yesterday,'' Kat said. ''He's only about twenty-five. Not too old, do you think?''

''What do you think?''

''At first I thought he was hassling me. Knowing my record and all. But he's been in the shop several times,'' Kat said, grinning. ''He always gets really pink, like he's embarrassed to be there. But he talks with Yvonne and then always wanders over to where I am and talks to me.''

''So did you go for coffee?''

''No. Maybe some day. But not just yet.''

''Go when it feels right.'' Stupid advice. It felt right with Nick, and she'd refused. Maybe Kat would prove wiser.

''Do you think?''

''I think the deputy wouldn't ask you out if he didn't want to get to know you better. Go and have fun.''

Kat sat silent for a long moment.

''Is there something else?'' Ellie asked at last.

''Nick's leaving got me to thinking. My time's up soon. I'll be leaving, too.''

''Are you looking forward to that?'' Ellie asked.

Kat shrugged. ''Maybe.''

''Maybe you're just a bit apprehensive, as well. That's normal,'' Ellie said matter-of-factly. She'd been through this before.

''Is it normal?''

''Sure. But ask for help if you want it. Just because your time is up doesn't mean you suddenly become a nonperson. We like you, Kat. Alberta and I can help you find an apartment, if you're serious about staying in Jackson. We'll ask at the church for donations of furniture. The guys can help you move. And you'll have us nearby.''

"You made Nick leave and told him to never come back."

Ellie took a breath, feeling the sharp pain. "I know, but that was a different situation. You're welcome here whenever you wish to come. I hope you keep in touch and visit often. I care about you, Kat."

The girl slid her eyes sideways, looking at Ellie. "Yeah, well, you cared about Nick. We're not blind, you know. You're crazy in love with him, if your sappy expression was anything to go by most of the time. And you sent him away and did not invite him back. Excuse me for thinking I wouldn't be welcome either."

Stricken, Ellie turned to face Kat. "That's not true. I want you to view this as a second home. Come whenever, you are always welcome."

"And Nick?"

The girl didn't give up. Ellie tried to rally her thoughts, find a way to explain. But she couldn't. She wasn't sure she knew herself. Giving up, she just shook her head. "That's a different situation."

"Okay, then," Kat said, seemingly reassured.

"You'll do fine," Ellie said, reaching out to lightly brush the girl's arm. She wanted the best for Kat. Her earlier life had not been kind. Ellie hoped for a brighter future for her.

"I'm going to do you proud," Kat said suddenly. "I won't ever forget what you did for me, Ellie. I'll never let you down."

"I know, Kat. Thank you."

Score another one, Bobby. This one will make it, I know it. I wish you were here to see her.

I still miss you.

The next afternoon Ellie tried painting. A light breeze blew in through the open windows. The aroma of cinnamon and sugar floated in the air. Alberta was baking another batch of apple pies. It was still and peaceful. Conducive to painting, except Ellie had never felt less like being creative.

Hearing the footsteps on the stairs, she looked up as Margot burst into the room.

"I heard he's gone."

"Nick? Yeah, he left a couple of days ago. His time was up."

"I think you are a fool, *mon amie,*" Margot said impatiently. "I think you were falling in love with him. Why not keep him around a bit longer? See what developed?"

"Nothing was going to develop. He was *fond* of me. If I insisted, he might have married me. But he would not have loved me. And that's something I would like to have in a marriage, you know?" The hurt went deep; she sighed and blinked back tears. Would she ever stop crying?

"Give the man a break, *chérie.* He went through a lot. At one time he was never going to trust a woman again. Now you say he wanted to stay and make a life with you. Is that so awful?"

"Margot, three years ago he loved Sheila. Loved her so much he covered a crime and went to prison. So he's without a woman for three years. Then he finds a nice, willing woman who places no demands on him, and he fancies he wants to make his life with her. Given time. Maybe."

"So, what's wrong with that?" the ever practical Frenchwoman asked.

"First of all, it's not what I want." *Liar* a small voice inside whispered. "Second, he's not thinking straight. He's not even seen another woman in more than three years. It's hormones talking."

"He's thirty-two years old. He probably knows what he wants by now."

"It would never work." Was she trying to convince Margot, or herself?

Margot blew out her cheeks in exasperation, a frown

marring her features. Taking a deep breath, she tried again
"Maybe he is afraid to admit to love."

Ellie shook her head. There was more to it than that. I
he'd loved her, he'd have refused to go. If he'd loved her
she would have insisted he stay.

Margot paced restlessly. "I cannot believe you let him
go."

"There was no letting. I made him go. He needs to ge
back into the mainstream. Put the past behind him an
move on."

"And then, if he dates a dozen women, if he gets a jo
and a new life, and then if he still wants you, would yo
take him?"

"You've been writing too much fiction. It's never goin
to happen." But, oh how she wished it would. Just as Mar
got said.

"Bah, I cannot believe you! First you send him away
now you say it'll never work, yet unless I can't understan
what my eyes see, you yearn for the man. Which is i
chérie?"

Her friend was right. Ellie had seen this coming and sti
done nothing to prevent it. Their time together was ove
no use moping about it. Time enough to dream of wha
might have been at night when she was alone in her bed

Around the other people in her life, she would be brigl
and cheerful. Sending Nick away had been her decisio
and the right one. There would come a time when her hea
wouldn't ache so, when her mind would stop wonderin
what Nick was doing every minute, where he was, if h
was all right. Life did go on, one sunrise after another.

"I think he loves you, *chérie*. Perhaps he just doesn
realize it. And I think you love him. We've been frien
for a long time. What's going on?"

"I wanted to be young and pretty and desirable for hir
I wanted him to love me to distraction, be extravaga
overwhelming in his love for me," Ellie said passionatel

the hurt building. "But he told me he was comfortable here. He's *fond* of me. How would you like Philip to be 'fond' of you? You're right, I love Nick, but he doesn't know it. And his leaving is better in the long run. I'll get by and be fine one of these days."

In her heart she questioned it, but it was probably true. One day, when she was old and gray, she'd get over Nick Tanner.

Margot sighed gently. "I came by to tell you I heard from our publisher. He likes the latest book. Wants a couple of changes to the text and one more drawing. And he likes the proposal for the next one. Wants to know how soon we could deliver it."

"Great." Ellie forced enthusiasm into her voice. "What changes specifically? What does he want for the additional picture?"

They discussed their work, made plans for the next project, scheduled dates and drafted the basic outline and picture list. Ellie forced herself to pay attention, clung to the discussion as a means to forget the ache in her heart for a few moments.

Ellie felt better by the time Margot left. The work schedule they drew up was tight; briefly she wondered if Margot had exaggerated the need for haste to make sure Ellie had plenty to do and didn't brood. Whatever the reason, there was a close deadline looming over them.

Life settled into a routine. She spent time with each of her guests. Applied with Helping Hands for another to fill Nick's slot. If at each meal she remembered Nick's presence at the table, she mentioned it to no one. If when she gathered eggs she remembered the day the egg dropped on his head, she tried to smile through her tears. If as she sat on the porch and listened to the waterfall, and watched her ducks swimming in the pond she remembered every second spent with Nick Tanner, she kept the memories private.

At first she was miserable, but the memories were happy and they became easier to live with.

Her birthday came and went. Margot and Philip sent her flowers and a card. Her guests, abetted by Alberta, threw a party, with a huge cake and presents from each. Ellie enjoyed the day, but she couldn't help but think of all the birthdays yet to come. Other birthdays she'd spend without Nick.

Working on her sketches and drawings took a lot of time. The one additional painting for the book had been easy, sent in a few days after Margot's visit. Now the stack of paintings grew for the next book. A Christmas story. If they could make the deadline, it would be published in time for next year's Christmas list. She worked long hours, determined to meet the deadlines, glad for the concentration required. Focusing on work, to make sure she didn't think about Nick.

But during the long, lonely nights Ellie couldn't ignore the memories and she thought about Nick nonstop. She wondered what he was doing, where he was. If he ever thought of her. She missed him dreadfully. Missed him with a deep longing that so far showed no signs of abating. Surely this empty feeling would pass, given enough time.

Chapter Fourteen

Three weeks after Nick left, Ellie found a bright postcard in her mail, with a cheerful picture of an old-fashioned beach scene. Turning it over, Nick's bold scrawl jumped out at her. "Came home. Went well. Have started dating, as you suggested." It was signed only, "Nick."

Ellie stared at it for a long time. So much for protestations of wanting to stay and make some sort of future with her. Already dating again. She closed her eyes against the sharp thrust of pain the image brought. Nick smiling at some woman, holding her hand. Maybe even dancing.

They had never had a date. Never gone dancing, out to dinner alone, or even for a walk together. Now he was wining and dining other women. Women who probably would never love him as much as she did.

"Damn him," she said to Tam as he trotted beside her up the driveway. "He didn't have to tell me. He's gone for good, why write at all?"

She tore the card in half and stuffed it into the pocket

of her jeans. No sense saving it. It wasn't something sh
could share with the others—how would she explain hi
cryptic message?

She'd been proven right—theirs was not a lasting rela
tionship. She'd been wise to refuse him, to send him away
So why didn't she feel better, now that she knew her choic
had been the right one?

The next evening Ellie dined with Margot and Philip
During dinner, she mentioned the card.

"What did he say? Where is he?" Margot asked. Phili
stopped carving the roast as he awaited Ellie's reply.

Quoting the card, Ellie muttered sulkily, "Don't kno
why he sent it."

"I'm sure it was to give you the comfort that he is fine,"
Philip said placidly, giving his wife a wink.

"I assumed he'd be fine," Ellie said tartly.

"And I know you're happy he's started to see othe
women. You didn't want him on the rebound *chérie*. No
you know he's not pining away for you." Margot's prac
tical assessment only angered Ellie.

"Oh, yes, I'm ecstatic with joy."

Margot laughed softly.

"Shows he had no lasting feelings for me, doesn't it?"
Ellie murmured, fiddling with her water glass.

"Or he recognized defeat when he saw it."

That night in bed, Ellie questioned her stance. "I did th
right thing," she repeated as a litany.

A week later a second card arrived. This one had a scen
from Rehobeth Beach, Maryland. It was a typical Ea
Coast beach with a wide, clean, sandy shore and gentle sur
Viewing it, Ellie was suddenly, unexpectedly homesick fo
Georgia, for the southern beaches she'd known as a youn
girl.

Almost fearfully she turned the card over.

"Will be published again," said the boldly writte

ords. "Having fun. Beaches are great. Say hi to the gang.
ick."

Ellie's heart soared with the news his second book had
een accepted. She knew it must mean a lot to him. She
ished him well. So many other lines of work were closed
 him because of his past.

She reread the message. Was he still seeing other
omen? She looked down at the big German shepherd sit-
ng patiently at her feet.

"It's from Nick. He says hi to everyone, and that in-
udes you, old boy." She patted his head, a smile lighting
er face, her heart strangely lighter. At least he hadn't for-
otten her totally.

She shared the card at dinner. The others were excited
 hear from Nick and the news about his book. They de-
anded all the information Ellie possessed about it.

Ariel wanted more. "Did you get his address, Ellie? We
uld all write and then he'd write back. I've never had
ail before."

Ellie hesitated. But Nick had started it with the postcards.
"There's no return address on the card, but I'll see what
can find out."

"He'll want to know how the cattle are doing," Brad
id. "And that I'm still keeping up with the accounts."

"Maybe Alberta can bake him some cookies and mail
em. Remember how those cookies seemed to disappear
hen Nick was around?" Kat said.

"Yeah, at least there're more for us with him gone," Jed
id.

Suddenly Ellie was glad Nick wrote. How she wished
e could share some of the things around the ranch she
ought he'd like to hear. The new book she and Margot
ere working on; the way the ducks were using the pond;
enrietta's feat of an egg a day for over a week. How well
rad kept up the accounts. And the fact Kat might be dating
erself soon.

When the card made the rounds, Rusty handed it back to her.

She smiled wistfully as her fingers lightly traced the bold writing. This was from Nick. He'd picked it out and written.

The following weekend the entire ranch turned out move Kat into her new apartment. Her time was up a she was free. Yvonne had been delighted to have her sta on. Together Kat and Ellie found an inexpensive apartme in a nice complex—sublet at a reduced rate through a mem ber of Helping Hands.

By the next weekend, Kat had been back to the ranc twice for supper, and had gone on that coffee date wi Jimmy Monroe, the deputy who kept asking her out. S confided in Ellie that Jimmy wanted to take her to the sho on Friday night, and she'd accepted.

The following Monday, Margot called. "*Je suis fini!* I bring the manuscript with me and we'll match the word to the drawings and see what we still need."

"Good, come any time. I've blocked out all the pictur we discussed, painted a few of them. I'm still working the clouds on the swing set scene. Come over. Plan lunch. Alberta won't be here. She and Gus took off for couple of days. But I can make a great sandwich."

"I'll be there around eleven."

Margot arrived promptly. Ellie had scarcely greeted h before a bright pink delivery van, with Patty's Peta painted in large purple letters, turned into her driveway.

Both women stared at the van with surprise.

"Expecting flowers?" Margot asked.

"No. He's probably asking directions. I'll go see."

Ellie met the man as he climbed down from his truck

"Miss Ellie Winslow?" he asked, referring to his cli board.

"Yes," she said in surprise.

"Have a delivery for you. Please sign here," he said, indicating a line on his board.

She signed, feeling a hint of excitement. Who would send her flowers? She wasn't sick and it wasn't her birthday.

The man went to the rear of the truck, returning with a large pot of African violets in full bloom. The rich purple flowers spilled over the edge of the clay pot, the yellow stamens bright against the deep royal color.

"Thank you," Ellie murmured as she took the plant. Holding it out, she showed Margot.

"They're for you? From whom?" Margot asked, following her into the kitchen.

Putting the pot in the center of her table, a smile of pure pleasure lighting her face, Ellie reached for the card tucked discreetly to one side.

"Aren't they lovely?" she asked as she opened the envelope.

"*Oui, bien sûr.* But who are they from?" Margot asked impatiently.

Ellie gently drew the torn piece of paper from its small envelope. There was one word printed. *Will.*

"Who's Will?" Margot asked reading over her shoulder.

"I don't know. I don't think I know any Wills," Ellie replied, searching her mind for anyone she'd met recently called Will. Shaking her head, she looked at the envelope. Her name, nothing else. She looked back to the card. "Will?"

"So maybe you have a secret admirer who's soon to be not so secret," Margot suggested.

"Weird. I can't think of who it could be. But aren't the flowers beautiful? I do love violets. Maybe I can call the florist and find out who sent them."

She looked up the number and quickly dialed. Explaining her puzzlement regarding the sender to the woman on the phone, she was disappointed to learn that the woman had

not taken the order. Her partner had, and she was not work
ing that day. The shopkeeper promised to inquire upon th
woman's return.

Ellie turned to Margot when she hung up. "She didn'
know. Someone else took the order and won't be in unt
tomorrow."

"No matter. It's exciting, don't you think? A secret ad
mirer."

"I don't know," Ellie said softly touching the violet pe
als. "It's a little odd. I wish I knew who to thank."

Margot waved her hand in the air. "Enjoy. Come or
let's get on with the book."

Over the next couple of days. Ellie found her thought
turning again and again to who Will might be. She re
viewed everyone she knew—evening wondering what som
of the deputies who delivered her guests might be name
The woman at the florist had called, but had no informatio
for Ellie. The sender had paid cash.

Two days later when Ellie went to get the mail, sh
found a large box of candy stuffed in the mailbox with th
rest of the mail. It was filled with dark chocolate, carame
and covered nuts. She loved candy and wondered wh
would have sent them to her. The ragged note on the bo
only said "Ellie."

It didn't make sense. Who would send her candy?

Of course—it was Margot. Was this her way to keep he
mind occupied? Trying to create a mystery that would tak
up Ellie's time trying to solve?

She smiled at her friend's wacky notion to keep her fror
brooding. But she didn't need something like this to kee
her occupied. She was doing fine. The violets were lovel
and Margot knew she loved dark chocolate, but she didn
need to spend her money on such things.

Ellie called her.

"Margot, I got the candy. Thank you. But you mustn
spend your money on me. I'm fine. Really."

"Whatever are you talking about, *chérie?*"

"The candy you sent me. I appreciate it very much."

"I sent you no candy," Margot said, sounding sincere.

"First the violets, then the candy. Margot, it has to be you." Ellie hesitated a moment and then said, "Doesn't it?"

"No, Ellie, it was not I. So you got candy? Hmmm. This is getting interesting."

"A large box of dark chocolate, with nuts."

"And a card?"

"No card this time, just a torn scrap of paper with my name. I thought it had to be from you."

"No. Maybe from your mysterious Will?"

"If so, why not sign it?" Ellie wondered, frowning. She didn't know a Will, or William, or Bill for that matter. She had mentally reviewed every man she knew.

"Most intriguing. I'll ask Philip what he thinks. Let me know if you get anything else. How romantic."

Ellie hung up, wondering if she viewed it as romantic or not. If she knew who was sending the flowers and candy and liked him, she might think it romantic. Right now it was frustrating.

Another picture postcard waited for Ellie when she went to get her mail the next afternoon. This one showed the state capital building in Annapolis. Eagerly she turned it over. It read, "Condo sold. No more San Francisco for me. Still dating, have reached a decision. Nick."

Ellie's heart sank. She felt the world darken a little. He was probably planning to marry. She'd known it would come to this. She hoped he was happy. It was what she wanted for him. Only she hadn't realized how lonely, how desolate she'd feel. She couldn't believe she would never see him again.

And she couldn't believe he'd found someone so fast.

Ellie looked up at the bright-blue sky, hoping to find an answer to the ache in her breast. It was no more than she expected. She was glad for him—she would be glad for him, she thought fiercely. He was so precious to her and she wanted him to be happy, to have a rich and full life, especially after all the trouble he'd had the past few years. She blinked back tears.

She would be happy for him!

On impulse, Ellie went to the phone, dialing information in Salisbury. There were six Tanner families listed. The fourth one she called was Nick's.

"I'm sorry, Nick's not here right now. He's gone to see his girl," an older woman said when Ellie asked to speak to him. "Is there a message?"

"No, no message." Ellie hung up, feeling sick. The reality was worse than the speculation.

On Friday afternoon Ellie was in the corral, washing Penelope. The pig squealed and snorted as she frolicked under the hose. The cool water felt pleasant in the hot sun, though the dusty ground turned into mud with their efforts. Ellie laughed at Penelope's antics, forgetting for a while the heartache that was so much a part of her these days.

The crunch of gravel and Tam's barking alerted Ellie to the arrival of a familiar pink van.

"This is getting out of hand," she said with a lightness in her heart that belied her words. She ran the water down her legs to get rid of most of the mud, climbed the fence and headed for the delivery truck.

"Hello, again," the delivery man said, smiling and holding out his board.

Ellie signed and smiled up at him. "What do you have for me today?"

"The best," he said, withdrawing a long white box, tied with a wide gold ribbon.

Ellie felt her heart skip a beat. It had to contain roses. She'd never been sent roses in her life, but she watched

TV and recognized the box. With a wide smile, she thanked the man and went inside the house to the kitchen.

Opening the box, she drew in her breath. They were gorgeous. A dozen—no eighteen— long-stem red roses, nestled in greenery. Their fragrance filled the room. She couldn't stop smiling. She didn't know who was doing this, but it was wonderful.

Ellie stepped back a pace and studied the flowers. Their heavenly fragrance seemed to fill the room. Their rich color seemed to glow with a light of their own. Roses were too fancy for the kitchen, but she'd keep them here for now. Until the others had a chance to see them. Tonight, she'd take them up to her bedroom with her. Their fragrance would greet her upon wakening in the morning.

Ellie looked through the box, ruffling the tissue paper. Where was the card? If it wasn't Margot, who was extravagantly sending her flowers?

Beneath the green paper she found another scrap of paper. It had on it a single word and when Ellie read it her heart began to pound. For a moment she felt almost dizzy. Crazy dreams filled her mind, images and memories and foolish longings.

It couldn't be. It simply couldn't be. There was some mistake. A torn scrap had gotten caught up when they had been making up the order.

Despite the total illogic of the whole scenario, she went to the kitchen drawer and pulled out the two previous notes and arranged them in the order she'd received them. The ragged edges matched.

Will. Ellie. Marry.

He stood just outside the screen, watching her. His heart pounded as he waited for the moment she'd see him. He didn't know if what he'd done would work. But something sure had to. He couldn't keep going like he had these past few weeks.

She looked sexy as hell in those short shorts, her legs streaked with mud. He'd seen her from the road when he'd pulled over after following the delivery truck out. Her top was skimpy and he could see her breasts outlined where water had splashed against the fabric. She wasn't wearing a bra and he could feel the once familiar tightening in his gut, the longing wash through him for her. She was so pretty.

He'd missed her so much.

He was staying now if he had to pitch a tent in a neighbor's field.

Nick opened the screen door quietly and stepped inside, watching her read the pieces of paper, his own heart so constricted he didn't know if he could carry this off. If she refused again, he didn't know what he'd do.

"Will Ellie marry Nick?" he said quietly.

She whirled around.

"Nick?"

He nodded.

"What are you doing here?"

"Making sure the last delivery arrived."

She looked at the papers, the roses, the man.

"You sent all this?"

"Traditional, don't you think?" he said.

"Traditional?"

"For courting. Flowers, candy." He hoped he wasn't making a hash of this. Why didn't she say something? Or at least look slightly glad to see him?

Suddenly, without notice, she flew across the room and launched herself against him. He caught her in a crushing embrace. She was here, where she belonged. With him.

Eagerly his mouth sought, found hers. She tasted like ambrosia, like heaven and earth and Christmas all rolled up in one fantastic package. He couldn't get enough.

His lips demanded. Hers responded. Ellie held nothing back as she returned caress for caress, pressure for pressure, demand for demand. When his tongue plunged into the warm welcome of her mouth, she opened for him, her tongue dancing with his, moving to taste him, feel him with all her body, her hands roaming over his shoulders, up the column of his neck, threading into the softness of his thick hair. Had she missed him as much as he missed her?

Ellie couldn't believe it. Nick here! She couldn't explain it. She'd only just received his card saying he was through with San Francisco. She'd called his mother to find out he'd gone to see his girl. What was he doing in California?

As his kiss deepened, she knew she didn't need to understand. She only wanted this moment to continue forever. For his kiss to never stop.

She pressed her small body against his as if she wanted to become a part of him. She could not get close enough. She had missed him so desperately. She only wanted to savor the solid feel of Nick as her arms tightened as if she'd never let him go.

"I've missed you." Nick moved to kiss her neck, her throat, across her cheeks to claim her mouth again and again. His arms were like bands of steel as he held her so tightly she could scarcely breathe. Still it wasn't close enough.

"What are you doing here?" She asked, kissing his jaw. "I got your postcards," she said, nibbling against his neck, and taking a deep breath to inhale his scent. Her fingers threaded in his hair, relishing the thick waves, the heat radiating from him. "Oh, Nick, I've missed you so much!"

She exclaimed, pulling back a little as sanity returned, "Nick, what are you doing here?"

"I had to come. Now I want you to tell me after this exuberant greeting that you don't love me. That you really do want me to leave and never return." His eyes narrowed as he stared down at her, daring her to lie.

"I…" Ellie tried to pull away, but he wouldn't let her move an inch. She could feel the strength in his muscles has he molded her body to his, her breasts pressed against him, the heat of his arousal hard against her belly.

"I can't marry you," she said forlornly, her happiness fading as the reality of the situation crashed around her.

"That's not what I would have thought after those kisses. Do you kiss all your casual friends that way?"

"Of course not. Let me go, I can't breathe," she said. When he complied, Ellie frowned. She already felt as if a part of her had been wrenched away. But one of them had to maintain a modicum of sense.

Nick roamed around the kitchen, studying the herbs on the windowsill, peeking in the cookie jar and snitching one of the fresh cookies Alberta had recently made. He leaned against the counter and let his gaze run over Ellie from her curly hair, to those mud-splattered legs.

"Still wearing indecent shorts, I see," he teased.

Ellie raked her hands through her hair. "Oh, Nick, I look a mess. I was washing Penelope," she said, looking down at her muddy legs in horror.

"Sweetheart, you don't look a mess, you look great." He reached for her again, but Ellie fled across the room.

"Tell me what you're doing here," she said again, holding on to the back of a chair as if for support—or a barrier.

"Where is everyone?" he asked instead.

"What?"

"The others, where are they?"

"Alberta's resting. She'll be along soon to start dinner. The men are out working, Ariel is in town. Kat's been released. She has an apartment in Jackson."

"So it's just you and me right now."

Warily Ellie looked at him and said, "Yes." Why did his words cause her heart to skip, to race?

"Pond working all right?"

"Perfectly."

His gaze slowly roamed down her body, pausing as he watched her nipples peak and push against the damp

splotches on her top; moved to the swell of her hips, the
tan legs showing beneath the short shorts. He met her eyes,
want and hunger evident.

Ellie felt as if he'd caressed every inch of her. Her heart
pounded; it was hard to breathe, she couldn't get enough
air. For a moment she let responsibility and rules fly from
her head.

"Why don't you fix some lemonade? We'll sit on the
swing and talk," Nick suggested.

"You fix it. I'll go freshen up," she replied, her eyes
blue against the light tan of her face.

"Just don't change the shorts," he ordered.

Ellie dashed up the stairs. Quickly showering, she
changed into fresh clothes. She could hardly believe he was
here. Yet she'd seen him, felt him, tasted him. Her heart
swelled in delight and joy. She had thought she would
never see him again and now he was here!

Brushing her hair she didn't recognize herself in the mirror. Her eyes were bright, luminous with happiness. Pink
color rode high in her cheeks. She had a silly grin on her
face.

Her heart began tripping rapidly as she started down the
stairs.

Will Ellie marry Nick? echoed in her brain.

Some of her excitement faded as she remember nothing
had really changed. All the reasons for refusing before were
still there. For a brief moment, she'd let her logic be
swayed by the joy at seeing him, but she knew they were
in the same situation. How could she bear for him to leave
again?

And what about all those dates he'd been bragging
about?

She gave a deep sigh, fighting tears that suddenly threatened. She squared her shoulders and pushed open the
screen door. She would see what he wanted, enjoy his visit,

then bid him farewell. At least she hoped she could do i
a second time.

Nick sat on the swing as he'd done so many times before
petting Tam. The big dog had his head worshipfully or
Nick's knee, soaking up the attention. Nick looked up smiling at Ellie as she joined him on the porch and moved to
slowly sit beside him on the swing, leaving at least three
feet between them.

Nick said nothing, but his lips tightened at her action.

"Lemonade?" he asked, reaching for the pitcher.

"Thanks." She took the glass he offered, glad for something to do. The strong current of awareness that ran up her
arm at his touch alarmed her. Her hand shook slightly as
she raised the glass to her lips. Stalling for time, she sough
words to begin the conversation.

"I shouldn't have let you shower," Nick began, his
voice grim.

Ellie looked up, startled. She hadn't expected that.

"I put on shorts," she said.

"But washed away the glad-to-see-you attitude."

"Of course I'm glad to see you, Nick," she replied
primly. "How are things going for you? You seemed to be
back in the swing of things."

Nick slammed his glass down on the tray and snatched
her glass from her, slamming it down as well.

"I didn't come three thousand miles to talk polite ba-
nalities," he said, reaching for her, his hands hard on her
shoulders. "Maybe we should start over."

Before Ellie could react, he captured her mouth with his
drew her to him, her soft breasts pressed against his strong
chest, his hand creating shimmering waves of delight and
desire. His mouth evoked remembered longings.

Ellie never thought of resisting. She'd as soon resist living. She loved Nick Tanner. She would not willingly turn
again from his embrace. This was where she belonged,
where she had longed to be for so many long lonely nights.

When at last Nick drew back to gaze down at her be-mused expression, she felt cold, bereft. She swayed toward him again and he caught her around the shoulders, drawing her up close beside him on the swing. His thigh was hard and warm against hers, despite the denim of his jeans. His hand was hard on her arm, holding her tightly as if worried she would try to escape.

"I came to talk. Are you in the mood to listen to what I have to say?" he asked gently, lacing his fingers through hers, resting their linked hands on his thigh.

Ellie nodded.

"I want you to marry me," he started.

Ellie turned to see him clearly. "We've been through this before."

"No, hear me out. I've been gone for almost six weeks. During that time I don't think there was a single moment that I didn't think of you. Of us. I admit I handled things badly before, so I want to do it right this time."

"But..."

"Shhh. Just hear me out." He cleared his throat and gazed out toward the pond. "Sheila and I dated, went to dinner, the theaters, parties. I've never taken you to things like that. How are you to know you're being courted if we don't do that kind of thing?"

"Nick, I never expected to be courted."

Liar, her heart cried.

"I should have done more. I'm here now to make up for that. The flowers and candy are only a start."

"I loved them. I didn't have a clue you sent them. I thought it might be from Margot to cheer me up." Should she tell him she'd never received such gifts before?

"Why did you need cheering up?" He pounced on her careless statement.

"I...uh..."

He smiled at her obvious embarrassment. At the implication of her statement.

"As I said, the flowers and candy are a start. Now we can continue. Dinner, dancing. Maybe a weekend in San Francisco, just the two of us. We can drive up to Reno to see a show."

"Nick, I don't need things like that," she interjected softly.

"Ellie, I want to give you the world. I want to have you remember our courtship as one of the happiest times of your life. Because I want it to lead to a happy marriage."

She shook her head, but he didn't stop.

"I've spent the last month doing everything you asked of me. Just to prove to you that we should marry."

"But..."

"Hush," he said, kissing her lightly. "I took your advice and went to see Mr. Roberts. It wasn't easy even getting to see him. But he finally agreed. I told him exactly what had happened and why. I apologized." Nick was silent for a long moment.

Ellie knew it could not have been easy. "And?"

"I felt better. He said he could understand it, though not condone it. I'm glad I went, Ellie. I still wished I'd never done it, but it helped to talk to him about it."

"Then you went home to Maryland. Did you tell your folks?"

"Yes, and that was damned hard. It shook them. But what surprised me was how much it hurt them that I hadn't told them at the time. We had a lot of long talks. I know them better now and they know me better. So you were right again. A person's family loves him no matter what damn-fool thing he does. I hadn't told them about the books, either. They were proud of that."

Ellie smiled somewhat smugly, but said nothing. *Oh, Bobby, another one who benefited.*

"I stayed in Salisbury. Seems to me I visited everyone I've ever known. Saw all my cousins, aunts, uncles, my grandfather. I didn't tell them all about being in prison, but did tell them about my books. It was nice to go home for a visit."

"I'm glad."

"I've also tied up all loose ends financially. Sold my condo. Got a contract for this second book. And came up with another idea for a new book. I have money in the bank, can go wherever I want, do what I want." He paused.

She remained still. Waiting.

"The acceptance of the book didn't mean as much to me until I could share it with you. Everyone in Maryland was excited, but you're the one I wanted to tell. I knew you'd be thrilled for me. I needed to share it with you to make it real for me."

Ellie smiled wryly. "I was thrilled when I got your card telling me. And mad at you for not giving me any way to contact you. There was so much I wanted to say," she said, hope beginning to build. There had always been so much to say with Nick.

"Exactly my point. We belong together, we complete each other."

"But..." she began.

"One hang-up you have," he continued as if she had not spoken, "was my having been out of circulation for a while. I fixed that. I've been out with ten different women. One even twice. They were pretty, friendly, interesting, funny. A couple were downright sexy. But I never found one that could begin to replace you. I tried, Ellie, really, if only to please you. But there was nothing between us. I want you."

Ellie said nothing, conscious of her emotions ranging from jealousy to joy as he talked.

He dropped a kiss on the corner of her mouth, holding up a finger to stop her when she would have spoken.

"I know you want to be an independent woman. I can accept that. Marriage doesn't end that. You are who you are. Nothing I can do will ever change that. If you'd take me on, I guarantee it'd be an equal partnership. I like being on the ranch. I can help out even if I'll never know as much as Gus or Rusty. But I can pull my weight. And do the accounts," he slipped in slyly.

She groaned softly. "I hate that part."

"I know. But you don't hate the rest, do you, Ellie? Don't say no, not this time."

"Nick, there's more at stake than just the accounts." How much more could she stand? She wanted to say yes, wanted to have him stay forever.

"I know, my record," he said grimly.

"No, that doesn't bother me."

"Ellie, don't keep saying no! I love you so much." He pulled her against him, his face buried in her soft curls. "I've missed you so much, wanted you so much. I'll fix every objection you give me, make everything come right, court you all you want, *only don't keep saying no!*"

Holding her breath she replayed the words in her mind.

"You love me?" she asked breathlessly. Her heart pounded before it began to take flight. She wanted to believe. She remembered Margot's urging, her own desires. She remembered how lonely and empty her life had been these past weeks without Nick to share it.

"Yes, I love you. I love you more than I thought I could love anyone. I want to marry you, sleep with you, love you. Wake up together in the mornings and plan our days together, our future together. I want you to be the mother of our kids, to be my companion when I'm old. I'll learn more about the ranch and maybe write a book or two over the years, but not without you there. What do you say, Ellie?"

"I thought you were fond of me." Saying the words still hurt.

"I blew that. I didn't want to fall in love again. I made such a mess of things over Sheila. But what I feel for you is nothing like what I felt for her. I love you deeply, lastingly. It's based on good things, not false expectations."

"You never gave me any indication. I thought you didn't trust me."

"That was a man fighting against feelings he was afraid to trust. I was drawn to you the first day I saw you. Your efforts to make me comfortable and at ease were almost too good to be true. I love your sweet Southern drawl, the kindness you always show, the silly notions you get, like a pond for ducks to swim in. The patience you show the kids, the genuine delight you feel for the ranch. I think I fell all the way in love the day Henrietta's egg fell on my face. Later you learned about so many parts of my life, never condemning, only encouraging. But I had been very badly burned in trying to love. I fought against trusting you, against loving you."

"But now you're sure?"

"Absolutely. Say yes, Ellie."

Ellie began to smile. Her heart pounded in fearful anticipation, overflowing with happiness until she thought she'd burst.

"All life's a gamble, sweetheart. We don't know how much time we have, let's not waste a minute of it apart. I want to spend all my tomorrows with you. I hope we'll share sixty years or more together, my love, starting right now."

She took the plunge.

"Yes, please, Nick. I'd be honored to marry you."

His exulted yell surprised her, but before she could even blink at his reaction, he stood up and swung her into his arms, twirling her around and around on the porch. Tam barked in the background, confused with the sudden activity.

The back door banged shut and hurried footsteps could be heard through the house.

"What's going on?" Alberta asked, bursting out on the porch. Stopping at the sight before her, she grinned.

"Ellie's going to marry me!" Nick said, setting her down on her feet.

"Well, about time, I'd say," Alberta replied, nodding.

Epilogue

The party was in full swing as the afternoon faded int
evening. It was Ellie's thirty-third birthday and Nick ha
thrown a big surprise party. Alberta and Jenny, one of the
new guests, had baked steadily for two days to prepar
Margot and Kat had decorated the downstairs until ever
room looked festive.

Gus had ferried guests from town, smuggling Nick's pa
ents, several neighbors and Nick's friends from San Fra
cisco into the house while Nick had made up a shoppir
excursion for Ellie in Jackson.

Ellie had been surprised when walking into the hous
upon her return. Surprised, pleased and flustered. Sh
sought her husband's loving gaze as her eyes filled wi
tears of happiness. In the months since their marriage, Nic
had done so much to show her over and over how muc
he cared for her.

"I've never had a party before," she whispered as sh
reached up to give him a quick kiss.

"I remembered you saying that," he said, smiling. 'Happy birthday, my love."

She greeted her guests, friends and neighbors, Matt and Steve and Sally from San Francisco. Pete and Consuela, both former guests in the Helping Hands program. Jed, Ariel and Brad all returned to wish her well on her special day.

Delighted with the party, she moved from group to group, talking with friends, discussing everything under the sun, catching up on "her kids." The food was excellent, the warmth of her friends made the celebration special.

Ellie was surprised to see her in-laws, greeting them with warm hugs. She had hit it off with Nick's parents when she first met them on her honeymoon and they had instantly drawn her into the warm embrace of his family. Since then Peggy Tanner and Ellie exchanged long newsy letters each week.

"So, *chérie*, it is a happy night, *n'est-ce pas?*" Margot asked her at the punch table.

"I'm so happy! Isn't life wonderful?" Ellie's gaze sought her husband across the room.

"May I say I told you so?" Margot asked slyly.

Ellie laughed and turned back to her friend. "Why not, you throw it up in my face all the time, why should today be any different? But you were right and I'm so happy I don't even mind you reminding me, *again!*"

"Ellie?" Nick's voice reached her over the sounds of the party. She looked around and saw him on the stairs. She hurried over.

"Come and see to little Bobby, can you? He's fretting."

Ellie smiled as she ran up the steps. Her son was so precious.

"Why can't you..." she began as she entered the nursery. "Oh, of course."

"I can only do so much at one time, and Annie was

crying,'' Nick said, gently tending their infant daughte
while Ellie went to pick up the fretful twin boy.

She nuzzled his soft cheek as she went to stand by he
tall husband. Her heart swelled with love and happiness a
she surveyed her family.

''How'd you get so smart?'' she asked as she watche
him deftly change their daughter's diaper.

''What do you mean?''

''This marriage is wonderful. I've never been so happ
in my life. You said it would work, how did you know?'

He leaned over and dropped a quick kiss on her lips
''Some things are meant to be. I'm happy, too—more s
than I probably deserve,'' he murmured as he pulled u
their daughter's ruffly rubber pants.

Margot appeared in the doorway with Nick's mothe
right behind her.

''We'll take care of these two. You go enjoy the party,'
Margot said, taking Annie as their grandmother picked u
Bobby. ''We'll settle them then come back.''

Nick drew Ellie into the hall, pausing before descendin
the stairs.

''Thank you for everything, my love,'' Ellie said smilin
up at her husband.

''My darling Ellie, you're the one to be thanked. You'v
brought so much happiness to my life.''

He took her in his arms and kissed her soundly.

''Maybe the party wasn't such a good idea, after all,'
he said against her soft skin.

''It was, too. Why ever wouldn't you think so? I'm s
excited. It's great!''

''If all these people weren't here, we could slip into ou
room now and make passionate love all night long.''

She laughed, shining up at him.

''We can do that as soon as they leave. I do love yo
Nick Tanner.''

''And I love you, Ellie Tanner, and always will.''

* * * * *

Looking For More Romance?

Visit Romance.net

Look us up on-line at: http://www.romance.net

Check in daily for these and other exciting features:

Hot off the press

View all current titles, and purchase them on-line.

What do the stars have in store for you?

Horoscope

Hot deals

Exclusive offers available only at Romance.net

Plus, don't miss our interactive quizzes, contests and bonus gifts.

PWEB

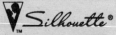